NIGHT
OF THE
BOOK MAN

BOOK ONE OF THE SURF MYSTIC SERIES

CASTLE BRIDGE MEDIA
DENVER, COLORADO, USA

This book is a work of fiction. Names, characters, business, events and incidents are the products of the authors' imaginations. Any resemblance to actual persons, living or dead, or actual events is purely coincidental.

SURF MYSTIC:
NIGHT OF THE BOOK MAN
© 2020 Jason Henderson
All rights reserved.

ISBN: 9798680297346

CASTLE BRIDGE MEDIA
Denver, Colorado, USA
castlebridgemedia.com

Cover by In Churl Yo
Photo by Kanate/Shutterstock

No part of this book may be reproduced, stored in a retrieval system, or transmitted in any form or by any means, electronic, mechanical, photocopying, recording, or otherwise, without the prior written permission of the author, except as provided by U.S.A. copyright law.

CHAPTER 1

Brutal things happen on the most beautiful days.

The sun no longer beat down on Moro Ridge Road at 6:15 in the afternoon, instead hanging over the ocean to the west, glaring at intervals from behind jutting ridges of bleached rock and gnarled coastal scrub. Crystal Cove State Park was empty because it was Easter Sunday, and Frances Cohn—Frannie to Noreen Swail, her only companion today—figured they were the luckier for it. If they made bikes that could go off the concrete road and up into the rocks she would have veered off with Noreen and zoomed down the ridges, zipping around scrub like a skier around trees. She pictured the descent, the jolt of rocks and the swoop of tiny hills and valleys and picked up her pace. It was their twenty-fifth mile.

Maybe Noreen was getting tired, but probably not. Every Sunday, the

Laguna Beach Girls Cycling Club rode thirty to forty miles, starting at the Laguna Beach High School and heading up Ocean Highway, past giant cars swaying with their own bulk on the road, then up into the park, as far as the paved road would take them. Noreen was one of LBHS' strongest athletes, and Frannie competed with her for who got winded the least.

Cycling was the *most*.

Usually there were ten or twelve girls, but for Easter everyone had begged off except Noreen. "Believe me, Frannie," she had said. "By the afternoon I'll be wanting to get out of there." Noreen had five little brothers and a forty-mile ride was just the thing after a day of Easter egg hunts and decorating.

"So, what about egg soup?" Frannie asked.

"What?" Noreen asked, pulling closer. The wind was picking up, unseasonably hot, flying in from the Mojave, the Santa Ana winds that made the hairs on Frannie's arms itch as the sweat boiled right off.

"Do you do egg soup?"

"No, for Pete's sake. All the eggs are boiled."

"So egg salad."

"Egg salad, absolutely," said Noreen. "Come over tomorrow and I'll give you a couple casserole dishes of it."

"Deal." Frannie gave her pal a thumbs-up sign and dropping into 4th gear as the road pitched up for a quarter mile. She had a Passover meal with her folks and her uncle, but she'd make a stop at Noreen's somehow.

At home, Frannie thought, her mom probably had a whole feast for her pop and his students from the University who were all over to talk about literature—he had been waving around a gray canister of *The Golem*, a crazy old silent movie he loved to show, and she figured he would show it and talk legends. She had been to a couple of these parties. About now, in the old movie, the old wizard would be asking a risen devil to breathe life into a big lump of clay, to make a hero to protect the chosen people.

Not a foolproof plan, unless the old wizard wanted a big clay Frankenstein lumbering around scaring people.

Frannie preferred a ride over a movie any day. "I'll have my mom send a bunch of knishes."

"Well, I knew we let you in the club for something."

Frannie laughed and thanked God that they had let her in the cycling club. She had been in California for two months and this was her reason for living now, riding the hot mountains with girls on bikes.

They turned right as they topped the ridge and a rabbit zoomed across the road, daring them to flatten it. "Thank you for coming out today," Frannie called, watching the white tail disappear behind some rocks.

"You talking to the rabbit or me?" Noreen called.

"Both."

A state park truck, a white Ford Ranger with a California seal, appeared far below and started moving up the road towards them. Noreen pulled in front then, making a single file on the right side of the road.

"Ah, I wouldn't let you do it alone." Noreen pumped those legs of hers that made her so famous at school and that would surely do her even prouder on the beach. Frannie had never seen a California beach in summer with all that entailed. She wasn't looking forward to it. She felt like a living scarecrow next to Noreen, skinny and small. Thank God for friends who didn't care about that jazz.

Without Noreen, Frannie wouldn't have known what to do in a school that was so different from Brooklyn that she may as well be on Mars. For a moment Frannie looked out at the concrete road, long and blank and waiting. Like it was nothing until she rode over it, like her life was blank and it could be miserable and alone or a friend could walk in and then it's full of adventure and sun.

Whiteness filled her vision and she blinked it away.

A deep mechanical bleating burst through the air and Frannie looked down the hill to see a motorcycle come flying over a hill, looking to connect with Moro Ridge Road. Frannie saw the rider's brown helmet and arms wobbling as he entered the road and the state pickup veered left instead of right.

Noreen gasped and went off the road and hit a rock and for a moment Frannie saw Noreen tumble headlong. A split second's image of blood, flying in a spattering arc. Frannie felt a surge of shooting empathetic pain, her skin tingling under the hot wind. She tore her eyes back to the road, too late. She had a brief moment to brake and then she was partly stopped and partly flying.

The white hood of the truck filled her vision, blankness stretching endlessly before her body came to a sudden halt.

CHAPTER 2

She saw the Golem of Prague.

Frances Cohn soared across a space of white, endless and undulating. She cast a shadow that flowed over the whiteness and made visible recesses, the shadows licking letters into view, lines of writing she could not read, until the meaningless writing went away and one word floated, white on white: *Emet*, truth.

A figure, the golem, rose up in her vision, gray and crackling like old film, standing in the sea of white. He was a man of clay, his arms wide, and the word *Emet* shone on his forehead and his eyes burned and spewed out curls of white smoke.

Here to save us, she thought, *here to guard us, here to lead us out of the darkness*. The golem watched her, and she began to tumble, drifting. The sea of white had an edge now and she was sliding towards it.

Come back, the golem said. *Come back to the truth. Can you hear me?*

She felt her feet hit the white ocean and she was sliding, sliding towards the edge, reaching back to grab on to nothing and the edge was coming fast, nothingness.

Another voice: *your story is done. There is no shame in closing the book when the story is done.*

But the golem was still in her view, reaching down, the whiteness splashing around his giant clay hands. *That voice lies. That voice fools. Come back to the truth. Come back to Emet.*

Can you hear me?

Frannie, can you hear me?

And she awoke.

CHAPTER 3

"Frannie, can you hear me?"

"Yes, I hear you." Frannie blinked and rubbed her eye, wincing as the stitches on her forehead throbbed. She focused on her mother at the edge of the hospital bed and turned a little away from the sun pouring through white window shades. The calendar and the clock on her nightstand saw that it was Tuesday, two weeks after the accident. "I was just sleeping." She cast her eyes over her mother. "Your blouse is pretty."

Sally Cohn pursed her lips in an apologetic half-smile, smoothing down her cream silk top. "I'm supposed to give a lecture later." Mom reached out a thin arm and brushed back a few strands of Frannie's hair. "Oh, that's looking good."

"Thanks."

"What were you dreaming about?"

"I don't…" it was fading, fading into white. She had no idea what she had been dreaming about, but now, as usually happened, she was thinking again of the white truck, and of Noreen going end-over-end by the road. "Noreen."

"Oh, Frannie. You do remember." Her mother brought her hand to her mouth. "Right?"

"I… No, I do." Frannie said, all of reality washing back in her mind.

She had even seen Noreen's mother, briefly. The woman had come in and sat by her bed and hadn't said a word. That *had* actually happened, hadn't it? Frannie felt tears come to her eyes.

"Hey. They're going to release you." Mom sat on the edge of the bed, filling the space in Frannie's mind where Noreen's mom had sat a few days earlier. Her mother couldn't stop touching her, her eyes searching, inspecting the land that was Frannie. "Hey, it's okay."

Frannie sniffed. "I saw her mom. Noreen's mom was here."

"Don't think about that." Her mother nodded, squeezing Frannie's hand. "Did you hear what I told you? They're gonna let you out. Tomorrow. Do you feel good?"

Frannie drank some water, fighting away the thought of Noreen's blood. "I feel fine."

She did feel ready. She was wasting time here. She needed to get out.

To stop reading and staring out the window and get some strength back. She wanted to get out and hit the road, get some distance. Maybe not get on a bike. She searched her thoughts and that one waved back at her defiantly. Yeah. Maybe not a bike. But she had to get *out*.

"How's your vision, still bleary?"

"I see fine." For the first few days she had had blurred vision, but the doctor had said that was the least of her worries. That she had survived without breaking her neck was a miracle. She had bounced off the hood of the truck and come this close to getting crushed under the wheels as it screeched to a halt. She ran her hand down her side, feeling along an agonizing roadmap on her hip, knees, elbows, where she'd skinned herself so fiercely that they were warning her about persistent scars. Contusions. sprains and a hairline fracture to her thigh where she'd gone under the bike. And for all that she was the lucky one.

Her mom kissed her forehead. "I have to get to the University," Mom said. "summer physics; I don't know why I bother getting dressed. The students are all asleep. But your pop will be in later. Then tomorrow you can come home, okay?"

Frannie nodded. Hell yes that would be okay.

"Your uncle's here," Mom said as she moved off, touching Frannie again. "The old *fantayzor* brought you some books."

"Oy," Frannie said, looking towards the door to see a short, powerfully built bald man come into view. Mom patted Uncle Saul's shoulder as she passed him on the way out. Frannie called to her uncle, "You're killing me here."

"What, you don't have time to read? What else ya gonna do in here?" Uncle Saul wore a pair of gray slacks and a black t-shirt that showed off his biceps. He took the chair next to the bed and reached into a leather bag he carried. "You look good."

"A man should watch his lies when he reaches a certain age."

"Ah. Here." Saul produced a small stack of books and lay them on the bed next to her, then snapped up the stack on her nightstand. "You done with these others?"

"I finished the Connie Blair mysteries. I could use more," Frannie said, indicating the mystery novels in the stack. "And the Bullfinch Mythology, that was kind of fun."

"Not the Norman Mailer?"

"You're kidding."

"Eh, we try," Saul said. Uncle Saul had opened a new place, a coffee shop sort of like the old Café he used to run farther up the coast. Frannie hadn't seen that one because it was closed by the time her family moved here. "You gotta see the new place, Frannie. It's a great spot. You can throw a baseball and hit the beach if you don't bean one of the jokers in the hotel across the way. And we got books."

"People read books on the beach, huh?" Frannie was looking at the new stack. She saw a couple more Connie Blairs—so Saul *did* know her poison now—and some science fiction.

She grimaced. *"Invasion of the Body Snatchers?"*

"Science fiction not your thing?"

"Not last I checked."

"I mean, your pop would like it; he'd say it's actually about communism."

"He thinks everything is about communism." Frannie came to a black book without a title. "What's this?"

Saul was flipping through the Norman Mailer book and looked up. "Huh?"

She held it up. "No title."

Saul froze for a second, his brow knitting under his tan cue ball head. "Uh… here, lemme see that."

"Sure," she said, and Saul took it—snatched it, really. She sat up a little more as her uncle's demeanor shifted, getting stiffer, and he turned slightly away, flipping the book open just a crack. He mumbled under his breath. "How the hell?"

"Uncle Saul, what is it?"

"It's nothin'." He forced a smile. "I don't know how this got in there. Somebody ordered this." The book was already back in his bag.

"You sellin' illegal books in that place?" Frannie asked. "That something you're supposed to keep in a plain brown wrapper?"

"Don't worry about it," Saul said. He brought the leather strap of the book bag over his shoulder and rose, going to the window. He stared out of it for a while, his hand on one of the strands of the blinds.

"Thanks for the mysteries," she said. "I'm getting out tomorrow."

"Good," Saul said quietly. Now he looked like he was searching the outside, squinting into the sun. He clapped his hands and turned back to her. "Good—come to the café when you're out. I'll fix you up with something nice."

"You got a deal."

She got out of bed and watched at her window as Uncle Saul got to his car in the parking lot. Watched him look in every direction, even up at the roof. Watched him quickly make the sign of the *kina hora* and drive away.

Kina hora: the evil eye.

CHAPTER 4

At 9:30 in the evening, the North Texas air swam with humidity and heat. Sunlight had soaked into the concrete and the metal of cars all day, and hours after sundown, Verna Brody's cotton blouse stuck fast to her back and shoulders and perspiration beaded at her temples and brow. God, if it was like this in the building, what would it be like outside?

She locked up the Nu-2-U consignment shop at the Lancaster Town Square Market with a jangle of keys and an unconscious humming she'd picked up from the shop radio.

Verna liked to stay after hours doing the books and puttering around rearranging blouses. The shop was her life's dream and at sixty-seven years old, it was a lover she hated to leave. Now the last song of the evening stayed with her as she left by the front entrance of the two-story, red-brick building. Verna's baby-blue sedan was the only car in the lot.

The car door was still warm and the seats sticky. The heat would keep pouring on as she drove home, she knew, driving itself up from the ground, and it would do so until 5:30 or so in the morning, when finally having exhausted itself, heat would finally give way to cool—just in time to greet the sun.

Verna Brody drove out of the Town Square past the closed cafes and the limestone bank building. Bonnie and Clyde had rousted the place when she was a little girl, and she smiled at the idea though she had no memory of it. She drove past live oaks that gave shade but no respite, singing the last song, a Johnny Cash number about fire.

The fire itself started like a mouse at home, tiny and snuggled, a beating heart of life that breathed shallow and grew slow for many hours. It began deep within the wall behind the consignment shop. By 11:30 on May 1, 1958, Verna was two hours gone from the place, and it was hidden but well underway.

The Book Man knew the fire was coming so clearly that he might as well have set it himself.

He knew it was coming because his whole body—this strange body, really just a skin he had acquired and was now only somewhat used to—prickled with the anticipation of what food would fuel it.

The Town Square Market Building boasted plaster floral arrangements in an arch around the entrance and a central court where one could enter and choose a store or take an elevator or flight of stairs up to even more. The fire started on the second-floor northeast corner with an electrical short in the walls.

At 11:30, three men—the brothers Dave and Dicky Lome, plus their high school soccer coach, Tom Hoag, were entering the Tri-Arms Sporting Goods store on the first floor, north*west* corner, putting them a story down and a floor across from a fire they did not know was there.

As the Book Man smelt the fire on the wind, the ridges of his fingers sharpened and vibrated. His nostrils flared. He turned the wheel of the grey, stolen Morris Minor pickup, with its pinched nose and wide-mouthed, hungry face, and pulled over on the shoulder, considering it, the fire and what the fire would be. He was twenty miles away.

He whipped the pickup around and sat for a moment at the intersection, the red light above him swinging in the wind like a condemned man. Condemned. The building would be condemned, the Book Man realized, as he held his hand out the window, his flesh rippling with the wind. He could taste the fire and more. He waited until the light turned green and began to roll.

The three men entered the sporting goods store through a metal door and stood nervously in the golfing section. "We should get golf clubs," Tom said, because he was ten years older than the other two and had a notion of the value of golf clubs.

"Basketballs," the wiry younger Lome brother Dick said. He ran now, giddy with risk, and grabbed a basketball off a big red-and-yellow Wilson rack and began to dribble the ball on the linoleum.

"Cut that out," Tom hissed.

"There ain't no guards," the other brother David said. "Mister Whit had his stroke and they ain't replaced him."

Tom took David's arm and Dick stopped dribbling this to listen. "I don't care if they vowed it in the paper never to have a guard again. Breaking into a place and making a bunch of fool noise is stupid." He changed his tone, softening—a coaching technique, and one the boys responded to. Snap, and then smooth. "Now, get two shopping carts from the front and let's start filling them. The most expensive stuff first, golf clubs, equipment, anything metal."

"Yes, coach," the boys said.

A loud creak—the opening of a door, for sure—emanated from the back of the building and all three of them froze and looked up like startled deer. Tom grabbed a golf club—a putter—and motioned the other two to follow him.

They had come in through the employee break room in the back using a stolen key. Dick worked at a hardware store, and he'd lifted it when the manager of the whole building had come in to have some new keys cut. Tom had that key out in his hand now.

They walked back into the break room and saw beyond the card table and punch clock that the door was hanging open. They could see the parking lot beyond where their pickup waited next to a concrete flight of stairs.

"I thought we closed that," Tom said. He pulled the door closed and heard it latch. "Let's get what we can." It bothered him that the door had popped open like that. He set to stealing things.

Above them, the fire that had begun in the walls of the consignment shop had crept through, born and breathing but still silent, and had emerged in the Western Section of the Tattered Wisdom Bookshop.

Only the Book Man, now ten miles away, would know that the first volume to feel the lick of fire would be *The Light of Western Stars* by Zane Grey, the flames cutting the edges of the paperback and curling as the book fluttered from the shelf, and the fire hissed and shot glue-and-paper-fed plumes in all directions.

The Book Man's nostrils flared as he drove, the asphalt a blank screen in his vision against which he watched the eating and hissing of *Ligeia* and *Rebecca* and *Peyton Place*, shelves and pages and wallpaper licking with flame that spread across the floor and began to pry itself into the boards beneath the stories. He stepped on the gas.

On the first floor, Tom looked up as a glass upstairs broke while he and Dick were maneuvering a basketball goal into a cart. It sounded to Tom like a full pitcher and he exchanged glances with the two boys. "That was upstairs," the coach said.

"But what if it's someone coming?" Dick asked, and Tom made a gesture that said *just get going.*

"If it is, they're awful clumsy," Tom said.

"But if they're coming…"

"Then we need to hurry," hissed Tom.

The Book Man, rolling inexorably towards his meal, could tell anyone listening (if he chose to speak to mere mortals) that the glass breaking was in fact a kerosene lamp, more ornamental than useful, that sat that evening next to a rocking chair where just the week before Truman Capote himself had sat next to the lamp and read *from Breakfast at Tiffany's.*

By that time, the fire had spread across a fifteen-foot area of the second floor, and now the papers and rugs mixed with kerosene widened and deepened the fire.

Smoke finally made its way downstairs and Tom felt an animal urge to run. But he held it together and looked at the two high school boys he was escorting through a burglary and told them they should finish up and leave. They started making their way across the store back towards the rear entrance with their carts, though Tom had a time trying to maneuver his, weighed down as he was with 300 pounds of golf materiel. David's was less unwieldy but nearly as heavy, loaded with free weights he had stolen from below the beaming visage of Charles Atlas, the fitness guru. They were now making their way past just such a black-and-white standee scarecrow of Mister Atlas when the roof of the store caved in.

Tom watched Charles Atlas disappear in a falling avalanche of wood and paper, Shakespeare and Homer felling Atlas as one, *The Sands of Iwo Jima* landing in Atlas' face where the cardboard fell.

Tom gasped and Dick shrieked like a child as it began to rain fire. Dave was in front of them and turned around and his face was streaming with blood, and he staggered and fell, and a flaming rocking chair came down and stove in his face. Just visible for a moment, though. All was on fire.

Dick and Tom were screaming, still alive, running, abandoning all and every man for himself, and they made it to the break room and stopped.

A vast wooden bookshelf had fallen through a flaming hole in the ceiling and now lay lengthwise in front of the door. They took in this information instantly, amid the smoke and darkness and the flames on the books, and Tom could see the metal door he'd just shut a few moments earlier, and he and Dick ran for it. They clawed away books to try to reach to the shelf.

Tom also became aware that he and Dick were both calling for help, out loud, as they kicked books away and tried to reach the bookshelf, and their clothes were catching fire.

Then a flowing mass of rug on fire from upstairs landed at Dick's feet, and Tom turned and saw Dick screaming, his flesh melting and his arms flailing.

For a moment he was waving his arms and books were fusing to him and his clothes, *Charlie and the Chocolate Factory* and *The Scarlet Letter* lodged in his shoulders and chest.

A metal crunching sound burst out and Tom tore himself away from this terrible sight to see the door flying away from its hinges. Tom had a thought, like Jimmy Olson on TV: We're saved!

And the hero who stepped through the door was barely a shadow in the smoke, and as he came near Tom, he reached out a tweed-sleeved arm and patted Tom's shoulder. And Tom realized all feeling in his shoulder had gone away.

He looked down and saw blackness where a body should be, and the hero had crouched and was sifting through paper and flesh at his feet. Dick had gone silent, but Tom stayed standing, and swayed.

The hero stood up, and now his face was visible, a face with a smart beard under a Fedora and crinkled, whimsical eyes.

The man in the fedora (there was a feather in his cap!) showed Tom what he had picked up: it was a copy of *Remembrance of Things Past* by Marcel Proust, a paperback student's copy. Partially burnt, but a little wet and shiny.

"That's you," the man said, running a finger along the pages as he showed Tom the soaked pages. "Tomfat, I guess. How do you like that?" And as he came close, it looked like his face slid around of its own accord when he moved. He seemed most unnatural, did the hero, thought Tom, as he swayed on his feet.

The man bit into the Proust paperback like a sandwich, and the human fat dripped over his chin.

Tom looked down and his legs were gone, and he was falling, and it was raining books again.

The Book Man thanked a long-abandoned God for his good fortune and ate well.

CHAPTER 5

"The sea makes a heck of a racket," the surfer boy said as he dropped into the sand, folding his legs under himself and holding two beers. He was probably nineteen, a college boy she figured, and Deborah Aegean nearly didn't hear what he said because he was right: it was noisy as heck.

Deborah rolled over in the sand, switching which side would catch the most heat. All around her there was a chattering of boys and girls laughing, slapping one another around, tossing stuff into the bonfire to make it pop. Laughing to fill the air and compete with the noise of the waves, so the air grew thick with undifferentiated sound.

Above all she heard the roar of the ocean, steady and rhythmic to her right, the Pacific undulating in nighttime retreat. That way was cool. After turning over and staring at the sea for a few seconds, the skin on that side of her body had to be 8 degrees cooler than her other side, where the bonfire roared. The bonfire licked yellow and sent sparks into the black night.

"What did you say?" she asked the boy dreamily. He was tan as her father's desk, even in the fire-lit dark you could tell his skin had taken on a deep bronze that only came from living on the beach. He had brown eyes and black hair in a crew cut, and not a jot of fat. All these boys were built that way here, the skinny legs and arms and a giant back, as if all strength were being re-routed to his latissimus dorsi.

He held out a beer, offering it to her, making his voice sound deeper than likely was real, which tickled her. "I said it makes a big noise all the time over here."

"Does it!" she laughed.

"No, I mean—that was what Chumash beach dwellers said about this place. *The big noise*, they called it."

She took the beer and sipped it, wanted to gag for a second. She hated beer. She cast her eyes to the boys and girls dancing, and some of them had sodas; she would have been fine with a Coke. But she drank.

"So get this." The boy turned, lightly tracing loops across her shoulder with a fingertip. "They had a word for the whole phrase, 'It makes a big noise all the time here.' And you know what that word was?"

"What?" she asked, entranced.

"*Mall-a-wu*," the surfer boy said. "Malibu. So technically, they mean

Malibu. But it's still true here in Laguna Beach."

"I'll say," she said, having lost the plot of what the bronze person was saying. Divided by heat and chill, wet and warmth, she looked past him at the boys and girls with their beers and soda bottles and drank in the feeling. She looked back and laughed again.

This was what it was to be at a beach bonfire, a real bonfire like they showed in the photos of the beach magazines—really just rags they printed up to put around ads—that she grabbed at the entrance of the Piggly Wiggly with her mom. When you're sixteen you can go to the beach, her mom had said. And here it was! Almost, anyway—it was May 5, and she wouldn't technically be sixteen for two days, until May 7 of 1958, but that was close enough.

"What's your name?" the boy said.

"It's Deborah," she said. "I live in Oakmont."

"Oakmont, oh," he answered, smiling.

"That's what everyone says," Deborah said. "*Oakmont, Oh*, but it's not that bad. The houses are a little older, but..."

"I don't know anything about Oakmont," he said, by which he meant not that he wanted to hear more, but that he meant nothing at all and wasn't all that interested. "I'm at Northwestern. Chicago, you know? But for the summer it's this, every night."

Come with me, a voice sang in her head, like a distant bird. *Come with me and swim.*

"Come with me and swim?" she said aloud, and the boy seemed to startle for a second, as if what she had said was an alien suggestion. He looked at his half-full beer bottle and nodded. "Yeah, okay," he said, and swigged back the rest of the beer.

She rose, dropping her cutoff jeans to the sand and tossing her white men's shirt, feeling the chill of air against her bare belly. She felt so scandalous! Bikinis were—what did the magazines say? *Bitchin'.*

The boy wore long trunks loosened below the belly in what she thought a pretty scandalous display itself, though when they reached the water, he cinched them up, tugging the draw string and tossing his sandals as they began to walk to the surf.

She shivered when her feet touched the water, and he started running. "Best to run and just dive, doll!" he said, and he did, leaping fast and heading into the water, looking like a bronze fish disappearing into the surf.

She followed, ignoring the cold as it hit her and leaping into the air, arms forward. She plunged into the water, feeling the salt as much as tasting it. She swam through the waves a few feet and came up, looked around. She saw the boy waving a few yards further out and she headed that way, diving again and coming up.

Sing with me, a voice said. Under water, her eyes came open and for a moment there flickered a white image that glowed, something she couldn't make out through strands of seaweed.

She came up to the surface and the boy was nearby, swimming towards her, laughing. "It's beautiful, ain't it?" he cried.

"Yes!" she said, and it was. The white image drifted from her mind. She looked off towards the beach and saw the bonfire, high and yellow and gorgeous. "They look like a painting," she said.

He smiled—his smile was crooked, that was what made it always look like he maybe wasn't smiling at all. He looked back at the bonfire, turning away from her. He floated on the water, one of the many young gods of the sea.

She was watching droplets of water fall from his hair onto his dark shoulders when a white-skinned woman rose from the waves between them. Deborah saw angry dark eyes and long black hair. She started to scream, and the woman's fingers closed around her throat, catching the sound before it could escape. In less time than it took for the boy to look back, she dropped beneath the waves and all went black.

CHAPTER 6

Frannie Cohn wound up at the beach because she couldn't say *no* anymore, even though it was Carol Dolenz at her door, who had never paid any attention to her before Noreen and Frannie's accident. Carol had asked three days in a row and here she was back again, ringing the door at 9 in the morning.

"I'm glad you're here," Carol said. "I thought you'd be out riding."

Frannie shrugged. Carol was one of the ones who hadn't been on the ride *that day* because of Easter eggs and all. She come by the hospital, too, and in the last couple of weeks of class had brought Frannie some homework to try to get caught up. And Frannie had said how much she wanted to get back out on the road, get some soreness back in her legs, get moving. But of course...

Carol wore a long white cover-up over a bathing suit, and her battered 1930 roadster—the kind all the kids favored and probably on loan from her pop's car lot—rumbled behind her in the driveway. Three other girls back there, sunglasses and cover-ups, all staring.

It should be Noreen. Frannie wanted to shut the door but couldn't bring herself to be that bold, and she started to shake her head.

"Come on," Carol said. "Come out with us."

"Are you going for a ride?" Frannie asked.

"We're not biking, Frannie," she said. "It'll be fun."

"I don't know."

"Frannie, come on. You need to get out. We'll stop by Noreen's mom's and say hi and head to the beach."

"You really think," Frannie mumbled, shaking her head, "that she wants us to drop by? On the way to the beach?"

Someone honked. Carol looked back at the roadster and held up a finger, curtsying a little before turning back. "I don't know. Maybe we don't if you don't think that's right. Maybe that's stupid. I'm sorry"

"No, it's not…"

"We just don't want to see you waste away."

Frannie sighed. She felt tired. All the antsy energy of the hospital bed had left her the moment she got home. She wanted to listen to the radio and sleep. "What's at the beach?"

"*Boys*, Frannie." Carol laughed, not harshly, a sweet laugh. "What else would be at the beach? Come on, you're gonna be a senior. We gotta get you out there."

Frannie sighed.

"Do you have a bathing suit? Get it."

A bathing suit and a white men's shirt for a cover-up. She was sixteen and a half and built like a long-haired boy, and as she rode in the convertible, she folded her arms around the white button-down and squinted into the sun.

"Hey gang," Carol called as she zipped through the streets, headed towards Ocean Highway. "Frannie's never been hunting!"

Frannie Cohn reached Laguna Beach for the first time in her life on May 15, 1958.

Carol parked the roadster in the sand at the side of the road behind a dozen other cars up the road a ways from a wooden sign that said MAIN BEACH.

"Seven miles of pristine sand, ladies," said Noreen as she unloaded towels and suntan oil and other accoutrements onto her crew. Frannie took an armful of towels. "Let's find the local fauna!"

Frannie squinted hard, wishing she'd brought sunglasses or at least a hat, and the sun baked the sand along the side of the road and heated her toes through her canvas shoes. Already she felt her pale skin frying as she and the girls found the wooden stairs down to the sand.

Frannie regarded the beach, struck for a moment by the curve of sand and the waves crashing to the cliffs, drowning out any traffic sounds from above. The pickings for mammals of the human male persuasion seemed a little slim, and that suited her fine.

They were halfway between the road and the water and Frannie spread out a towel and watched a few kids leaping in the water, tossing a Frisbee to their dog, and they all seemed to leap the same, like a school of fish trying to escape the ocean. She smiled to see this and thought maybe it would be the kicks to drag her parents out here. Her father would likely lecture her about Pinder and how water was the Greatest of All or some such and he'd miss the beauty of the thing itself. Still, she liked the idea of seeing her pop on the beach.

In the other direction there were some boys in the water, too far away for distinction so they looked like an army of bronze slashes in the bright day, human daggers, lean and running into the water carrying enormous slabs of wood. She'd heard of surfing but had paid it no attention.

Nadine Morley whistled behind Frannie and said, "That's the idea," and she and Carol made quick work of moving their whole campsite down the beach a little closer to the surfing gods. They sat down and started arching their backs, ready to be admired.

Oy. Frannie trudged after them and Carol said, "Sit, Frannie, you look like you're either stalking us or about to take our order."

"What can I get you?" Frannie grinned, pretending to write on her palm with a pencil she mimed pulling from behind her tied-back mountain of black, curly hair. "A slab of man-meat, perhaps? That comes a la mode."

"Oh, she can be crass," marveled Carol, as though she liked this change in Frannie. "Sit, Frannie."

A thought came to her: her uncle, looking around nervously at his car as she watched through the hospital room window, making the sign of the evil eye. That was funny, because he had never struck her as the old-world type.

Come by the café when you're out. I'll fix you up with something nice.

Frannie frowned, looking down the beach. The surfers caught her eye again, bobbing in a long line far out on the water for some purpose. The sea sparkled as she looked farther out, until her vision filled with long waves and countless glistening points of light, all of it working like a blanket over the noise in her mind. Distantly a word moved through her, spoken by the golem in the dream: *Emet*, truth.

That made no sense to her at all. But she knew she didn't want to lay here getting a sunburn.

"No," Frannie mumbled.

"What do you mean, *no?*"

"I mean, before I get situated—my uncle has a café up the road,"

Frannie said. "I promised him I'd visit when I got out. I might get a soda; I could bring you something."

"Okay," Carol said, with a look of concern that reminded Frannie of her mom. "I guess you could bring us some sandwiches."

There was a time, way back before she could remember but so she'd been told, that they'd even lived with Uncle Saul. But that was when she was a baby, when they'd first come to the States. There were no slide shows of all this, and they never really talked about it. She did have a Polaroid of all of them, though—her mom and pop looking so young as to be strangers to her, and Uncle Saul in a tuxedo. He had this wavy hair and he looked like an emcee at a nightclub, which was exactly what he was.

"Ooh!" shouted Nadine. "Bring me a Yoo-hoo if they have them!" she fished a quarter out of a coin purse in the shirt she had wadded up beside her. Frannie dutifully took the two bits and hit the trail before any more requests could be lodged.

She walked back up the stairs, up to the sandy path next to the parked cars. The traffic on Ocean Highway beyond the cars was sparse enough that the cars seemed to be rolling out from the horizon as if announced in a fashion show for fins and giant lights, the bigger cars swaying with their own weight, rolling on their suspension and reflecting brilliant gleams of light as they passed.

Frannie read and followed street signs aiming her towards the 200 block, where she knew the café lay. She made out a hotel on the cliff side about a quarter mile up, white with huge balconies and a diagonal elevator carrying tourists down to the beach.

Across from the hotel was a low-slung black building with a great statue in front, holding something in its arms she couldn't make out. From a distance it looked like kind of thing you saw in front of a muffler shop.

That couldn't be it.

Come back.

As she walked along the sidewalk between the cliffs and the street, the place drew closer.

A hot Santa Ana wind blew, making her tingle. For a moment, the café shimmered, and she blinked as the image of whiteness filled her vision, and filtered away as soon as it had come.

That was strange. She blinked away the concern that welled up inside her, a deep, whispering fear that maybe she was suffering from some unknown after-effect of the concussion. She felt fine.

When she reached a hotel on the right, she turned and looked across the two-lane highway.

It wasn't a statue of a mechanic holding a muffler. The stone statue, its mouth stretched wide and its blank eyes wide open as it reared back its head, was a Greek god in a loin cloth, and where its muffler should be it held a long, muscular infant. Frannie recognized it: the statue was Kronos, about to eat the infant Zeus.

A sign leaned against Kronos' feet, black wood painted with white.

CAFÉ MONSTRO. FEED FOR YOUR BODY AND MIND.

Another tingle. It wasn't a concussion coming back to bite her. It was something else. She didn't recognize the feeling; she wasn't that old-world kind either. But the tingle was something more than curiosity, something beckoning, like a voice in the crackle at the end of a record.

Come in, Frannie. Come home.

She tried to blink this away as well. Because that was crazy. Places didn't whisper at you.

Her uncle had asked her. For a moment she wondered if it were possible that the free will they talked about in Hebrew school could fool you, take a hike and say, something else is running us for now, but we're going to just pretend. Was she pretending?

A squat, ugly building with black walls and glass doors. Just two cars in front.

And a tiny voice, dimly remembered: *Come back to the truth, to Emet.* She felt herself shrink.

Enough. She was wigging herself out. Stop it. She put the toes of her sneakers on the edge of the curb and made a decision. She was tired of walking slowly. She was gonna *bound*, now.

"*Cafe Monstro*," Frannie repeated.

She began to move like the athlete she was and had been running from, and determined she would drag her feet no more.

As Frannie reached the door, a woman was coming out of the café and nearly ran into her.

CHAPTER 7

At about the time that his niece was just laying out a towel on the beach and deciding not to soak up rays after all, Saul Cohn heard the door chime in the café.

He emerged through the beaded curtains of the book section to see a silhouette of a woman entering, backlit by the glass doors. The woman stood there for a moment near the reception stand in the dim light, her elbows out and her hands clasped. Saul could make out a jacket and skirt. Not a beachcomber.

At the wall near the stage, Saul's business partner Kurt Macintyre looked at Saul and then at the door, and shrugged. He had a paintbrush in his hand and was hunching his long, lean body over a two-foot tall statue of Donald Duck, applying the eyeballs. Donald was in an executioner's robe.

"Don't stop what you're doing on a visitor's account," Saul said, tipping back the baseball cap he wore.

"You're the people guy." Kurt was already focused once again on his duck statue.

"Yeah." Saul walked with a deliberately jaunty step towards the stranger.

The woman looked about thirty-five, neatly put together with a hat and matching jacket and skirt. Her light hair was pulled back and glistened slightly in the near darkness. She seemed to be taking the place in. She saw Saul, but her attention seemed drawn to one of Kurt's pieces of art. She opened a hand and gestured at it, as though about to ask a question about it but not sure if she should start right off. She moved towards it and Saul offered, "Do you like it?"

"It's... a statue," she managed.

"Mixed media, actually." Saul smiled. Next to the first booth in the cafe, a sculpture stood some eight feet tall. Most of it was a figure in iron, the Frankenstein monster as envisioned by Hollywood, right down to the flat head and little electrodes in his neck. The monster's arms and chest were bare and scarred, its eyes cast upward in St. Stephen-like ecstasy. He was being crucified on a cross of wood, real redwood, polished deep and so silky looking that patrons were tempted to dig their fingernails into it, and sometimes children did. Out of the cross grew tendrils of colored glass, separated in chains of glass and lead, until the tendrils met up with a stained-glass window that hung suspended from the ceiling. The stained-glass window showed the monster again, crawling up a hill, an army of torch-bearing peasants behind him.

"Um," she said.

"I'm Saul Cohn. How ya doin.'" He offered his hand.

She turned away from the monster and saw his hand, said "Oh!" as if suddenly remembering the rituals of society.

Kurt, apparently moved by a possible patron of the arts, had dislodged himself his work and was walking towards them. Saul said, "Kurt, we have a visitor looking at your work." But he couldn't tell if the lady were at all pleased to be here.

If she *wasn't* pleased to be here, then she was here for a reason that wasn't that pleasing. Everything felt just slightly off, Saul thought. Normally when someone came in between lunch and dinner, they made a beeline for the counter where a sign said, "Call us and we'll find you a SPOT!" Or they headed to the book section in the back. This woman was idling like she had walked in and lost her way.

"This is Kurt Macintyre, my partner," Saul said. "He does the art."

"Right." Kurt's pinched, hand-rolled cigarette danced in his mouth as it had for as long as Saul had known him. "I do the art."

"That makes him the useful one," Saul said. "Me, I'm here to class the joint up."

"Of course," she said, cracking a slight smile. "I'm Kali."

"Oh, the goddess of destruction," Saul said automatically.

"I'm sorry?" she looked confused. "Callie, um, Caroline. Caroline Stevens." He heard the spelling to it now.

"Did you want to order lunch?" Saul said, tilting his head towards the booths. "We don't really have the kitchen going but I can get you a sandwich, or sandwiches if you're taking it to a... group."

"She's here about the statue, Saul," Kurt said, a hint of anger in his voice. "Am I right?"

"Ah," Callie said. "Well, as it happens, yes." She clasped her purse in front of her with both hands. "I had to see it for myself."

Oh, Saul thought. "Of course, you saw it in the weekly?" That would have to be the place.

Callie nodded, pulling a folded, crude grocery store weekly from her purse and unfolding it. She looked down at the paper and read in an awkward dullness, "'Hey you *go-heads*, don't forget to cast off your cares and whatever else you like with a sandwich and a beer at *Cafe Monstro*, now open right next to Markie's Trunks and Gear. There's *grub* in the front and books in the back and all manner of daytime nightmares and dreams, and while you're there check out the crucified monster. Proprietors Kurt and Saul call him *THE STATIONS OF THE MONSTER*, but we just call him...'" and here she looked up, "...'swell.'"

Saul winced. "That's not exactly how we would have written an ad."

"The Stations of the Monster?" she asked.

"That's what it's called," Kurt said.

"Like the Stations of the Cross?"

Kurt took a drag without removing the cigarette, smoke billowing as he talked. "That would make sense, wouldn't it?"

"Does it?" she snapped, as though something had escaped from her and she clamped it back. She blinked mightily against the smoke.

"Kurt, take that *meshuge* thing to the bar," Saul laughed. Kurt shrugged and turned, crushing the cigarette in an ashtray on the bar a few yards away. Saul went on, "Like most artists, Kurt doesn't like to talk about the meaning of his work, but I think it's safe to say it's a... you know, a clever commentary on popular culture."

"There are other pieces," Kurt said, gesturing at the walls. Callie's eyes followed his indication to the long line of paintings, not really taking them in, which was just as well. Saul let his own eyes drift across the canvases, some of them abstract, some of them clear nightmares, witches on the gallows, and some that he was hoping she wouldn't see at all.

"Mr. Cohn," she said.

"Saul, by all means."

"Hmm. I have to tell you I represent the Laguna Beach Decency League."

Saul nearly laughed out loud, touched his lips. "I'm sorry?"

Kurt did laugh. "You're *kidding*. What?"

"The Laguna Beach Decen—"

"Is there really such a thing?" Kurt asked.

"Oh, there is," Saul said at once, because though he had never heard of such a preposterous thing as the Laguna Beach Decency League, he could tell that there was one, and Kali the Goddess of Destruction was their long-knived vanguard. In his mind he saw her in full regalia, six arms, a sea of skulls at her feet.

"There is, I have to tell you," Callie said. She stepped back as though they might lunge for her, these two men who Saul thought were probably objectively as threatening as Abbot & Costello. "I have come here to tell you, formally tell you, that the League has lodged a formal complaint with the City Council about this... this piece of sacrilege."

"Formally?" Saul said, amused that she liked the word enough to use it twice so close together. She was probably using it over and over in her mind: be formal. Be strong and formal, Caroline. He peered at the tiny new crow's feet near her eyes and felt as though he could sail past them, and there she was, nervous and tiny, making a speech at the public library, wanting desperately to win a... an elocution ribbon? That seemed right.

Saul didn't think of that as any kind of big magic trick. The ribbon, the need, all of that was true, but he knew it for the same reason he'd been able to make it in the Catskills before he'd found his true calling: he could spin a yarn about anyone he met. Just using what he saw in people. The stuff that lay there for anyone to see.

She wanted so desperately to be formal, did Caroline Matthews, and he probed no further. He was full of warmth for this dangerous woman because he was charmed by her. He reminded himself that that was often a mistake. Many times he underestimated the danger of adults because he wanted to protect the child within them.

"What does a formal complaint entail?" Saul held up a hand to stay Kurt, who he sensed was going to say something a lot less helpful.

"Well," the woman said, relieved to be answering a sensible question. "There will be a hearing, and I have to say the most likely result is that it will need to be removed."

"When is this to be?"

"We haven't set a date, but I would expect a notice before next month's meeting," she said solemnly. Which was no answer at all.

"And, for the sake of argument, what happens if we don't agree that this... I'm sorry," Saul said, trying to find the right track. "It's not sacrilegious, first, but even... I don't even know what that means in a private restaurant."

"I'm sure you can make that argument," she said. "You are free to attend during the open part of the meeting."

Kurt shook his head. "You're asking us to throw it out?"

She shrugged. "Mister Macintyre, I'm sure your business can sustain itself with one less piece of work."

"And what if we say no?"

Callie smiled. "Let's not get to that," she said.

Saul could see it, though, and it didn't take a mind reader. There would be more complaints, and raids, and probably one of the kids they might accidentally sell beer to would turn out to be a cop's son, and there goes the liquor license, and oh, yes, there were lots of ways to take down a local business.

He nodded slowly and shrugged, putting his hands in his pockets. Friendly, like it was all business. "Okay, then. We'll be at the meeting and see how it goes. Now, is there anything else? Would you care for a soda pop?"

She looked at him as though she wasn't sure if he were teasing her. "Actually, there is. Could I have a look at your book section?"

He smiled painfully and nodded, leading her back past the booths. As he glanced back he saw her shaking her head at the paintings, stopping for a moment to stare at Kurt's painting called Massacre of the Ushers, which featured several naked people (with theater usher hats) fleeing a crumbling house afire. It was just abstract enough that you couldn't really see anything, but the imagination did everything one needed to be appalled if you were Kali the Laguna Beach Goddess of Destruction.

They reached a doorway with a beaded curtain, and Saul held the beads back so that Callie could step through them untouched. She wrinkled her nose at the beads as though they were alive with disease.

Beyond the beaded curtain was a room of bookshelves, rather messily arranged but with hand-lettered signs for different sections: TRAVEL and PHILOSOPHY and MYSTERIES. He even stocked best-sellers because travelers often picked up something to read on the beach. Saul swept a hand. "Here we are."

"Hmm," she said, stepping towards the nearest shelf, seeming to idly peruse the volumes. "Where is..."

Where are the banned books? He wanted to say for her, wanting perversely to help her destroy him because the girl inside wanted so much to do well. "What was it you were looking for?"

"I don't know," she said honestly, then caught herself. "Um. DH Lawrence?"

"We don't have any *Chatterley*, I'm afraid," he said. "I wish, actually, because it would sell."

"Well," she laughed. "It would be illegal, though, wouldn't it?"

"You want something illegal?" Saul shrugged. "Sorry."

He tried to picture what it was she was expecting. Maybe some sort of pornographic display, anything but the Agatha Christie novels and *How to Win Friends and Influence People* staring back at her. He turned around and went to the back corner.

"You know, Callie, I may have something for you anyway." Saul looked up at the top shelf, which was lined with a series of unlabeled, brown-leather books. He took one from the end and turned around. As he glanced down at it, the pages were blank.

She took it without thinking, and as she peered at the cover he saw that it now had a gilded title on it. Quickly he read the words upside down: *The Girl Who Spoke Too Late.* Interesting.

Callie Stevens opened the book and looked at the title page. Then she scanned the first page, which Saul saw was printed in a nice and well-kerned font as though typesetter had toiled over the book for weeks.

The words written there were a mystery to Saul, and he did not try to see them or even listen to the persistent thoughts that washed at him off the pages. That *was* more than Catskills storytelling. But he merely watched as the woman ran her hand down the page. After a moment she seemed to sway.

Callie she shut the book, clapping it loudly down on a nearby shelf. "I don't..."

"Is something the matter?" Saul asked.

She touched her head, caught in the half-moment as though awakening suddenly. "I'll see you soon," she said.

"Go safely," Saul stepped out of the book section after she burst through the beaded curtain. She was at the front door before he the curtain had stopped swaying. The bell on the door rang as she tore it open and light streamed in. As Callie/Kali went out, a younger girl was coming in. The girl, another silhouette, stepped out of the way before Callie could run her over. It was his niece.

CHAPTER 8

Frannie nearly ran into the woman coming out of the restaurant. The lady, pretty and dressed like she could easily be a friend of Frannie's mom, seemed all huffy and threw her a look to kill just because Frannie happened to be coming in the door as the lady was going out.

Frannie walked in and immediately saw a whole menagerie of oddness at once: for one thing, there was a crucified Frankenstein monster in mixed media stuck off to the left, and next to it she saw her Uncle Saul and a wiry guy who looked like the kind of artist Gene Kelly was pretending to be in that *American in Paris* movie. The cafe was dark and smoky, with shimmering reflections coming from the tables and booths, and the microphone stands at the humble proscenium far behind them.

Whether it had really whispered to her or not, she loved the

Café instantly.

Uncle Saul and the artist were mainly watching the invisible wake left by the woman, and their look was not pleased or awestruck, which Frannie would have accepted because she'd seen that lady—but more like someone had told them they had six months to live.

Now they both seemed to regard Frannie as though they couldn't believe their show was over and something else was on, like her mom got sometimes when *Edge of Night* went off and then all the sudden you're listening to *The Lone Ranger*, and who in their right mind liked the *William Tell Overture* anyway?

"Hi, fellas!" Frannie swept her hand in a wide arc.

Her uncle looked into the dimness and recognized her as he snapped out of it. He smiled widely and walked fast, sweeping her into his arms. "Hey, little lady! Lemme look at you. Good to see you up and at 'em."

She loved the way Saul talked. Unlike her father, who had grown up in Germany—just as she herself had been born there, though she had no memory of this—Uncle Saul had spent most of his life in the States— first Brooklyn, then the Catskill Mountains, the place where he was the emcee with the wavy hair, all of *that* gone now. Because she had stayed there as a baby, Frannie's mom said Frannie was infected by the lingering chutzpah in the air, "like a fungus." Vague memories. Nothing to hold onto.

Saul sized her up. "Last time I saw you, you were in bed. So what are you, anyway, Frannie, like five foot?"

"That's what I tell people," she said. In fact she was four-foot-ten-and-a-half, and likely to stay there. "Let's just leave it at that."

"Smart," Saul said. "So look! This is the place. Not bad, huh? What can I get you?"

Frannie looked around and before she hit on the lunch counter, some of the paintings caught her eye. She hadn't seen anything like this except in some survey books her pop kept around.

"Saul, this place is—*hey,* what do you have here?" She went past the skinny guy and crawled into a booth, checking out one painting. On it, a man in a red cape was falling off a skyscraper, and a long line of frames in the air followed him down, and through each frame, the background was different, sometimes detailed and sometimes just a swath of murky color.

"I'm supposed to get sandwiches," she said, putting her hands on the back of the booth and kneeling in the slick seats. "You got a real German Expressionism thing going on here. You got egg salad?"

Saul said, "We don't have egg salad between the rushes, it goes bad."

"What do you mean, German Expressionism?" the artist said.

"Okay, what do you have? You got peanut butter and banana?"

"We can do PB&B." Saul said, shrugging. "I think we got ham."

"Nah. Actually—come to think of it, yeah, one ham, but not for me I swear."

"Spare me the put-on *frumkeit.*"

"Yeah, okay. Anyway: one grilled cheese, one peanut butter and banana, one ham and swiss for the shiksa—who *drives* I might add, and boy is she a looker. I should bring her in; she'll brighten up the place." Frannie felt herself motoring on as she bounced out of the booth and checked out more of the art. This place was amazing. She nearly bumped into a table in the center and turned around to see an over-sized sculpture of a telephone, its mouthpiece off the hook and a large, bumpy tongue sticking out.

Forget her imagination and the crazy idea that she was drawn here. This place was the *end*. Why in heck hadn't she thought to visit him before?

She spun around, internalizing that the artist had asked something. "German Expressionism—because of the color, and the odd angles, and then general feel of wholesale unhappiness. Like the unhappiness makes a texture on the painting of the world, like. And that's a little too deep but that's the way with the old GE," Frannie said.

The wiry guy stepped forward, his cigarette dancing in the corner of his mouth as he shook Frannie's hand. "Kurt," he said. "I'm the artist."

"Of course!" Frannie shook his hand and turned back to Saul, who was slapping sandwich fixings on the counter in the dimly lit cafe. "Uncle Saul, I—this place is *neat.*"

"Heh. *Menace to society* I've heard. *Contributing to the delinquency of minors* I've heard. *Neat* you don't hear so much, but great."

"So when you visited me, you said you'd fix me up with something nice."

He looked at her. "You come around some more; I'll put you to work."

The bell hanging on the door rang and someone else came in.

Frannie held her uncle's gaze. "Put me to work? Really?"

"Hey! Who's this?" a male voice said.

Frannie turned around. Standing in the entryway, reaching up to grab an apron hanging on a coat rack, was a boy of about eighteen, lean and muscled, with wide shoulders and cheekbones and shiny eyes. A dream, stepping forward. For the first moment of the last ten minutes, maybe of her life, Frannie was struck dumb.

She decided to step backwards to look cool; she bumped into a booth table and grabbed it behind her, then tried to look casual swinging her knee up to kneel again on the booth seat. But halfway through the maneuver she suddenly felt like she must look like she was about 8 years old fussing around in a restaurant booth, but she was already half committed, so she climbed into the booth and propped her arms again on top, and felt like she was sticking up out of a rabbit hole.

"Frannie Cohn," she said.

"Newpup," the boy said.

"New what?"

Saul, behind the counter, waved a knife between slicing sandwiches.

"*Newpup.* Oh, it's his beach name."

"Surf name," the boy corrected, with a raise of his eyebrows.

"Okay, yeah, he has a surf name. You know, like a code name," Saul said. "In case he gets captured by the Germans or somethin'."

Frannie eyed the boy. "That so? You have a German POW name?"

"What? No," Newpup said, with the most adorable amount of red entering his cheeks. He had a sweet voice, very smooth, like he was a singer. She wanted to hear him read the menu of every place in town. "It's a name—you get a name from the gang when you become a Legionnaire."

"A Legionnaire?"

"That's our surf gang."

"Really?" Frannie said. "That is cool. So are you a waiter?"

Kurt laughed out loud at that and Frannie was about to ask what the gag was when Newpup corrected her all on his own, with a note of annoyance. "I'm the *manager*. These guys just own the place."

"Oh, okay," Frannie said.

"They count on me," Newpup insisted.

"When he's not surfing, we count on him," Saul said.

"But you can call me Newp for short. Everyone does."

"Do they really?"

"So what's up, Saul?" Newpup changed the subject.

"The Laguna Beach Decency League," Kurt said.

"What is *that?*"

Saul slapped several brown-wrapped sandwiches on the counter. "That is trouble, my son."

"This is amazing." Frannie slid out of the booth, waving an arm. "I count three employees and not a soul in the actual restaurant."

"Oh," Newp-for-short turned to her. "It's not always like this. Come back tonight and I'll show you."

CHAPTER 9

And she did go back.

This was a surprise; she had no reason to. She had returned to Carol and Nadine with the sandwiches and made excuses she'd already forgotten, and then after an hour of whistling at the surfers they all came home. At four in the afternoon, she was quite comfortable reading a Connie Blair novel (*The Green Island Mystery*, in fact), and her mother was in the kitchen, humming absently as she fussed with a chicken and half-listening to the problems of the actors on THE EDGE OF NIGHT, which was just coming on.

And it began as a tickle in the back of her head like the early static at the start of a sickness, a tickle that made her fussy and unable to concentrate on her book, unable to find a comfortable way to lay on her bed, unable to relax among the lime-green throw pillows of the couch.

Frannie wandered into the kitchen and sat at the table, listening for a few minutes to her mom's soap opera.

Vus machs da, Frannie, her mother asked. And then a phrase that loosely translated to *you have your head in the clouds.* She concluded with: "Why don't you help me with the potatoes?"

Frannie grabbed a knife and started peeling, and as she cut into the first potato she said, "I'll help—but I'm going out for dinner, Mom. The girls are meeting up Uncle Saul's place near the beach."

"You're seeing your Uncle?" her mom shrugged. "How do you like that? He never visits us, but he gets to see our daughter twice. Maybe he's busy."

"Never can tell," Frannie said.

At five o'clock she got her bicycle from the back yard and pedaled seven miles to the beach. All told, it was a 45-minute ride, not much worse than if one of her friends had driven if traffic had gotten up.

She wore blue Capri pants and an oversized white shirt stolen from her father, and blue sneakers. She parked her bike in front of Cafe Monstro, next to a cactus and snared in the long twilight shadow of Kronos the god-eater.

The parking lot was full of cars, including some truly ancient Model A's, which seemed to be super-popular in the area. Surfboards were stuffed everywhere, sticking out of the back of old Caddies and stacked in the convertible Fords.

Frannie felt a vibration in her collarbone, a fuzz of excitement running up her arm as she approached the darkened glass of the front of the cafe. As she put her hand on the door, she felt the vibration and pulse of the music.

She tore the door open and entered another world.

#   #   #

First there was chatter—countless boys and girls gathered at the counter and sprawling all over the booths. She saw Kurt the artist personally whisking a tray of empty soda glasses towards the sink, and behind the counter, Saul was taking orders and slapping them onto a turnstile that spun around into the kitchen. The conversation was loud and full of laughter, and my god, she saw more giant backs and shoulders than she had ever seen in her life. This was not a no-shirt-no-shoes kind of place.

And then there was music. Frannie stood for a moment next to the crucified monster and found herself transfixed by the singers up on the stage at the back, just opposite the beaded curtain on the door that said BOOKS 4 YR ENJOYMENT.

On the stage were two girls: one was a trim, tall black girl in a pink dress with white gloves like one of the Chiffons. Her white-skinned partner was strange, though; wearing a red-patterned full flannel nightgown, her hair done in a big helmet of blondness. On reflection, going out in a flannel nightgown might be all right.

They were singing a song Frannie didn't know, but everyone in the audience seemed to, because when Newp suddenly called from the middle of the room, "Everybody!" everybody did.

The Old 49 is Coming

The Old 49 Won't Stop

It's Gonna Be the One for Us

It's Gonna be the One.

Newp emerged in her vision as if bursting from a vase. "I told you it would be different." He took her hand and dragged Frannie towards a booth where a group of four boys and a pair of girls all listened to the music and generally dug the scene. The boys all had that same surfer look that Frannie had to admit made her stomach flip.

One of the boys had black hair buzzed real short, and he pounded the table as Newp led Frannie over. A basket of fries near his fists jumped. The fries jostled and fell back to earth. "Hey, you bring us some fresh meat?" he called as Frannie sat in the space across from him.

"Lay off, T-Bone," Newpup said. "This is Frannie, she's a nice girl."

"Speak for yourself, cha-cha," Frannie said, trying on as wisenheimer a voice as she could manage. One of the girls—about eighteen and stacked in a lavender swimsuit—jostled the boy next to her over so Frannie could take a seat.

T-Bone laughed heartily and howled, and next to Frannie, another boy who had his hair bleached nearly white, like a lot of the sand bums did, slapped a high five with T-Bone. When he dropped his hand, he let it brush against Frannie's shoulder, a little close like he was really reaching for a feel, and Frannie squirmed. She got up, making eye contact with Newp, who was coming back from another table.

"Thanks, Newp, but I gotta go."

Newp threw the boy next to her a look. "Creasy, you hassling the young lady?"

"So who is this kid?" the girl next to Creasy asked.

Newp smiled. "Ah! She's the new waitress, is what Saul said."

"What?" Frannie looked at Newp. "What are you talking about?"

Truth to tell she wanted a job, but just like that?

"But not tonight," Newp told her. "Saul wants you to get to know the place. Hey, have a seat. Sheila, get between Frannie and your animal boyfriend, all right? Jeez."

"Who are those guys?" Frannie asked. In another booth were two gentlemen, both in their late twenties or so. They dressed square as Frannie's pop and maybe squarer; they worse slacks and long-sleeve shirts, and though they had no ties on, they seemed to Frannie's mind to be regretting it. They drank coffee.

Saul was setting a plate of fried pickles on the table and said, "That's

Mutt and Jeff."

"Mutt and Jeff?"

Newp bent closer. "They're undercover police officers. But it's okay; they tip all right and they don't make a scene. I think they like the place."

Sheila turned to Frannie and gave her shoulder a squeeze. "So where are you from?" Her voice was high but full and warm.

"We live in Laguna Beach," Frannie said.

"Born around here?"

"Nope, Germany. But I try not to tell people that because they like to ask if I was a Nazi."

"People are maroons," Newp said.

Frannie couldn't stop looking around the room. Shadows danced off the sculptures and the paintings, the air pungent with fried clams and fried pickles and fried potatoes. She smelled vinegar and catsup, fish and suntan oil.

"Who's the band?" Frannie asked, "They're the most!"

"Mm," Sheila said, pointing a languid hand past Frannie at the singers on the stage. "Okay, so Newp puts the band together and manages them. Sometimes he plays guitar. The blond girl in the nightgown, that's Betty—she's Newp's sister—and the colored girl is Truly."

"Newp's sister?"

"Yeah."

"She looks…" Frannie studied the freckled blond and tried to find the word.

"Odd? Don't let the nightgown trip you up. She just… likes to wear soft things."

"Like all the time?"

"Far as I know."

"Likes to or has to?"

When the girl shrugged Frannie said, "I don't know, I was gonna say she looks… sweet."

Truly and Betty were in perfect harmony now, working their way through a Les Baxter song that Frannie had heard playing on some of the radios in the hospital.

O Sinnerman, where you gonna run to all on that day?

New music was full of a heck of a lot of this Christian judgment day talk, which was strange and exotic to Frannie. But God it was beautiful.

The Lord said Sinnerman, the sea will be a boilin',

O Lord won't you hide me all on that day?

Something caught Frannie's eye—Uncle Saul was standing at the beaded curtain in the back, talking to a man in a tweed jacket and tie.

The room through the beaded curtains shimmered like a liquid pool for a second, an illusion that Frannie shook off. Over the door, a sign said BOOKS FR YR PLEASURE.

She rose, walking towards the back.

\# \# \#

Frannie stuck her head next to her uncle's shoulder and spoke softly. "What is this?"

Saul moved out of the way and Frannie looked past him to see what she expected from a book section: high shelves lining a small room. Books crammed in every corner, but less messy than some little book shops she'd wandered into.

The man in the tweed jacket was browsing and suddenly gasped, grabbing a book off a shelf that said Performing Arts. He held the book up. "*Look* at this."

"What'd you find?" Frannie asked.

"This, my dear, is a novelization of Val Lewton's I WALKED WITH A ZOMBIE. That's a real rarity," the man said, scratching his moustache and adjusting his thick glasses before continuing. "I haven't seen this since— well, I did see one once." He trailed off.

"Where?" Saul was trying to sound mildly curious, but Frannie could hear an insistent tone just at the edge.

Family. Every inflection tells a history. She didn't know what it meant, why anyone would care deeply about someone's random memory about something so minor.

The man thought for a second as he looked at the cover, which showed a woman walking through the woods in a billowy, shimmery dress like Frannie had never actually seen a person wear except in old movies. The man's eyes searched the book and seemed to look past it, holding it as thought it might disappear into dust if touched incorrectly. "Paris," he finally said. "I saw it in Paris. That's funny because it's in English, you know? I mean, there weren't a lot of English bookshops in Paris. Not standing."

The man looked up. "I'm sorry," he said suddenly, reaching out a hand. "It's Forrest. How rude of me."

Saul shook his hand. "You collect books, Mr. Forrest?"

"Forrest is my first name." the man said. "But my friends call me Forry."

"Are you from around here?" Frannie asked. She didn't think so.

"No, gosh," Forry said. "I come from back East."

"What brought you to LA?"

Forry's eyes twinkled. "All my friends are here."

Frannie gasped. "You make movies?" Her pop was a screenwriter sometimes. She was fascinated by all that jazz.

"No, I do a little journalism here and there." He waved his hand as though it were too complicated and wearisome to talk about. Frannie found this fascinating about adults. Ask a kid who they are, and they tell you; ask an adult and it's all just too much.

Forry looked around. "This is a heck of a collection."

Saul said, "You know, I may have something you'd be interested in."

He nudged Frannie and brought her to the back shelf.

Frannie took the opportunity to whisper to her uncle. "Did you tell Newpup that I'm gonna be waitressing here?"

"Well, aren't you?"

"I don't recall ever discussing it."

"What, your summer is so exciting that you can't work for your uncle?" Forry said, interrupting. He smiled, looking like a jolly middle-aged elf.

"Maybe I just want to work around the books," Frannie said.

"Why don't you hand Forry one of those books there," Saul said, pointing at the top row. "One of the black ones."

Frannie pulled one down (this took some straining, but she managed it) and turned back to Forrest. As she did so she caught the smell of pipe tobacco and, oddly, pumpkin pie. The book had no title. A notebook? Maybe Saul had Forry pegged for one of those writers who hung out in cafes all day. He was that, but he was too square, really, with the black slacks and jacket and tie. She handed the blank book to Forrest.

And then she swore that as Forrest opened the book, words appeared on the pages. One moment they were blank—exactly like the notebook she expected—and the next, there was writing there. Forry was reading as though he saw nothing odd at all; he was skimming a book someone had handed him. But no doubt about it: Frannie saw the writing fall into place.

Forry ran his hands down the title page and read aloud: *"All the Good*

Monsters in Hiding." He froze for a moment, and uttered a tiny, sad little exhalation of breath.

Frannie stood as close as she dared and looked at the pages, and then the world at the edges of the page disappeared and she—

CHAPTER 10

Because now we are, now I am in Paris, actually just outside the city, and I am freezing.

I am a tired and worn Private First Class in the US Army infantry and the cold emanating from the streets of Paris freezes our breath, freezes the sweat on our tongues and makes it hard to talk. My feet are numb, and my toes are in agony because I stepped in a puddle and the water has frozen through my boot, and somewhere far away I realize I will feel this cold somehow for the rest of my life. Some things will never go away.

Snow piles high at the curbs. Bombs have not fallen here this evening and townspeople move about, scurrying to local merchants who stay open to sell bread and cheese and sausage. The Germans still hold Paris, but they are falling even now, and these are the ugliest times. The bombs still fall, and the result is always ugly.

I am walking past a park with snow against rosebushes and pass a small church, and then I hear the whistle of bombs and run for shelter. I burst through a church door and find myself in a stairwell alone, with the church basement below. In the cold stairwell I get the feeling of people waiting because generally you get that after a while, and when I get to the basement, I expect to see men and women and children but instead I see monsters.

The Frankenstein Monster, tall and lean and patched together, the Wolf Man, the Hunchback of—the Hunchback of Notre Dame! Alive as late as 1945! The Phantom of the Opera. A seven-foot golem, surely not The Golem of Prague, but who can say?

"We came here to escape the bombs," the Monster tells me in English. He speaks many languages. "But now we fear to leave this basement because the townsfolk will murder us. Is it not so?"

What is it about Monsters? Not the ugly kind we see each day, the Nazi commandants and the perverted teachers. But these Monsters—the ones I know and would die for. As bombs fall, we set at a church table and drink wine that Hunchback liberated from somewhere. These monsters have been forgotten because horror is all around us, we have supped full with horrors and these Monsters lurk not in our darkest recesses. They only reflect our innocence now.

What will we do?

The next day I must leave, and I tell the Monsters so. "Come with me, I will smuggle you out," *I say, reaching for the ridiculous. But the Frankenstein Monster refuses for his clan.*

"I will remember you," I say. Already I hear the whistle of more bombs and I must go. "I will never forget you. I will preach your gospel; I will make hearts sing of Monsters."

The Frankenstein Monster nods. The Phantom looks up, hearing the whistle of the bombs. He sings, then—Sea Drift, a lovely modern opera, O Soul of sea foam and death, death, death.

The golem lights a cigar and gives me one, and I take it from the giant clay man and go.

I find my way back to barracks by evening and sleep like the dead, dead, dead. When morning comes, I am roused awake—and I feel the rest of my life coming. Months later I return to the church, but it is rubble and husk.

I will sing of the Monsters forever.

CHAPTER 11

Forry didn't say anything after what Frannie and he saw together. At once she became aware that he was walking out through the beaded curtain; he kept going until he was out of the cafe.

"What do you think he's going to do?" Frannie asked Saul.

Saul turned to her after the front door finished chiming and sighed. "Something wonderful."

"What, uh, what just happened?"

"Did something happen?" He cocked his head and it glistened in the darkened room.

"I can't describe it."

"Blanks," Saul said. "The books are called Blanks."

"I thought—I could have sworn I saw things in…"

"In the blank pages. I wondered, ya know," Saul said. "But I could tell. Your pop, he doesn't see it. So it goes. Do you want to work for me?"

"What makes you think I want to work *here?*"

"You want to know more?" Her uncle looked at her and she found herself nodding.

"Come on, what is it?" she asked. "Is it a parlor trick?"

"Can you start tomorrow?"

She thought of the vision and the man leaving to do something wonderful, it was all jazz, but it was jazz that dared to be something more and happiness washed over her. "Absolutely! Marvy—I'll be here."

She wandered out of the book section and into the restaurant, the music filling her ears; Truly and Betty were singing another Kingston Trio song, "Ballad of the John B," but Frannie was lost in the reverie of the blank books and the story she had heard, whispering in her head like someone on her shoulder, reading a book to her. The restaurant was swinging, and she barely noticed it as she stopped by a sculpture of the 12 Apostles re-imagined as versions of Vincent Price in *The Fly*.

"Hey!" the girl Newp had introduced to her as Sheila yelled out, and at first Frannie thought the girl was calling to her, but there was an edge of anger in the voice, and as Frannie looked over she saw the girl pushing a guy she hadn't met yet, a boy in a letter sweater like Archie Andrews, who snarled as Sheila drenched him in grape soda.

Newp was running from the stage towards their booth with a towel over his shoulder.

The boy howled and called the girl something ugly.

"Hey, Dick, language." Newpup waved his hands with some theatricality. "This is a family place. Why don't you have a seat and I'll get you something?"

"Who the fuck does she think she is?" the letter-sweater boy called Dick said.

"Really I have no idea," Newp answered. "And again, language."

Dick grabbed Newp by the collar of his white work shirt, "And who the fuck do you think *you* are?" He dragged Newp towards him, stepping back as he did so. Frannie stuck out a foot. It seemed like the logical thing to do.

Dick went sailing backwards into a tray of Coke bottles and straws.

Mutt and Jeff, the two undercover cops, rose, and then looked at one another as they realized there wasn't really a reason for them to get involved in a drunk teen falling over himself. Frannie and Newp both gave Mutt and Jeff hand-waved permission to recede once again.

Dick was flailing in a rage on the floor and Newp immediately reached forward to help him up, and the boy shook off his help, crawling up and wet with coke, red in the face and staggering drunk.

Dick shook a finger at Newp and pulled off his letter sweater, then put up his fists, ready to go for Round 2. Frannie put her hand on Newp's chest to hold him back and also kind of because she really wanted to.

"Out, Mr. Stewart," came the voice of Uncle Saul, who grabbed Dick by the shoulder and steered him towards the door. As they went Saul winked at her, and Frannie could hear him telling Dick he was welcome to come back when he was sober.

Frannie took Newp's towel and dropped to start to sop up the soda.

"That was crazy!" said Betty, who came down from the stage and crouched next to Frannie.

"You don't have to do that," Newp offered.

"No, I feel like it's my fault."

Betty looked at Newp. "Did you see what she did? She sent him across the room."

"She tripped him is what she did," Truly agreed as she arrived.

"Is that normal?" Frannie looked up as Truly and Betty and Newp started stacking fallen glasses. "The drunk part."

"Eh," Newp said. "But hey, you haven't even had a shift yet and you know how to run the place."

"Well, I have mean cousins," Frannie said.

"That's a lie," Saul said as he returned with a tub and a broom for the broken glass.

Betty looked at her brother. "You're gonna do something nice for her."

"O…kay," Newp said. "I can get you something."

"No, you goof," Betty said. "Surfing. Take her surfing."

Newp nodded. "Okay." He turned back to Frannie. "Tomorrow, before work. We take you surfing."

CHAPTER 12

Forrest, the man who had had the vivid memory of his time in France, pulled his jacket closer about him, still shaken and haunted by what he had read in the book. He walked for an hour along the beach, then strode slowly back to his car amid the big noise of the waves, and drove away.

Nearby, a ghost stalked once more.

There was no bonfire tonight, but there were a bunch of kids hanging out by and in their cars, perched near a hot dog stand not far from the Laguna Riviera, on the cliff above the beach, across the street from the Cafe Monstro.

At 11:45, Darla Delaney, who wore her black hair short and up like a Busby Berkley swimmer, sipped a coke that one of the boys had brought her. Hooky, a lean, bronze-colored surfer who seemed older than everyone else but whose voice gave her shivers, chatted her up until she broke off from the cars and they wandered down the stairs next to the hotel and out near the water.

"So you're a student?" Hooky had his muscular arm around her shoulder.

"Mm-hmm," she said, tiptoeing in the sand, her shoes in one hand and the other brushing against his flat stomach, walking so close that she could feel the hairs of his brown legs against hers.

"What do you study?" They stopped at the edge of the water and he kissed her neck, the surf crashing so loudly she could hardly hear him.

"Sociology," she said, and breathed as he kissed her jaw. "You?"

"I'm studying right now," he said.

She pulled away, laughing. "Let's swim."

They ran into the waves, Darla dropping her shoes and laughing giddily as foam lapped at her legs. She dove and swam, and came up again, and after a moment Hooky broke through the surface. He held her waist and kissed her, their mouths searching, and then they broke away and dove like porpoises.

Darla swam through dim light, seeing Hooky's muscular legs pumping in the water away from her. She hung in the water for a moment, letting the bubbles go from her mouth, sinking a little.

A faint shimmer rose in the water far below her where the sand swept away into the dark. She floated, brushing her arms sideways to keep her place, transfixed by the strange glow as it came closer.

A girl with long, black hair and glowing white skin rose towards her. Her hair floating around her like an undulating mane. She had black eyes that glimmered in the dark and as the stranger reached out her arms, Darla had visions of an octopus she had seen in a film in grade school.

The stranger's shape began to flow and change. Darla screamed as it showed its razor teeth and pulled her into the deep.

CHAPTER 13

Frannie pedaled home far later than she had expected, bursting with energy—she had been offered a job and a surfing lesson in one night! She barely noticed the miles go by, the busy Ocean Highway giving way to quieter streets with white-washed houses, people turned in for the evening. There were still a few kids, real kids as opposed to the ones on the beach, playing in the street, but any moms calling them home had fussed and given up hours ago. summer yielded soft discipline in the suburbs.

A job and a surf lesson. It was as though the people at her uncle's place had just handed her a life.

"Over my dead body!" her father wailed. Marc Cohn, who had come to the United States as an adult, spoke fantastic English but was a great student of clichés and tried them out on Frannie whenever he found one.

He would tell her daily to *not take any wooden nickels,* and disappointments were *cookies that crumbled.*

"Who are these people?" her mother looked at her from the kitchen table, her wire-rimmed glasses up over her head. Sally Cohn was a serious looking but seriously beautiful woman. She had a past that Frannie only vaguely understood. Now she was a professor of physics at the same place where her pop taught.

The scientist and the literature professor looked to Frannie like tired old people who didn't have the faintest clue why their daughter was bouncing up and down and chattering to them about Saul and the Legionnaires and the singers and the beach. Pop was eating an egg and onion sandwich and he set it down, waiting for Frannie to answer the question.

"They're *Uncle Saul's* people," Frannie said. "Come on. He wants me to work for him."

Pop shrugged. "That's not so bad. A girl should work for her uncle; it's good business."

"I'm saying," Frannie said.

"What kind of place is this?" Mom asked. "Marc, don't get ahead of yourself. We've never even been there."

"We've only been *here* a while," Frannie offered.

Mom continued, "Well, Saul had that other place up the coast when he was married. I went there once before we moved here. But this new place.

They don't have dancing girls, do they?"

"Yes," Pop asked. "Do they have dancing girls?"

Frannie wrinkled her nose. "What, are you crazy? It's a cafe that sells sandwiches and teenagers sing in bands. But I'll be sure and make the suggestion." She changed tack. "Come on. You were at me all month to get back out of the house." This was true, she realized, even though ever since she'd run to Saul's at the beach she'd felt so… *energized* that she had barely thought about the accident.

"We need to ask your brother to come over," Mom said to Pop. "In thanks at the very least."

Pop offered up a hand, *Sure.*

Frannie jumped again. "It's the neatest cafe in Laguna Beach."

Mom eyed her. "You know all the cafes in Laguna Beach?"

"They have coffee and music and sculpture and books and *ooh*, it's just fantastic," Frannie said.

"I'll bet there's a boy," Mom said.

Frannie was stumped by that.

"Of course," her pop said. "A surfer boy and they probably all go around shirtless in that place."

"Darling, do the boys wear shirts?" Mom asked.

"I think it's a rule," Frannie answered solemnly. She was careful not to mention the fight that had started and that she had actually gotten involved in, or the undercover cops, which didn't seem to speak well of the place. Or the sculptures that had everyone all tizzied up. "Mom, look, this is a great summer I'm talking about. I could spend it following my friends to the beach or I can work for Saul—I know I'll get more out of the cafe, I just know it." She couldn't help that when she got worked up, she started to shriek a little bit, but there it was.

"Well," her mom said. "Just be careful. Saul's okay and he can look after you. But Frannie," and here she leveled a dishrag at her, "a lot goes on around the beach, and you don't know what people really want from you sometimes."

She was up with the chickens to pump it out to the beach. She realized she had no idea when she was supposed to meet Newpup, so she got to the beach at 8:30 and wandered around the curve of cliff and sand below the Hotel Riviera. She could have thrown a baseball high and hard up the cliff and over Ocean Highway and hit Saul's cafe, she figured.

Newp and his friends showed up at 9:30 and immediately started hitting the waves, all of them with those lean looks that made Frannie practically swoon. But Newpup stayed with her and led her back to a bunch of boards at a little workshop area next to a wooden hut. He chose a board and began walking with Frannie back towards the waves.

"Saul knows people," Newpup said, as though answering a question he'd asked himself. "If he wants you as a waitress, that's good enough for me."

"What are they doing?" Frannie asked, looking out at the surfers in the water. She and Newp had stopped at the water's edge. There was a wide expanse of choppy water, and then beyond that, where the water got calm, all the surfers had lined up, sitting on their boards, looking out to the horizon. To Frannie they seemed like a string of jewels, the facets of their shoulders sparkling with water.

"Looking for waves," Newpup said. "Come on."

They waded out to the water and Newp dropped the board down and straddled it. Then he swiveled back and gestured to her. "Climb on."

Frannie got on the board—it was more buoyant than she expected, and smooth, all covered in fiberglass like a boat. She held on with both hands as though it would start bucking in a second, and he tapped the section of board between them. "Get closer," he said. "Against my back."

She slid forward until her chin was sideways against the middle of Newp's shoulder blades.

This was a little closer to this boy than she had anticipated being this particular morning, and she felt dry in the mouth, sure that he could hear her heart beating against his back muscles.

"Okay, Frannie," Newp looked back and stopped, watching her face. "We're gonna paddle. Paddle fast because we gotta get over the breakers."

She dipped her hands into the water and mimicked Newp as he leaned over and started paddling hard and fast with his hands scooped. She paddled the same, the water splashing around her legs. The little breaker waves started coming, hard and galloping. She paddled on, hearing Newp breathing hard.

"A few more yards!" Newp called, and she paddled, but for a second she closed her eyes to listen to the chopping sound of the water. Finally they broke over and slid across the water, into the calm beyond, not far behind the line of surfers looking out west.

Frannie sat up and turned to look back towards the beach and the hut, and the Riviera Hotel a few hundred yards beyond that.

"You're not even winded," Newp said.

Frannie looked away from the beach and smiled at Newp. "Why should I be winded?"

"This paddling is a —it's tough," he said, awkwardly avoiding some curse or another.

"Boy are you a chauvinist," Frannie laughed. "If you must know, I'm a pretty avid cyclist, and my mom made we swim ever since I was born. Plus a lot of cross-country skiing. So no, I'm not winded. *Oy.*"

He raised an eyebrow and waved his hands in surrender. "Okay."

They paddled until they got in next to the line of surfers, about ten or twelve of them. Newp seemed to know them all and they all hooted at him.

"Hey, Newp, who's the guppy?"

"You bring one for me?"

"Does she have a sister? I mean like a *big* sister."

"This is Frannie," Newp said. He turned back to her. "You have a sister?"

"Not around here," Frannie said. She did have a sister, Dolores, who was off in Chicago.

"You robbin' the cradle, Newp?" one of the boys said.

Newp waved his hands. "Nah, she works for—"

"Surf's up!" another boy shouted, and Frannie looked out to the ocean to see, indeed, a wave rolling in.

"Okay," Newp said. "Hold onto the board. We're gonna paddle and grab it."

"Grab it?" she said. "But we're facing it."

He bucked in the board and they started to turn sideways. "Paddle sideways to it, come on." And they were paddling southward as the wave rolled, unbroken, a swell that even now was starting to lift them. She felt the power of the rolling water as it pushed them and everything around them five feet higher.

"Okay, stay there," Newp said, and he tilted and paddled and now they were pointed back towards shore, the wave lifting them, and Newp suddenly sprang to his feet, one foot in front of the other, arms spread for balance.

They were riding on the wave. Frannie heard the water smacking fast against the underside of the board as Newp guided them down.

It lasted just a few seconds, sliding in towards shore, until they reached the chop and then her toes were touching the sand below them.

"Ha!" Newp jumped into the water and held the board. "How's *that*."

She laughed and looked back at the waves, which shimmered and sparkled. She wanted to feel the waves again. "That was... "

"You want to go again?"

"*Do* I!" She laughed.

But just then there erupted a bunch of cheers, all the gang making agitated sounds and even beating their chests. They all were running to shore.

Newp's eyes traveled back to the beach to the little hut next to the shaping tables and he and Frannie walked the few yards to the sand in silence. Someone had emerged from the hut and stood there in silence, drinking in the sand and the sun.

"What's going on?"

"Someone for you to meet," Newp said.

Her first thought was that he looked like Tarzan, golden-tan and brown-haired, with shoulders and back muscles like a Corvette and blue eyes that blazed and flashed, sad and wise. He wore a straw hat and cutoff denim pants, no shirt, and a necklace of shells and shark's teeth.

Several of the guys had fallen to their knees and were stretching out their arms, saluting him like a tribal chief. "He is awakened!" one of them said. "Lo, he approaches!" this guy, who had coke-bottle glasses and blond hair, was the same joker who had called her *Guppy*.

The fellow in the straw hat didn't respond, but held out a hand and someone almost magically put a beer in it. He tipped the beer and caught sight of Newp and Frannie about twenty feet away. He winked. The joker *winked*, like Superman.

Frannie had had enough of this absurd display. "Newp, are ya gonna introduce me to your friend?"

"Oh, sure, Frannie," Newp said. "This is Hooky—short for *Hookele*, but we call him Hooky."

"Hookele?"

"It means great chief," the coke-bottle kid said. "Hookele is the chief of all the boardsmen, the lord of the surfers, he travels the world looking for waves. He toils not but for the surf and eats not but to sustain his surfing."

"Well, Byron," the great chief said, "I don't know about all that."

"Are these your worshippers, Lord Hookele?" Frannie said. She was nervous as he turned the slightly crinkled eyes—*how old was this guy?*—towards her, and it came out in toughness.

"They're my friends," he said, and his eyes caught her teasing, but it all slid off like water on fiberglass.

"That's right, we're Hooky's Legionnaires," said Newp. "Hooky, we're teaching Frannie here to surf."

"That's nuts," one of the boys said. "We don't bring dates by day."

"I'm not a date," Frannie said. She looked at Newp, smiling. "I'm *not* a date, am I a date?"

"I—you," Newp said. That was helpful.

"Girls don't surf Laguna," one of Hooky's boys said. "That's just the way it is; this is peaceful ground."

"I don't know," Hooky said. "How'd you wind up with this loser, Angel?"

"She works at Cafe Monstro and made some friends and some enemies while helping me," Newp said. "I owed her one."

"So you're gonna pay in surf lessons." Hooky concluded. He tilted his head, studying Frannie's entire four-eleven frame. Then he turned to another boy, who had been silent all the while. "Go-Go! We have a board for her?"

Go-Go pursed his lips. "Maybe. I made one for my nephew. It's banged up, but eh."

"Throw her back, Hooky," one boy said. "We got a good thing here and she's too small yet."

"Hey," Hooky snapped a finger. "Respect." He looked back at Newp and Frannie. "I guess we'll see what you can do."

Frannie throbbed with relief and hadn't the slightest idea why.

Hooky continued, turning to another boy, "Go-go, see if we have a board that will fit. Something light. It needs to—"

A scream cut across the beach.

While everyone else had startled or jumped, Hooky had merely grimaced and started to run towards the scream. Newp was next and the pair led the rest of them along the cliffs.

Frannie was close behind, wincing with what felt like hundreds of tiny cuts from shells in the sand. When they came around the bend in the cliffs, she saw Truly, the girl from Newp's band.

Truly was crouched in the sand with her hand over her mouth, and at her feet was what looked at first like a mound of seaweed until Frannie saw a girl's arm stretched out from it. It was a girl, all right, her blanched face looking out from below her own hair and a mound of weeds.

Truly grabbed the girl and lifted its shoulders, crying, and when Frannie saw the body's bare breasts she ran forward to put herself between the body and the boys. It just seemed like the thing to do. A terrible thing to be exposed like that, the least you can hope for is someone to stick up for you.

"We need to call the police," Hooky said.

Frannie turned back to Truly, sitting right next to this dead body. *That* wasn't freaking Frannie out yet, but the white lips and the blue skin would come back hard to her later, she knew. "Truly," she said, looking away from the body. "Who is this, do you know this girl?"

"It's Darla," Truly said, her voice shaking. "She's a college girl, I've talked to her, you know, a lot. *Ugh,* my God, she was a swimmer, she was a good swimmer."

Newp had come closer. "Well," he said, "you and I both know that even a good swimmer can get caught in seaweed or get confused, get caught in a riptide, I mean, you can get bonked on the head by a boat."

"I'll call from Saul's," Frannie said. She ran up the first stairway she found and then headed south on Ocean Highway, past blinding chrome fins and cars. She reached the Hotel Riviera and ran across to the Cafe, the asphalt burning her feet. She burst in and found her uncle and his phone. Someone was dead.

The next few hours were a blur for Frannie. The police came in giant black monster cars that seemed like surfboards of their own, black uniforms that couldn't possibly be comfortable in this heat.

Above the beach, Frannie waited at the side of the highway with Newp and Hooky as a crowd gathered on the beach. Newp had called for his sister, and Betty was with Truly now.

Saul had gone down to the beach since the call had come from his place, and now he looked up the cliff and gestured for the three up there to come down.

"You see anything?" one cop asked Hooky. Hooky said no and showed the cop a card he pulled from the back of his cut-offs, probably his driver license, and it vaguely struck Frannie as funny to imagine Hooky waiting in line at some DMV somewhere. "You a little old for this crowd?" the cop said.

"Twenty-eight," Hooky said. "Is that too old?" Then he glanced at Frannie and she felt a little dirty for him.

"What happens now?" Truly asked, stepping forward and away from Betty.

The cop turned to Saul, which Frannie took as a sign that the cop was done talking to kids. "I think she'll be taken to County—do you know if there was anyone…"

"She has a brother in the Army," Truly said. "In Alabama."

The cop addressed Saul. "Maybe we can get the info."

Saul said, "You know, just because you ignore her does not mean she ceases to exist," he said, tilting his head at Truly.

"You're busting my chops already?" the cop said. "You got a restaurant up there? I can have some people check it out."

Saul shrugged. "I hear ya."

Soon the coroner's station wagon arrived, brilliant white and so low-slung it nearly scraped the asphalt. Serious young men in white coats emerged and made their way down to the beach and soon had the body on its way back up in a litter like Frannie had seen before only in movies like *All Quiet on the Western Front*. These guys worked fast.

And then they were gone and so was most of the day. Frannie realized she hadn't even worked out a schedule yet, but when she went to her uncle, he patted her shoulder and said he'd see her tomorrow.

Her bike turned out to be busted. Probably a cop car had clipped it; the rear tire was flat, and the rim seemed like it was a little crooked, to boot. Newp came out of the cafe and found her near the Kronos statue with her sorry wheels. Hooky and a bunch of the Legionnaires were heading into the cafe, and Frannie looked at them expectantly, not sure whom she could ask. Newp was quick, though. "You have a ride?"

The pack stopped. T-Bone looked back and said loudly, "I'll give her a ride," and Hooky cut that off with a swipe of his hand.

"I don't have a car myself," Hooky said. His face looked dark and distant. "Newp can give you a ride, maybe."

Newp nodded and gestured for Frannie to follow him. His apron flitted in the breeze as he walked towards his car parked at the edge of the lot next to the highway. She started to follow, then noticed Truly standing in the lot next to Betty, upset to the bone still, swaying like she was about to fall over. Frannie took Truly by the hand and they found their way to Newp's car.

Newp had a nearly new Corsair convertible with a big trunk, and Frannie tossed her bike into it as she told Newp where she lived. Then Betty rode in the front while Frannie and Truly rode in the back in silence. As they pulled out, Truly looked out the window and Frannie leaned her head on Truly's shoulder. Truly started to cry.

Newp looked at them through the rear-view. "You know, I saw her. Darla. She was at the bonfire the other night."

"Does that really happen?" Frannie asked. "People just get caught in seaweed and drown?"

Newp shook his head, not *no* but *who knows*. Betty still hadn't said a word, but she turned in the seat and put her arm back, laying a hand on Frannie's arm. When they got to Frannie's place, it was dark, and Truly was sleeping.

Frannie pulled the bike out of the trunk of Newp's car and began to wobble the poor thing up the walk.

"How you planning to get to work tomorrow?" Newp asked.

"I don't know," Frannie said, bone-weary.

"First real day," Newp said. "Can't miss that."

"Yeah."

Betty stuck her head out. "Oh, I'll drive her." She rolled her eyes, but she sounded warm. Newp and Betty, Frannie realized, always sounded warm.

The porch lights flickered, and Frannie saw that the lights in the kitchen were on. It was around eight o'clock. "But you don't work in the morning," Frannie said. "And neither does Newp."

"Well," Betty got out, leaning on the car door and putting a hand on the ragtop. "Riding with my brother wouldn't be proper, would it? Just let me, Frannie. Truly will come too. It'll be our pleasure."

"Where does Truly live?"

"With her," Truly spoke up, having woken up. "For the summer while we work on the band."

Betty said, "You see? We're already on an adventure. Let us take you to work."

Frannie ran back to the car and hugged Betty. Frannie walked towards the house and rummaged for her keys. All of this felt so strange, like she had barged into someone's diary. She didn't feel like one of them, more like someone who had fallen into their laps.

"Hey," Newp said as she crossed the headlight beams of the convertible. "Don't look like it's something you did. It's sad; that's all. It's just something sad and it doesn't have to make you feel anything more than that. Now we'll see you tomorrow and that will be great."

She was gonna bound. That had been her decision when she had spotted the Café Monstro for the first time. No more convalescing. She was gonna bound. Frannie turned back to him at her door. "Okay. You got it."

She entered the house where her parents waited.

"I don't understand," Pop said. To Frannie, the form in the living room chair resembled the lion in Aesop's fables, lying in wait. The cherry of his cigarette at the end of his hand was a glowing claw.

Frannie's mother wore her robe with a collar that shimmered in the moonlight as she leaned in the kitchen doorway.

"Don't understand..." Frannie responded.

"You left on your bicycle," her mom said. "You don't call all day. Did you work?"

"Of course I did," Frannie said, flushing.

"Why didn't you ride your bike home?"

"My bike got hit in the parking lot," she said. Just a moment, there, where she thought through it all. She looked in her mom's face and saw only worry, and she looked at her father and saw he was no lion. There would be secrets to keep, but this was not one. She realized she was going to tell them the whole story of the police who ran it over, and the girl found on the beach.

# # #

Hours later in her room, Frannie tossed and rose, standing in the dark, the reflection of her blue nightshirt flickering in the window. She turned on the radio and for a moment looked out the window and swore she could hear the ocean as the Everly Brothers sang "All I Have to Do is Dream."

Then something in the driveway caught her eye. Something that was about pencil length, maybe, and at first it sparked, or glowed, she wasn't sure, and then went dark again. *What the heck?* She pressed her face against the window.

It looked like a flute, or something like that. Whatever. She should go back to bed. She had to work in the morning and--

She put her sandals on and crept down and outside, off the porch and around the bushes, to the driveway, listening to the rustle of wind in the palm trees all over the street. She could hear someone else's radio down the block, playing "All in the Game."

Many a tear has to fall…

But it's all…

In the game…

She tiptoed out to where Newp's car had been parked hours earlier.

It was a piece of bamboo about a foot long. It must have been caught on some part of Newp's car and been deposited here. As she picked it up it barely shown in the moonlight, the glow must have been a trick of the light. She rolled it in her hand, it was thicker than a flute, more like a spyglass. Bermuda grass and "All in the Game" still droning from a distant window.

Spyglass. She put it to her eye.

Someone else was looking at her through the other end.

Frannie saw the blink of a black eyeball and threw the stick instantly, watched it sail into the street. Then she thought better, running in her sandals to retrieve it. She picked it up, but she didn't look through it again.

# # #

Who sleeps tonight?

Mid-May, a hot night. All across town most folks are finding their way to sleep, tossing off blankets and pajamas. Frannie's parents wander to bed, satisfied that their gentle lectures, to which their daughter had paid no more attention than any of us ever did if we told the truth, had had great effect. Really, they know in their hearts: what will happen will happen. No pounding of fists against the walls of a study will reshape the panels there.

Mutt and Jeff the undercover policemen are winding down their day, writing up all that they have witnessed at Cafe Monstro, which is very little. They sit now at the checkered card table of Jeff's apartment in Reseda, one typing and their other reading and correcting what the other has typed. They know what all undercover cops know, that what will happen will happen.

Kurt the artist is not working anymore in his studio above the cafe, he stops, pulls off gloves and sweeps up some shavings of wood as he clicks off the radio.

Saul, now, he is standing in the grass on a cliff overlooking the beach. He watches the sea and can feel the statue in front of Cafe Monstro watching over him, until he turns to go and close up.

Hooky, whose real name is Cliff, is supposed to be just getting started at his nightly rounds. There are campfires along the beach, kids singing, and he is eyeing the college girls he can chat up. But it's not good tonight, he has drawn back to his hut, the roaring ocean calling him to sleep.

But when Hooky closes his eyes on his cot it is not Hollywood-ready young starlets in waiting that he sees but Korea. He sees his altimeter and pressure gage, he sees smoke, he sees blood and fire. He opens his eyes and closes them again; it is hot and so is Korea, so is the fire and the beach he is roaring down toward. What will happen will happen.

He awakens and rather than go find a campfire to hit up one of the college kids for a beer, he dusts off his pants and walks up the wooden steps, across the highway to Cafe Monstro.

CHAPTER 14

Saul was thumbing through an old book at the bar as he saw the man the kids all called Hooky come in. It was 1:30 and the place was empty. Truthfully, he could probably kick the two students who were drinking coffee at one of the booths out and close up now and no one would raise a fuss, just as on any given night he might stay open extra hours because who really cared? Even the undercover cops had given up and gone home.

Hooky wore a shirt so bleached and worn that Saul could not tell whether it had once been red or blue; it looked drained, darker lines at the seams carrying an old and forgotten message to the eye. His jeans were cut off at the calf and faded to pale blue, and his skin was walnut brown, hair bleached. He had deep recesses around his eyes; the kid was turning to leather.

Saul raised a half-hearted salute as Hooky came and sat across from him at the bar. As they shook hands Saul asked about his name.

"Yeah, Hooky, or Hookele."

"What's that?" Saul asked. Though of course he knew because Saul read a tremendous amount.

"It's a Hawaiian thing," Hooky said, looking down as though now, discussing it with another real adult, an older adult, he felt foolish. Well, let him. We all have to be confronted with ourselves from time to time. "It means Big Chief."

"Ah. Saul."

"Pleasure to know you, Saul."

"So what's your real name?"

"Cliff."

"That's a good name."

"It ain't bad."

"You know, it's funny," Saul said. "My niece Frannie started working here and as far as I can tell, she runs back and forth to the beach twenty times a day or somethin'. But I don't think I've ever seen you in here."

Hooky rubbed his fingers together. "I live a pretty lean life. I mean nothing by it. But beer costs money and I gotta make mine stretch." He looked down, suddenly seeming more ashamed than Saul thought was called for.

"What do you eat down there?" Saul said.

"Oh, you know, crabs and abalone. Whatever I catch. I put 'em in a coffee can and cook them over a fire. Pretty good, really. Monotonous."

"It sounds both those things." Saul said, turning around and disappearing to reappear with a beer and a bowl of pretzels. "On the house. You want to see a book?"

Hooky had picked up a pretzel and stopped. "What?"

"I just figured," Saul said with a shrug, "that there's no excitement here but let's see if we can find you a book."

"Is this some kind of code—to"

"It's code for would you like a book. A nice book gets you through a lot."

Saul led Hooky back through the beaded curtain to the back.

Hooky seemed impressed. "I hear you guys are getting hassled by the Decency League."

"You hear that, huh?"

"I still can't believe that's a thing."

"Can you believe that? So how'd you hear about that?"

"I hear things." Hooky was scanning the shelves and took down a copy of *Lady Chatterley's Lover*, which as it happened was the forbidden book that the Decency Lady had wanted to get her hands on and would have found if he'd let her spend any real time in there. Hooky put *Chatterley* back and went on, "All I gotta do is sit still down there on the beach, and sitting still is this irresistible attractor. People come by and tell me what's up."

"I got the same deal." Saul walked to the back shelf and took down one of the blank books. "Here."

Hooky took the book and glanced over the blank cover. "This a notebook?" And then he looked back down at it and there was a title on the cover after all.

Saul couldn't see what Hooky was reading and he didn't want to move and spoil it. Hooky told him a lot, though, his eyes dancing with confusion, and then narrowed to angry slits. Hooky straightened up, squaring powerful shoulders and slapping the book down on a shelf. "What do you know about it?"

"What do I know about what?" Saul picked up the book, turned it over. No title.

"Look, no disrespect. I appreciate the thought," Hooky said, with no hint of irony that Saul could detect. "But I'm just... I'm here now, okay?"

Saul nodded. Play it safe. No idea what the kid was talking about and he hadn't seen the title fill in. He had some basic guesses. The kid was no kid, he was late twenties, pushing thirty. Certain things tear everyone up, but he was too young to have been in Europe or the Pacific or Africa. So the kid could be torn up by Korea, maybe, but God knew it could be prison or the foster system. Most of the people who came to the Blanks had a story and not a pretty one.

"You're *here* now?" Saul repeated.

"Yeah—you know. It's an okay life. I don't tell anybody what they have to do, and no one tells me."

"I can understand that," Saul offered. "I got things I don't like to go into myself. Less than some, you know. It's worse for my brother. That's how it works." It was indeed. Saul had come to the US and lived in boring working-class safety for decades while his brother and sister-in-law had to flee the Nazis with a baby.

But Saul wasn't working on that now. He had a man standing in front of him who needed something. And it was Saul's job to find that thing. He eyed Hooky carefully. "But let me ask you something. What do you think brought you in here today?"

Hooky had turned to look at one of Kurt's paintings, this one of Jesus raising a green, ghoulish and zombie-like Lazarus. "Your partner is insane, you know that?"

"Everyone needs a partner who's a little insane."

"I was with the dead girl the night she drowned," Hooky said.

Saul spun through a bunch of responses and chose none of them. The story didn't make sense yet. The Blanks usually called people about old wounds and future narratives. That was just how it tended to be. So far, this didn't fit. Maybe Hooky had a sister who drowned.

Hooky went on. "I mean, we hung out at a bonfire that night and went swimming." He looked up at Saul. "I do this a lot. I meet girls and we swim."

"It's good work if you can get it."

"I lost track of her."

Saul rubbed his bald head. "So you're telling me you saw the girl and she disappeared."

"Yeah."

"Well, I don't have to tell you, Cliff, but you have a dangerous hobby. Swimming at night. People do drown."

Hooky really seemed to want to find the right words when he said simply, "I felt… despair."

"Mm. Well, if you lost track… I can see despair. You look for someone and don't find them and that's what despair, is, actually. When you lose hope for what you're trying to do."

"No," Hooky said, meeting Saul's eyes. "It was thick. It was despair like—like a wave. Like an arm, tugging at me."

Saul couldn't grab onto anything the kid was telling him. He wanted to force the book back into Hooky's hand, but it didn't work that way. It had to be invited, even silently.

But the kid *wanted* to reach that story. He could tell it.

"Okay," Saul said, thrusting his hands in his pockets. "Let me offer you this. Despair. That's real. Keep your nose clean. That's all anyone can do.

Look, you live in a shack on a beach with a bunch of teenagers. I can relate, I operate a business that relies on them and one false move can get me shut down by the local Puritans. So: keep your head down. And it wouldn't kill you to find a job."

"I'll ignore that last bit." Slight smile.

"It's up to you." Saul patted Hooky on the shoulder and started leading him out of the book section.

They passed under the beaded curtain and Saul stopped to admire the stage, the microphones. He liked what the kids could do. "So what did the book say, anyway?"

"How does it work?" Hooky asked.

"That was the title?"

"No, I mean, how does it work? How does it just make a title like that?"

"It makes a whole book, but the how is a mystery."

"Korea," Hooky said. "It was titled Korea."

"No offense, but that doesn't surprise me."

"I'm a cliché," Hooky said.

"One of the best. One more thing."

"What's that?"

"Watch out for my niece. She's too young to be your type so I'm thinking this is a safe mitzvah to ask."

"Watch out for Frannie?"

"Yeah. I got a feeling. Watch out for her," Saul said.

Hooky nodded.

CHAPTER 15

Callie awakened with slow awareness to the dry winds coming in through her window, drifting into consciousness with the sigh of wind through the palms. She turned over in bed, reaching for her husband's shoulder, feeling her hand fall to the mattress.

Mort had cracked up against a palm tree one night two years before and she found her most likely time to forget all that was the middle of the night.

She was six blocks from the ocean, hidden in a cul-de-sac, but at this hour she could hear the sound of waves and the clanking of lines at the marina.

Music wandered in from the ocean, too, jaunty kid's music that she thought of as doggerel. Music like that was ugly; she was thirty-five, but she was far enough from youth to think that music turned young people into animals and broke down the natural order of things.

She was awake now, My God, were they still playing music on Ocean Highway at 2 in the morning? What kind of town did they think this was?

Ugh. That old man who ran the café, he was the one responsible. The guy couldn't be over fifty, and he carried himself with a sensual sort of confidence that Callie found intrusive, his hands in his trousers and his bald head squared over densely packed shoulders.

Who the hell cared about Saul Cohn, anyway? Except that now he had gone and broken the law again with this music, she was sure of it, and Callie would have to deal with it, would have to because tomorrow her phone would surely be ringing off the hook with complaints for the Decency League to deal with.

She rose, her feet cold against the floor even through her socks, which were all she wore as she went to the window. She turned on the radio she kept on a table next to the window and "All in the Game" began to play.

She found some clothes and within minutes she was driving.

CHAPTER 16

"I need to get some sewing patterns. Is there anything you'd like me to make?"

Frannie stared out the car window and didn't respond. She was thinking about how there had been a girl looking back at her through the bamboo stick. She carried the stick in her purse all Saturday morning at Temple and now she had it out, absently turning it, feeling its hard knots as she rode with her mother. She became aware that her Mom was talking to her.

Frannie looked down at her dress. She had no idea if she wanted her mother to make anything. "I'm fine with jeans, Mom," she said.

"You should wear a dress to work on Monday. Or at least a skirt."

Frannie sighed. Actually a dress was better for wearing her bathing suit under and running across the highway to surf. That was okay. She made a noncommittal sound.

She wanted to bring the stick to her eye again, wanted to see if the eye was looking back at her again, but she looked out at the passing buildings.

She couldn't wait. She brought it out of her purse and up to her eye to look through it at a Clifton's Cafeteria, and the cafeteria only looked back, the baby-blue Studebaker reflecting in the windows of the building they passed next. She put the bamboo away, watching the stucco columns of the bank they were passing now.

As her mom parked on the street, Frannie had the sudden urge to burst from the car and run from downtown, take a right on any of the arteries that headed straight to Ocean Highway and throw herself on the waves. The waves felt right there. She could reach them in minutes, and she saw herself building a hut like Hooky had and living off of abalone and crabs, content forever.

"Frannie," her mom said as she cut the car off. "Come on, let's do the marketing." Frannie nodded and sullenly followed her mom through their errands. She swayed to the sound of waves in her mind while they stood in line at the bank, the druggists, and she started to feel herself coming awake only when she was standing in the fabric store. Or as she called it: Thirty-Seven Billion Bolts of Cloth.

Her mom was fingering a greenish fabric and said, "You not get any sleep?"

"Oh, I did." Frannie was running her hand across a bolt the color of the ocean. The bolts against the beige shelves looked like the surfboards leaning on the hut and she thought of Newp, taking one and sizing it up.

"Is your uncle open today?"

"He's open," Frannie said. "He didn't *ask* me to work Shabbos."

"But he works," Mom said.

"You're sewing," Frannie clucked.

"I'm picking out fabric, that's not work."

"No no, pure joy, Mom."

Mom picked her cloth, some patterns and a few new thimbles. She was known for sewing even during her visiting hours at the university, and her pop had joked that she had made each of the scientists at Los Alamos a sweater. At three in the afternoon they were back on the sidewalk.

Frannie could smell salt air even miles inland, and she wondered if Hooky and Newp were surfing now, or did surf bums take days off, take vacations from the endless vacation?

"Oh!" her mom said as they passed a bookstore called Linda's. "Let's go in."

"To the bookstore?"

"I want to get *Peyton Place*. Everyone's reading it." Mom tapped the glass and Frannie saw a stack of hardback books, a few of them faced out in the window, showing a little New England village.

"I hear that's pretty racy stuff."

"Eh, we can always hope."

Frannie peered through the glass and looked in, and the bamboo clicked against the glass as she did so. She hadn't even noticed it was in her hand again. She saw a few patrons checking out, but beyond that it was mostly shadow. "Mom, I *work* at a bookstore."

"Oh, that's right, Saul has books. A coffee place with books."

Frannie was ahead of her and turned next to the glass door to look back at her mom. "I maybe can get you a deal. Let me see if Saul has it."

Mom shrugged. "I guess it can wait a day."

Frannie turned, looking down to put the bamboo stick back into her purse, when the glass door of Linda's opened and the man stepping out ran right into her.

Her mom was behind her, not looking, and the man stood still, staring not at her but peering back into the store, the door he'd come through still open. Normally when someone ran into you, they made a fuss, a little dance, *oh how foolish* or *hey look where you're going.* She heard the bamboo stick clatter to the sidewalk.

Frannie called, "Oh, excuse me!" She sounded effusive and apologetic.

The man turned and Frannie thought *professor.* Felt hat with feather, tweed jacket with leather elbows. He wore thick-looking, warm khakis with a coating that sort of shimmered; it reminded her of the fabric you find on a pup tent. He had a gray beard and a thin shirt and glasses, and she could have sworn as he stared into the bookstore, half turned to her, that his nostrils were flaring angrily and filled with… smoke. How could that be?

"Excuse me," Frannie said again, less little girl this time.

The man in the tweed jacket looked at her now, raised a heavy arm, and placed his hand on her shoulder.

His fingers landed mostly on the strap of her dress, but some touched her skin, and where it did she felt the most peculiar, lemon-drop harsh burn. He managed a smile. "Forgive me." He took his hand away.

His touch reminded her of the tiny shells on the beach, leaving thousands of cuts.

Her mom had caught up to her and Frannie had frozen, staring at the man, who peered back at her with intense, amber eyes. A cloud seemed to pass through them.

"Yes." The man pulled his hand away and stepped fluidly around her and into the street.

Frannie felt the throb of his touch against her neck, which was crazy, and she wondered absurdly if he had acid on his hands, maybe, or something strange like that. She looked down and saw the bamboo stick and picked it up. She started to put in her purse again and then whipped it up to look at the man through it—a crazy idea she couldn't explain, but by the time she swept the bamboo up to where he should be, he was just disappearing behind a hardware store.

"Handsome," her mom said. "Frannie, stop fidgeting with that thing."

Frannie stared, put the bamboo stick away.

As they pulled away and started to drive home, Frannie rubbed her shoulder. The blaring late afternoon sun was giving her a sunburn worse than she ever got at the beach, and she shielded her eyes. She didn't feel right. She rolled down the window, laying her right arm out the door and rubbing her shoulder with her left.

As they passed a little park, Frannie was sure she saw the man standing in a gazebo just big enough for a small party, not far from the public library. He stood stock still next to the gazebo railing, looking out at the highway. Looking at her.

She rolled up the window and he turned as they passed, or rather turned and did not turn, as though he moved and did not move.

His touch is paper cuts, she thought. *That's insane. You're going insane.*

Her mother started nattering about dinner and having Saul over sometime and to be sure and get her that book, discount or no, and Frannie went into autopilot and answered and pretended to engage.

When she got home, she was awake again, the man's touch so drifted and forgotten that she was chattering herself abut surfing and Newp and the cafe and Newp. This was her mom's turn to pretend to engage. She forgot all about the man in the gazebo and the burning that went away, and even forgot the bamboo, which she should have put to her eye when she saw the man in tweed at the gazebo, but which instead she let fall into the floorboards of her mother's Studebaker.

CHAPTER 17

Frannie realized that Hooky and Saul seemed to know one another in her second week of work when Hooky came into the Cafe and sat by himself instead of joining Newp and the gang.

Betty and Truly were up on stage singing "Bay of Mexico" and Newp was in his usual place right next to the stage, half watching the crowd for their needs and half watching the performance, even taking notes sometimes to give to the girls in the wee hours, after most of the guests had gone and they'd done both sets.

Right above Newp was a new painting, *The Assassination and Persecution of Doctor Frankenstein*, and in it a man dressed in a surgeon's smock, with slicked brown hair and gaunt features, sat in a giant bathtub as knife-wielding cherubim snuck up behind him.

"Who's that?" Frannie asked Kurt when she saw him pass by, a bottle of rum in one arm and a bottle of coke in the other. "It doesn't look like the others." In all of Kurt's other Frankenstein paintings, the mad doctor, if he appeared, looked like the guy on the late show, with the square jaw and 40s-ish white smock. This guy with his steel eyes and rich hair looked as much like Sherlock Holmes as Frankenstein.

"Oh, yeah," Kurt mumbled through a cigarette. "This is the new guy; I caught him in the double this weekend."

"I think he looks like Sherlock Holmes."

"The guy played Sherlock once," Kurt said over his shoulder as he wandered back to his studio. "So good eye." Frannie saw Hooky come in then and took a seat near the book section. She started to approach him to see if she could get him anything (she reckoned anything but crab would work) but Hooky sort of waved her off in a gesture that said at once "don't bother me" but "it's okay." Saul came over and they exchanged a few words.

After a second or two they went off into the book section.

Saul had asked Frannie to help him in book section numerous times, but she'd never actually ventured beyond the beaded curtain without first being invited. She picked up a tray and carried it to the bar, bringing her closer to the beads.

Curiosity was going to get the better of her either way, so she may as well give in early. She peered through the beaded curtain, and as she drew near she was sure she heard sobbing.

In the corner of the book shop, Hooky held a Blank in his hand and was crying as Saul stood next to him, a hand on Hooky's shoulder.

Frannie backed away. Later, as she got off after the lunch rush, Frannie hurried across Ocean Highway and straight down the stairs next to the Riviera Hotel, the sun beating down the whole way and heating the asphalt so hot that it burned her feet through her sandals. The burning on her feet always felt glorious, a sore prologue to joy.

Frannie emerged at the beach next to Hooky's hut. She cast off her capris and work shirt as she spotted Hooky and the gang. They were all in a row beyond the chop, watching for waves.

Frannie grabbed a hard board from the shaping hut and paddled out next to Newp, who had taken off earlier to catch the waves. Hooky hung back more than usual, his face clouded by the shadow of the brim of his straw hat. Frannie let Newp go and paddled next to Hooky.

She wanted to ask him about the Blanks. She wanted to say, *it's the kookiest thing, Hooky, but my uncle is letting me in on his magic books and I have a knack for it, see, I'm part of a world you want to be a part of,* or something, and before she could say anything, Hooky started talking.

"Your senses go haywire," Hooky said. "If you stop and listen you can hear the way the air moves over the water and change around you, and beyond that you can hear the other surfers, and you can hear the highway. And these sounds are the same on every beach. Every beach. It's all the same."

What was this jive?

"You should enjoy your time at the cafe," Hooky said. "Your uncle is a good fella." And then he broke away, paddling as Frannie followed.

Commencing to surf was like coming to the edge of a whirlpool. You weren't part of it and then you felt the tug, and then you're suspended for a second and you're in it, no longer thinking, your mind occupied and unoccupied by the active work, the wave, skittering forward and bringing your feet up. Every day, every hour it was the same, one minute she was a girl on a board and the next she was a surfing thing, a floating piece of the wave, a mixture of sound, water on wax on fiberglass, toes on board, riding the wave, no thoughts, no mom or pop, no Saul or Newp, only this, and only this for hours until the sun was down.

Sa Frannie glided back to shore and began to walk, Hooky and Newp were there, and Hooky said, "You've really taken a shine to it."

She didn't flush, but just smiled and nodded with what she thought would come across like humility. "It's something else."

Newp put his arm around her as the three of them walked in silence. Then Betty called from up at the highway. "There's a call for you, Newp!"

"What is it?" Newp asked, but he kept his eyes on Frannie, like he was reluctant to look away.

"It's a guy called Newberry, Tom Newberry," Betty shouted.

"Okay?" Newp looked up, as in *so?*

"He's a booking guy for Ed Sullivan."

Newp froze. Ed Sullivan, that was the guy that Frannie's parents liked to watch on TV, along with pretty much everyone else in America. "Holy—"

"Go!" Betty said. "Truly is holding the phone for you!"

By the time Frannie got to the cafe Newp was already on the phone in Saul's office next to the kitchen. She pushed past Saul in the door and joined the crowd that was silently craning at Newp, who sat at Saul's desk amidst two mountains of ledgers. Saul's was a small, typical office, a madness of paper near which he took notes on a yellow notepad.

"Okay, we do," he said, as he absently looked from Frannie to Saul to Betty to Truly. "We have a set that—the Weavers, yes. Yeah, people love that." His snapped his fingers for a pen and Betty handed him one. Newp scribbled something and held the notepad up. LABOR DAY SHOW.

"No," Betty's eyes grew wide and Truly jumped, using Betty's shoulders as a handhold for her springing.

"But we're in California," Newp said. "How would—really? Okay." Newp was gripping his own forehead and Frannie found herself mimicking the gesture. Then Newp snapped at her and she came forward and he cupped the receiver as he rubbed her head. "I'm rubbing your head for good luck," he said.

"You really need luck?" Frannie whispered.

Newp said, "Okay—goodbye," and hung up. He was silent for a second.

"Well, come on!" Truly shouted.

"Out with it," Frannie said as she put her arms around Truly and Betty.

Newp leaned back. "We are —you guys are—not only going to be on TV. You are going to be guests on the *Ed Sullivan Labor Day Show."* He paused. "It's a folk thing, see. They said they read some notice in the LA *Times* and they want us to do, you know, Weavers stuff."

"But this is California, how do we get there?" Truly said.

"Well, covered wagon, Truly," Newp said. "They're flying us in. God, I never thought I'd use those words. We'll fly in to be on *Ed Sullivan*. ED! SULLIVAN!"

Frannie hugged everyone twice and then turned to Saul, but he was gone. Saul didn't come back for the rest of the night.

She got to her car and had a thought, a pressing need—she padded across the highway and this time took her time, sauntering through the Hotel Riviera, down the back stairs past the gorgeous Hollywood-star patios, and down to the beach.

She found Saul standing with Hooky at the water not far from Hooky's hut, holding up a fishing net.

CHAPTER 18

Saul had his hands up, a silhouette against the rolling surf, lit by the moon and the light coming off of the Hotel Riviera. He seemed to be shouting, but she couldn't hear him over the ocean. "Saul!" she called. "What are you doing?"

Another figure emerged from the dark and stood next to Saul, then looked her way. It was Hooky. Frannie gasped as he came towards her, looking distracted and alarmed. "Frannie, not now. Go home."

"What are you doing?" she asked, and the smile had gone out of her voice.

A whistle cut across the window. They looked back to see Saul gesturing for them to come back to him.

"Frannie." Saul looked strange, standing in the water with his pants rolled up to his knees and his sleeves rolled to his elbows. He held an item in each hand. The book in one hand made her think of TV preachers holding the bible up as they spoke, while in the other, he seemed to be holding a box. It was about shoebox size, with a long train of cloth or netting trailing from it.

"What's that?" Frannie asked.

"It's a box."

"What's the tail hanging from it?"

"That's a fishing net."

Frannie stared. "Nope. I was hoping that that would make sense, but it's not happening."

"She shouldn't be here," Hooky said.

"Oh, she can probably help," Saul said.

"I'm overwhelmed by your confidence, Saul," Frannie said. "Seriously. What is this?"

"Sometimes it's better to *do* than *explain,*" Saul said.

"But—"

"Shh, just watch."

"Do *you* know what you're doing?" She was beginning to wonder if Saul might have found his way to Kurt's special cigarettes.

"What did I say?"

"Okay."

Saul shook the box in one hand, the fishing net waving in the wind. "Clifford, now is the time to call your friend."

Hooky slumped his taut shoulders with defeat. "We don't know—"

"Call her now."

Frannie whispered, "Your name is Clifford?"

"What did your uncle say?" Hooky snapped.

"Said your name is Clifford, which is news to me."

"Shh. Saul, what do I need to say?"

"I don't think the words matter much, but you know what you need to say." Saul took the book and turned to Frannie. "Here, you hold the book; I'll hold the Dybbuk box." She could barely hear him because the wind was high, and the white hairs on his arms moved like grain.

"What's a Dybbuk box?"

He asked, "You sure you want to know?"

"Sure."

"It's a box for catching *dybbukim* and other invading spirits."

"Okay."

"Do you believe me?"

"This book is one of those Blanks, right?"

"Yes, it is."

"And I think we can agree that those are not your everyday books." She put her hand on her uncle's shoulder. "I'm trying to say I'm gonna roll with whatever craziness you get up to."

"Good," Saul said. "Clifford, look at the book that Frannie holds. Put your hands on it and open it. This book is your story. You started to read it before, but now is the time."

Hooky let Frannie keep holding it as he held the book beneath her hands and came around to read. Frannie watched him open it, feeling the warmth of his shoulders, watching his eyes search the pages.

Ink began to appear, and

CHAPTER 19

Hooky is holding a net. A fishing net. He is throwing it down as he trips onto the beach. He is coughing and tripping in the net which has caught him by surprise, the way a fish is caught by surprise, and he tries to crawl through it and scales from other caught fish slice into his foot.

The surf roars and red foam sloshes up as he tries to keep his head above water. He has lost his boots. It was only seconds ago but he was sure they were on fire and he is barefoot and pain wracks through him, a deep slice in his right foot singing with pain.

Crashed. He has crashed. Ol' Cliffy finally bought it, they'll say. Went down over North Korea. For a second his head falls under the water and he is in the cockpit again, shrapnel bursting through the engine and his sleeves are on fire and his legs and he is tumbling through the air. His face comes up out of the water again and he screams as he drags himself and his parachute to shore.

He awakens again after the sun goes down and a woman is standing over him. She is a blur to him, and he is burning with fever.

The woman chatters as she strips his parachute and his burnt clothes from him and the net he was tangled in as well. She seems to inspect him and clucks something that might mean he is not nearly dead, and he sleeps again.

The parachute and the tiny pack attached to it are a bundle now, under the small of his back.

It is later and mosquitoes are eating him, and he awakens with a mosquito biting his eyebrow and he hisses and swats it. He is awake. For the first time in days, perhaps, he's awake. He hears her voice in the darkness. The Angel.

The woman has come back, she has long black hair and she has brought him clothes, and he struggles to put them on. His ankle is badly sprained, and he wants to howl as he pulls the cotton pants she has brought. But he has his faculties now, and he doesn't howl. Because for some reason he is being helped by a strange woman and he is behind enemy lines. His head aches and he feels woozy. He realizes he has been cut over the eye. He moans and the world dims again.

The Angel drags him into the trees, and he is moaning his serial number. He looks down and she is binding his foot with gauze, and where she got the gauze he does not ask and has wondered many times. He nearly loses it over the pain of the binding, but he does not fall unconscious again.

She says something sharp and he looks at her, she has her hands palm-faced towards him; she is certain this means wait here, as though he has other plans. She drags great bamboo leaves over him.

He sleeps and dreams he is being captured and North Korean soldiers are doing terrible things to him with bamboo shoots and knives. Then they take a look at his foot and they get a pair of pliers and

He's awake again and the Angel has returned, this time with a cherub, a boy of nine or so and by the boy's tone he is skeptical, and Cliff has the presence of mind to think what the boy might be saying, are you insane? If we get caught helping him, he won't be the last one killed. But the boy and the woman move him farther up the beach, against a palm tree, and make a better work of his camouflage. He touches his head. At some point she has bandaged that too.

Clifford Carmichael, AF28 248 933, he says. United States Air Force. AF28 248 933. And then: why are you helping—

And she claps a hand over his mouth and stares into the distance. Hurriedly she and the boy cover him up.

The patrol of North Korean soldiers that comes through the jungle then emerges one hundred yards from his hiding place, and he's with it now, boy. He tries to make himself small. He shakes and tries to will himself to stop shaking. The palm fronds are rattling over him and he swears that they clatter like a xylophone, stop shaking. The patrol comes close, moving up the beach at the edge of the trees.

Through the palm fronds he can see them. Stopping just a few yards away, a North Korean soldier puts up a hand, listening as his men fall silent. He can see it: an American was reported shot down. Probably went in the ocean, but then...

Now one of the soldiers is wandering by his hiding place. The soldier steps on one of the fronds connected to the ones he is under, and the pressure lands on Cliff's foot and he winces in pain, whimpering inside.

A mosquito has landed on his cheek. He clamps his lips shut. His foot is throbbing and the mosquito is biting and he wants to scream. His heart is pounding and a half-remembered story flits through his mind, *Do you not hear? It is the beating of his accursed heart!* His breath is shallow, and he swears it is a clashing cymbal, a banging gong. The gig is up and in any second the soldier will plunge a bayonet through the fronds—

She speaks. Emerges from the trees and calls to the soldiers. Hey soldier boys. She is carrying a basket of goodies for the fighting men. She makes a showy presentation of the dumplings and fruits. They follow her.

Later she pulls the fronds away and she and boy—brother? Son? – sit *beside him as he shakes with the fever he is now certain he has. She says her name: Sang-ook.*

When they leave him he sees lights on the ocean. A ship.

He turns and digs up the bundle, tossing dirt aside and finding it, digging until he finds the tiny pack and the flare. He breaks the flare and fires it into the air. He will be seen by friend and enemy alike. He prays that someone can retrieve him and that the first ones to him are not the North Korean soldiers.

He will always remember the flare, pink and sparking, as it arcs into the air and pops like a firework. He is standing for the first time since he has fallen here, and he turns while the pink light still brightens the beach and sees the Angel at the tree line, staring at him with fear. He falls once more and waits, shaking with fever.

Gunfire wakens him before dawn and he hears American voices, and suddenly hands are grabbing him, throwing him on a stretcher, dragging him out. They came, his head falls back, you came, yes we did, boy, and we're gonna get you out of here, you just hang tight.

And oh god

She is lying in the sand, she and the boy and her head is a mess, her eyes nearly unseeing, clutching the boy, she is on her side and bleeding and staring at him, and he is losing sight of her, craning his neck, no, his Angel, wait, and she is dead and he is lost in the sounds of the boots of the men carrying him as they run into the surf for their waiting boat.

He has been rescued twice in three days and Clifford Carmichael will never be the same again.

It is June 3, 1952.

CHAPTER 20

Frannie felt as though a curtain had dropped. One moment she was in the scene, *live*, with the man she knew as Hooky living his own personal war movie, shot down and rescued no less, and then his rescuers shot out from under him, and then the curtain fell and she and Saul gasped with re-entry into the present world. Frannie blinked the vision—that was what it was, wasn't it? She got around her uncle's books and her uncle's strange tools, and somehow they brought visions out of her—and saw a woman rising from the waves.

Holy Christ, as the *goyim* said, but a woman was standing upright and coming in like a ship's mast, the water rolling in front of her as she stood stock still and sailed in. Her arms were raised and outstretched and her long, black hair trailed behind her and out like a black, blazing halo. She opened her mouth and hissed as she came straight for Hooky.

Am I seeing this I cannot be seeing this, Frannie thought, and weirder still was the changing *visage* of the South Korean sympathizer surfing in on an invisible surfboard. Her face changed as though she were a doll whose head can spin to reveal different emotions, it changed without moving, it changed in waves, she was angry and *swish* she was howling in pain and *swish* she was laughing deliriously.

"We hold here the book," Saul shouted, "that tells of a life intertwined with that of another, and of a tragedy shared."

The ghost slowed, hissing and swish listening, the woman tilting her head, studying him.

"What is she?" Frannie asked.

"Korean water spirit," Saul said.

"You have something for that?"

"I know your anger!" Saul addressed the ghost.

"You think she understands English?" asked Frannie.

He spoke sideways to her, "You want to try Yiddish?"

The ghost hung there, the face flicking in orientation, looking down at the book and straight ahead, the image juddering in the air.

Saul took the book from Frannie. "You feel a need to wail and cry, and the cry is so great, so thick with rage that you have followed this man around the world. And lashed out! And lashed out.

"But my darling, this man is filled with *pain* for you and your brother. The women you have dragged down cannot sate the pain you feel, nor his, nor anyone's. If you look to your soul, you will see this."

"This book is a special gift. It tells all one's life, that has been, that can be. If you will trust in what I saw you can have a look at that life you did not complete, and you can enter it. There are so many lives we lead, and our world is but a shadow of the many, many others."

The ghost hung over the waves, barely lit by the reflecting lights from the distant Hotel Riviera, and stared at the book.

"He calls to you, your brother. He grows up and grows older and you are with him, and you lead long and happy lives. Come see your book, woman of the waves. Come see your life and let this place of pain go."

She hissed and Frannie felt her body shiver in the cold. The roar of the ocean deafened her and suddenly there was a CRACK and the ghost plunged, like water from a pitcher, into the air before the book in Saul's hands, indeed into it.

Saul closed the book and moved in a fluid motion, slipping it into the Dybbuk box. He lay the box down and folded the net into the box after it. He knelt for a moment before the closed box. "*Kina hora*, no evil eye here." He looked at Hooky. "She will haunt this place no more."

Hooky looked at the box. "Is she trapped?"

"Eh. It's another world. You're wondering if I should have tried to get her to move onto the afterlife."

"Well…" Hooky wrinkled his brow.

"Korean rage ghosts don't work that way. I gave her a solid way out."

"So she *is* trapped."

"I'm hoping she remains in her vision of a better life. Either way, Hooky, she was drowning people."

Hooky nodded. "That book—is there another one that…"

"A book for you that is not entwined with hers?" Saul asked. "I think so."

"Okay."

"You can come in tomorrow and find one," Saul offered.

"Okay." He put his hands in his pockets. "I'm gonna stay out here awhile."

Frannie stood looking at the ocean and Saul finally turned to her. "You wanna talk?" He gestured with his head towards the Riviera and began to walk, and she followed him.

They trudged up the back stairs of the Riviera. They found seats on the deck chairs of a landing with big umbrellas and a perfect view of the ocean, which rolled perfect and black against the grey sky.

Frannie sat in a deck chair, stretched out like she should be getting a tan. Finally she looked at her uncle. "What *are* you, exactly?"

Saul laughed softly. "Just a man. But *what I am* isn't really the question."

"Okay," Frannie said. "What are *they?* The books."

"We call them Blanks," Saul said.

"Who are *we*?"

"Whoever keeps them."

"The Blanks tell the future?"

"Sometimes the past, sometimes more or less." Saul put his finger to his lip. "But don't get hung up on the past they show. The past is just a narrative, a way of showing the person how they got to what's next."

"Futures that could be, even."

"I say future, but it's more… I'm gonna sound like your old man, but it's more *potentiality*. Frannie, they tell the right stories to the right people. They show you what you become, amount to, strive for. Maybe it gives them a kick in the pants."

"And it all plays out like recordings of the past or future?"

"It plays out like the truth."

"Right, like they say in journalism, the who, what, where…"

"*Pssh*. That's not truth, that's fact. They tell your true story of potentiality. That's the best I can explain it. But for me, I don't *really* know how they do this thing they do. I only know that from the moment I beheld one, I became what I am."

"You said a keeper. A keeper of the Blanks."

"Some people even say *Blankguards*. And the reward is that we see the visions the books imparts. But keepers are drawn, *Frannie*. They have to have some vision already. You have it; I told you that."

"I mean, Uncle Saul, I'm your niece, I came into the cafe because I thought I'd check it out."

"Don't give me that." Saul waved a hand. "But hey, maybe there's a hereditary thing. That I can't tell you."

"How did you find them?"

"The Blanks came to me," Saul said, lying back on his own deck chair. "I found the first one in Philadelphia in a bookstore on a side street, all by itself. I had to have it. I knew it was special, somehow, even though it was just a notebook, at first glance. The old man who sold it to me saw it that way. Then I started a bookstore of my own in Boston. One day, by chance, I saw what it could do when I put it into the hands of a man and his life spilled out into his brain and mine. The true story, past and future, as ugly and great as usually is the case. He bought it and I *let* him because I realized I *had* to sell it to him. I had handed over my first Blank, and watched it walk out of the store."

"The next day, I found four more where that one had been shelved. I have never been short of them. Do you see? I think they are drawn to some and when they find a home, they are free to keep coming."

"Come on," Frannie said. "Do you think in the night four books just appeared out of thin air?"

"I actually think they flew in like birds, but who knows? I've never seen it happen." He leaned on one arm. "I keep them, I sell them. I am a keeper of the Blanks. And I have one question for you."

"What's that?"

"Do you want to be one too?"

She didn't hesitate, not that she was constitutionally capable of that. "Oh, yes."

"Good," Saul said, and he leaned back to glance up at the Riviera's plain white exterior and up, as though he could cast his glance like a stone over the hotel and across the road to the Café. "Because this place is special, Frannie. They're coming *fast*, now. As though they know they have found a special home, more than any place I've ever had. When we opened two months ago I had five."

"How many are there now?"

"At last count? Sixty."

Frannie started. "But why—why Café Monstro?"

"I know!" Saul laughed. "I should be insulted by that question, but it's a damn good one. Why does this place with its bonkers art and its folk music become a beacon for Blanks while my old place, a family place, not so much. But there it is."

"There it is," Frannie repeated. "Uncle Saul, I knew when I saw that place that I needed to be a part of it."

"Then take my hand and shake on it, niece," Saul said. "And we will change lives."

CHAPTER 21

Frannie was a runaway, now. Not from home—she still went there at the end of the day, still saw her parents and told them bowdlerized stories of the denizens of Cafe Monstro—but from the life that she had known before. She threw herself bodily at two waves, the Blanks and the surf, and slipped right in.

Saul arrived one morning with a stack of books and told Frannie he was going to stack them all on the table in the little rat hole apartment above the Café. "You can go there and learn them. If there's not a customer bell ringing, if those beaded curtains aren't chattering, that's your place."

"You want me to study."

Saul shook his head. "I don't want you to *study*. You don't study the Blanks, because there's nothing in 'em. And anyway, you don't need to study. You need to *learn*. The stuff you need to learn is in books, the Torah, the Mishnah, some of the Talmud."

"You're kidding."

"I'm not. How's your Hebrew?"

Frannie waggled her hand. "Saturdays."

"I trust you. But I'm not finished. Don't worry, I'll divide this stuff up for you." He brought out a sheet of paper and Frannie saw that he'd divided it up into a grid for days of the week and hours of the day.

"Oh my God, you're a maniac."

"Look here. You got your usual studies and then you need the *Zohar, the Sefer Yetzirah*, the *Shoshan Yesod ha-'Olam*."

"What's all that?"

He scratched his head. "Books to understand the Teachings of the Ari, to grasp what is needed to repair the broken world."

"Ohhh," she said. "Magic."

"Sometimes, but that's a tough word, magic. Sometimes you mustn't think of it that easy way. It's the received truth. The wisdom to reach beyond the *Assiyah*, the physical world, and begin to work with the *Atzlut*, the world of spirit."

"Is this something I need to talk to a rabbi about?"

Saul looked down and pursed his lips. "Some of them don't like young people... look, follow your *Chochmah*, your intuitive self on that. But I promise you as your Uncle, I won't steer you wrong. And Frannie, you need this stuff."

"Five days a week above your Café?"

"Well, six, but who's counting. But you need it because they're coming faster now."

"The Blanks."

"The Blanks. And so the people. And so the others."

"Like the ghost? She wasn't after the Blanks, she was after Hooky."

"Trust me: you need to get ready." He clapped his hands. "So. Two days a week on the Torah, three days a week on the Kabbalah, one day on *toykhekhe*, the curses."

"Curses?"

"You never know."

"And what language are they in?"

"It doesn't matter. You could use Latin. You got Latin?"

"No."

"Yiddish is just as good, but ya gotta learn it and feel it."

Frannie put up her hand and turned, walking up the stairs not far from the beaded curtain. She stepped through the door at the top. Inside she saw a small, dingy living room with a threadbare rug and an open window. She could hear the ocean outside. Sure enough it was just big enough for a desk and some chairs, and on the desk were notebooks and the small library that

Saul had collected. "Oh, Uncle," she said as he came up the stairs. "Saul, this is *nebekh* nuts." She picked up a scroll. "This isn't even a book."

He sighed, his hands in his pockets.

"You really learned this?" she asked.

"Learning. Still."

"And this is what it is to do… what we do with the Blanks."

"What we do *for* them." Saul said. "And God forbid the wrong guy gets to do the wrong thing *with* them."

"You're gonna make me a freak."

"*Gam zu l'tovah*," he said. "It's all for the best."

There were more Blanks appearing over the next month, and more stories coming to find them, sometimes three in a week, as though a secret call had gone out, a psychic sign had been put up that said Open for Business and people were responding without knowing what brought them past the statue of Kronos.

Frannie observed that no one in Los Angeles seemed to be from there. Some visitors came from across the desert looking for whatever was here. They caught a whisper that brought them up the coast to Laguna and Cafe Monstro, now just three months old.

Before work every day, the sea called to her. Frannie took to the waves exactly as Betty had predicted. She learned to read the surf, to close her eyes and hear the scrape of the board on the water and the whoosh when she shot the curl.

Surf. Work. Surf.

Carol and the girls of the Laguna Beach cycling club stopped coming around. Carol and Frannie shared a soda once and she looked at Frannie like she'd lost her way.

That wasn't it at all. This was the way.

She had seen a vision of the golem and the blankness of life. It had led her here.

A week after they socked away Hooky's ghost, Saul took Frannie off tables entirely and dedicated her to the bookstore. Most hours she served up bestsellers to vacationers who wandered over from the Riviera, people looking for something fat and meaty to read as they baked in the sun and tried to catch a glimpse of Victor Mature or George Burns whenever they happened to wander out on private balconies. But that wasn't the real work; the real work was the Blanks.

A twenty-something guy called Dan with a sport coat and ink on his fingers heard the call when he was new in town. He'd come in from Kansas, son of a drycleaner franchise man who shipped his whole family west when Jew-haters made their lives uncomfortable. But Dan was a writer and Los Angeles was where he needed to be, anyway, and the Blank he chose showed him all of that. Frannie saw Dan see a woman on a train, a lonely woman making a trip straight into a Gothic world of New England that never could exist. The guy was steeped in Gothic, looming houses and dark shadows and ancient secrets. The young man had a story to spin out, and when he left he was set, and it was going to take years. Frannie never saw him again, never saw any of them again.

A truly gorgeous Italian boy, seventeen years old and a headlining trumpet player at the Riviera, wandered in. Truly pulled her aside and said, "That boy has made lots of jazz records. He's famous." He stood in the book section, all knobby joints and greasy hair, confused.

"Like you're not sure why you're in here, right?" Frannie asked. She shook his hand. "The girls on stage really like you. Your name's Francesco; that's close to mine, Frances. Frannie."

"Frankie," he said, shaking back. He had a deep voice, she was surprised he didn't sing, too.

Frannie was seeing a lot of Newp but she wasn't above flirting with the people called by the Blanks. "You surf?" she asked. He had the lean look of an athlete.

"Nah," he laughed. "Tennis, but no time, really..." drifting again as he eyes found their way to the Blanks on the top shelf.

For Frankie she didn't really understand any of it. Flashes of the trumpet and those crowds, a million eager girls showing up at his hotel room since he was about 12, first sent away, later not sent away. Then the rest got weird, he was surfing after all but against a gray cement wall, which must be a dream or something, and there was a long-haired Italian girl, again and again in his life, but not a love, more of an anchor. On and on. He left stunned.

"See ya round, Frankie," she said.

She was taking all these visits herself, now. Saul wanted it that way. "I have years more to do, but maybe not so many as I hope." That unsettled Frannie a little because she didn't like to think about the future.

Because what was the future? The summer wouldn't go on forever, even though she felt lost in endless sun-washed days now. And Saul was talking not as if he would die—and who wouldn't? But that she was going to be here with these books and these Blanks when he was gone. That might be great, but it was jazz, just talk and she didn't want to think beyond the days right up to when she'd have to go back to high school. When the old man got maudlin like that, she'd hit the tables for a change, then head to the beach to surf out the last rays of sun.

On the beach she was one of Hooky's crew now, and they called her lots of names. Newp and Hooky tried to come up with one that would stick but Frannie defied all nicknames. She was the girl on the surfboard.

Sometimes the boys on the beach would give her the willies—there was a college boy like that who knew Newp from school. He came around for a few weeks, kept trying to get close to her, but he wasn't a surfer and when he asked her for a lesson he took the opportunity to get all hands-y while they were paddling out. She wished at that point that the Korean ghost were still around and would start expanding her tastes. And yet she liked the attention—what's sixteen for, after all?

One day Newp saw her nearly sock the guy in the jaw and then he didn't come around anymore. What happened to him and what was said, neither Newp nor Hooky would fess up.

The woman called Callie came back to the store once, and when Frannie touched her she got a flash of the many armed goddess of destruction the Indians worshipped. That wasn't even with the Blanks present. Because it was rubbing off, and she couldn't get enough.

Callie wanted a Blank. She had seen one before and run from it. She was very vague about it, but Frannie got the gist. Frannie showed her a Blank and when Callie opened it Frannie got flashes she didn't like to see and turned away from, of teen boys mowing her lawn and invited inside, of her husband dead in a car and her baby daughter dead in a pink blow-up swimming pool, and ache and ache and ache.

Callie didn't like Cafe Monstro or its power over her, Frannie could see that. The lady put the Blank back angrily and walked out, saying *this place should be burnt to the ground*. And then, under her breath, something worse, though Frannie had no clue why:

Before he finds it.

"Wait!" Frannie called after Callie as she ripped through the beaded curtain and headed for the door, the brilliant sun shining through the glass walls, lighting her blond hair so it shone like a golden halo. "Before who finds it?"

Callie turned. "What?"

"You said, 'before he finds it.'" Frannie had to raise her voice because Betty and Truly were setting up for the night and they and Newp were dragging equipment and making a crazy racket. "Before who finds it?"

"I said no such thing." Scowling down her perky nose, which wrinkled as she swayed a little. Rattled and confused. All of this wasn't so strange because the Blanks did a number, people who consulted them often seemed like they were waking up, forgetting half of it.

But this seemed important. She had as good as threatened them and then said something worse. "Before he, who?"

"I don't know what you're prattling on about, young lady," Callie said, sounding awfully haughty for someone who seduced every boy who mowed her lawn and then cried herself to sleep every night in a little cave of baby clothes in her closet. Frannie had the urge to hug her and smack her at the same time. Callie disappeared into the blinding sun.

And as she had studies under Saul, she unwound it all with her lessons from Hooky on the beach, lessons that were pushing her from enthusiast to something more, just as she was getting expert on the men and women who came in to see what Mary White had called *the big, terrible things they have done and the big, wonderful things they will do,* except sometimes it was the opposite and always it was true, either way.

For Frannie learned many things from the *Zohar* and the *Sefer Yetzirah*, and she learned of the worlds of man and spirit and the Ten *Sefirot*, the forces we all bring to bear, the will and wisdom and the judgment and balance—

But the surf helped her understand it, in the surf you barreled into the curl and you looked for the end and sometimes you sail on through and sometimes you wipe out and sometimes, sometimes, you die.

Hooky taught her to read the surf, starting again and again.

"Look at the shadows," he said, standing behind her one morning, Hooky towering over her and then bending down to match her eye line as he swept his sinewy arm across the ocean. "They show you where the wave is about to break. Look at them long enough and you see the patterns. The sea is not random. It follows shapes as solid and constant as the mountains—and of course that's what they are."

"I see it," she said.

"No jazz?"

"No jazz, Hook."

"It's the sport of kings, this is," he said.

"Kings?" The Legionnaires were a lot of things, but kings they were not.

"Absolutely. I know you think we're just a bunch of crazies doing a sport nobody's ever heard of, but surfing was the birthright of the kings of Hawaii, right over there, an ocean's throw away."

"You ever been to Hawaii?"

"Once," he said, as he picked up his board and she did the same. "I'll tell you the story sometime." But for now he was scanning the waves, and they paddled out. Beyond the breakers they stopped and floated.

"You pick it up in Hawaii?"

"First time, yeah," he said. "This was with a group who were bringing it back. See, when the missionaries came to the Hawaiian Islands, at that time there were nearly two hundred thousand natives, Frannie. This was a huge bunch of people. And they all surfed, but the greatest of all were the royals. The kings surfed these gigantic boards made of local oa wood. No fins, no nothing. Every king and princess. They were lords of the land and they greeted it each morning from the water. And then…"

"What? They stopped?"

"The white guys never understood. They thought it was obscene, the men and women surfing out there. Soon enough it was all over. But you watch, sister. The kings'll have their day yet."

Frannie reached behind her and pulled something out of the strap of her one-piece as they sat.

"There's a wave," he said, and started to go, and stopped when he saw her.

She was holding the bamboo stick, which she had found again in the floorboard of her mother's car. She was using it as a spyglass. She looked through it to see Hooky with that cowlick over one eye, smiling curiously.

"Whatcha got there?"

"Something that a poor girl reached out to me through," Frannie said. "I'm glad you're here to say goodbye to it."

She let the spyglass bamboo slip into the sea with a whispered prayer for the dead. Looked out to the horizon, reading the waves. A swell was building, and she breathed, the sun drenching her shoulders and filling her with the energy of kings. "You see it?"

"I see it."

"Go, man, go," she said.

They started to paddle. "I catch a better ride, I'll make you listen to more History of Surfing," he said.

"I catch a better ride," she said, "and I'll *make* you tell it."

All these things happened and June seemed to last a year, summer curling on with rhythm but no end, just getting better, the surf getting stronger, Truly and Betty's act getting tighter, calls from the Sullivan show in preparation for their appearance more and more frequent, Newp just bouncing through it all with glee.

But all waves curl and flatten away. Something else had heard the call and was already on the prowl.

CHAPTER 22

Frannie was half listening to Newp answer her question about how the Labor Day show preparations were going on as they bobbed in the waves, looking for the next big one. There were beads of water on his shoulders and she was tempted to lean over and touch them, to burst the tiny mounds of water, to watch capillarity fall apart and the liquid spread out.

He was looking away and now he turned his head towards her. "Right now we're mainly working on the set for the luau. That should get on TV and I know the Sullivan guys will be watching."

"Luau?" Frannie asked. She wasn't sure she'd heard of this. "When?"

"Oh, yeah, it's..." his face darkened, as though he suddenly realized he was in a chess game he wasn't expecting. "Fourth of July. But it's a drag. You know, it's basically a barbecue."

"I know what a luau *is* in general, Newp." She considered, *what are you suddenly nervous about* but decided to give Newp more time with this. "So you're going to be playing this luau on the 4th of July?"

"Yeah. Yes. Right. You know but forget I mentioned it."

This was definitely something to ask Truly and Betty about.

"Are you working tonight?" he said, and she could picture a tiny pilot in his head hitting a button marked *change the subject! Retreat!* Dig this: she was sixteen and he was eighteen and she could squish his ability to maneuver a conversation between her toes. Actually it was worse; he did it to himself.

"No, Newp, it's my night off, remember?"

"We're gonna head to the Rubidoux Drive-In, watch Steve McQueen. You interested?"

Was she. But: "My folks have been hassling me to spend more time with them," she said. "I gotta stay in."

He nodded, looking down.

"You understand, right?" she asked, forgetting all about whatever he was hiding earlier, now looking at his sulkiness and wanting not to be the source of it. "They keep saying I'm never there, like I've gone off to college while I still live with them."

"Sure," he said, and started to paddle. "Yeah, okay. Surf's up, Fran."

They paddled for the coming swell and Frannie cursed the *meshuge* plan her pop had come up with. Her old man had been hassling her to see a better class of people than these beach bums—their words, though they'd never met any of the Legionnaires—and Pop had set up a date with someone, the son of a friend, one of the Regents at the college. It was a total stay-in-and-die night.

At 4:45 they were carrying in their boards and they stopped by the stairs. "I'll see you tomorrow," Newp said. He put his arm around her, but too *ol' pal o'mine*, and she turned and looked up at him.

"Newp, what do you think—"

He was toweling off his head and he stopped, his arm up, waiting for her to finish this sentence.

She couldn't finish it. She didn't want to know what he thought *of* her or *about* her or if there was any such thought at all. She wasn't stupid, she knew that even if she could out-logic him, she loved learning from him and she ached with the need to get closer, to learn more, even as scarlet and dime-novel as that sounded. She wanted to matter to him the way these occasional girls that the Legionnaires brought down seemed to matter, the ones with the curves, the scarves and low-cut blouses and white capris. Those women seemed to exude sex the way a playground slide exuded fun. They were slides on a teenage roadside, promising dips and dives that Frannie couldn't even put on a postcard. Straight lines for Frannie, none of the curves or the exuding of anything but energy and muscle, now.

And usually it was okay, energy was good, she could fight with the Legionnaires when one of them stole her packed lunch and she threw sand and they would toss her around. But what was she? Whatever it was, it wasn't coming to the luau, whenever that was.

At 6 o'clock Frannie was pulling on a pink angora sweater that made her look like a fuzzy yardstick when the doorbell rang, and her mom called from the kitchen for her to get it. She was still staring through the pink when she got to the bottom of the stairs. She pulled it down and opened the door to find Uncle Saul.

Saul had brought a bottle of wine and some books for the parentals, and he looked around expectantly. "So where's the hunk?"

"My pop sent for the hunk," Frannie said, taking the wine as Saul set the books on the dining table. "So don't get your hopes up. I'm not."

"It's just as well," Saul said. "You're too good for him."

"We don't know him."

"I figure if you can see people's future, you're too good for anyone."

"Uncle Saul!" she whispered. Because they didn't discuss the Blanks. "Pop's in his study. Why don't you go bug him?"

Doorbell again. "That must be David," Mom said.

Frannie went to the door and she knew it somehow before she had the door open.

Newp, who was born David Barlowe apparently, stood in the door in a blazer exactly the color of the bottle of wine he carried, which was classy, but Frannie hadn't really taken that in yet. She stood with her mouth open as her mom wandered by.

"Ask him to come in," whispered Mom.

"Come in," Frannie found herself saying, lifting her left arm and letting it drift into the house indicating where *in* was.

Newp handed Mom the wine and shook her hand. Mom took the wine and suggested that Newp and Frannie sit with some nice cucumber sandwiches—Frannie had made them herself, Mom emphasized.

This news had the troublesome quality of being both belittling and untrue, because Frannie had taken so little interest in the evening that she'd spent the last three hours talking on the phone to Newp's sister Betty and listening to the Big Bopper, and her mom had been making the sandwiches. Frannie just shrugged. "Yes. It took hours."

They sat on a loveseat next to the polished little table, and as Mom disappeared Frannie hissed at Newp, "What are you doing here?"

"I don't know, Fran, what're you doing here?"

"I live here. I thought you were going to the movies?"

"Okay, well, my father called and wanted me to go to dinner at one of the professor's houses. Had a daughter he said."

"You're here to meet a girl?" Frannie frowned. "How could you go on a date?"

"It's a family thing, and it turns out it's *you* either way, so bag it, beachcomber," Newp said.

"So you didn't tell me because it was no big deal?"

"Well, I mean, I didn't want to make you jealous."

She put up her hands. "Okay, what was this girl's name you were gonna meet?"

"It was Fran... ces."

"God." She shook her head. "You couldn't even tell you were two-timing me with me."

"In all fairness, we're not—"

"We're not what, Newp?" She stared. "I mean, what are we? Are we pals, am I someone you teach to surf, like one of the college girls the guys bring down?"

"No way, you're a natural on the waves."

"So I'm your surf pal, one of the Legionnaires?"

"Frannie," Newp scowled. "Come on. I thought you liked Hooky. You know?"

"Ugh." Although he had a point.

"You can't give me a hard time," Newp said.

"Why not?"

"First of all," he whispered, "because that 'ugh' was pretty noncommittal, and second, I'm actually here, so if you want to leave—look, start over.

If I asked you out, would you go?"

"I have no idea."

"Well, good, then here we are. You don't have to answer. Let's pretend you said yes and hey look, you made cucumber sandwiches."

She leaned in. "Actually, my mom made those."

"My god, you lie when you fall out of bed."

"Newpup!" Saul called. The two men were coming out of Pop's study.

"Newpup?" Pop asked.

"It's the kid's name," Saul said. "They give each other nicknames. This kid, he works for me."

"Right, he's Tommy Barlowe's son," Mom said as she entered with more snacks. "He works with Frannie, of course."

"Wait," Frannie said, "you knew I knew him? Why didn't you tell me—"

"Well, I didn't know you call him Newp, which is passing strange," Mom said. "But I knew he was the boy you spend so much time with. So fancy that."

"You get all this without leaving the neighborhood?" Frannie said. "You're like the Nero Wolfe of Laguna Beach."

"Thank you; now if you'll all join me in the dining room, we're going to have the liveliest salmon crunch you've ever seen, if I do say so myself."

Everyone was on their best behavior. Uncle Saul and Pop entertained everyone mainly with war stories. Frannie had no memory of the war, of course, though she was born while it was going on. Pop didn't fight—he was a refugee most of the time, first in Sweden, then Switzerland, finally across the Atlantic. By the time they had come to the United States, Pop's brother Saul was out of the Navy and they were all crowded into Saul's little three-room bungalow in the Catskills where he was an emcee and sometimes a comedian.

"Wait," Frannie said, "I remember the place in the Catskills." She had a forkful of turkey and she put it down.

"Oh, dear, I doubt it," Mom said. "You wouldn't have been five."

"It's possible," Pop said.

Saul said, "You came to the show, once, Frannie. Those days they didn't let kids in the nightclub, but one time your Mom brought you in and stood in the back with you on her hip."

Frannie's mind was tripping back to a dark, smoky room, and her uncle skipping from one end of the stage to the other, stopping to patter with the patrons. Suddenly she could see it, he'd bring ladies up and have them do a dance, he'd turn to their date and insult his jacket. Some of this she remembered and some of it, some of it was beginning to soak in, because the Blanks had either unlocked something or had rubbed off on her.

"Better rugs." Frannie snapped her fingers. "I've seen better rugs..." she snapped again. "Oh, what was it."

"My God," Mom said.

"I've seen better rugs at a flea market," Saul said. He laughed. "That's a toupee joke."

"That's not a fantastic joke," Pop said.

"What do you want from me?" Saul turned back to Frannie. "Are you kiddin'? You remember that?"

"Yeah," she said. "I do."

"So," Mom changed the subject. "What's this business I hear about the… Decency Committee?"

"League of Decency," Saul said.

"We got a flier," Pop said. He took out a pipe and busied himself with filling it. "Apparently a complaint is going to be reviewed by the Town Council at the July meeting about the crucifix sculpture."

"Well, what are ya gonna do," Saul said. "It's Kurt's art."

"They're gonna eat us alive," Newp said. "And run us out of town."

"Who's we?" Saul smiled. "You'll go back to school either way. Nah. I think we'll make it. People can't be that backward."

Pop raised an eyebrow and lit his pipe.

"Let them come for the art," Frannie said. "Just don't let them take the books."

"Café Monstro is what it is," Saul said. "It's all connected, more than you know. Nah, I'll fight for every drop of paint and dollop of clay.

Anyway, we got allies."

"Who's that, Uncle Saul?"

"A sort of informal league all our own—every gallery and bookstore in the city and many up and down the state will be watching." He stopped, because the phone was ringing.

Mom answered the avocado-green phone on the wall next to the bar and then looked Saul's way. She walked the handset over to the table, the long green coil getting wet in the ice cubes that had fallen on the bar. "It's your business partner."

Saul took the phone. "Kurt, whatcha got?" He tucked the receiver and looked at mom. "Hope it's okay to give him this number." Mom waved him off as they all leaned forward as though this were a really great radio show.

After a moment Saul said, "Are you sure?" A dark look came over his face and he rubbed his bald head. "When, now? No. No, we should go help."

He said goodbye and rose to hang up the phone himself, drumming his fingers on the bar.

Frannie bit. "What is it?" She was picturing a mob from the Decency League with pitchforks and torches, attacking the Kronos statue in front of the café.

But Saul was already in the hall getting his jacket. "Maxine Wolf's Book Nook is on fire," he said.

Pop shouted. "On fire? Well…I mean, they called the fire department, I assume?"

In fact, out the open kitchen window Frannie felt sure she could hear the distant sounds of sirens, but that was probably in her mind.

"No, it's—I mean, yes, sure," Saul said. "But you gotta understand. The book merchants call one another because the fire department, they'll save people and put out the fire. But getting a whole store of supplies destroyed. There's no insurance that really covers it, not really."

"Maxine's? My God, we were just there about a week ago," Mom said.

Yes, Frannie thought. And so was he, the man whose touch was paper cuts. *Before he finds it.*

"So we're gonna go, even if there turns out to be nothing to do," Saul said.

Pop nodded gravely at this. "What do you aim to do?"

"Drive by, see if Maxine is okay, maybe see if we can help save her stock. Maybe take some and store it for her. Water damage, my God." He jangled his keys.

"I want to come," said Frannie as Newp nodded. "We'll come."

Saul looked at Mom, who shooed them. "Of course. But you stay out of the worker's way and do what your Uncle tells you."

The three of them bundled into the front of Saul's panel truck and rolled downtown, following the sound of sirens.

"Okay, what's the real story, Saul?" Frannie asked as they made their way down the block. She was sliding around the bench seat, alternately colliding with Saul's elbow and landing in Newp's lap. The truck had zero suspension.

"Just helping a merchant."

"More than that," she said.

"Maybe it's nothing."

"But you don't think so," Newp said. They were passing the Kronos statue in front of the Café and turned off Coast Highway, the gleaming lights of the Riviera Hotel behind them. Up Main, and now the emergency lights flickered bright over the dark streets.

"Yeah, there's been scuttlebutt about some oddball has been hanging around the bookstores," Saul said.

"Not someone like an arsonist?"

"What does an arsonist look like?" Saul said. "Nah, no one describes him. That's why I think he's something else."

"What do you mean something else?" Newp asked. "Not someone."

Saul frowned into the windshield. "We call them collectors. But this one. The one who likes fire. That's the Book Man."

"And not the kind looking for a first edition of *Leaves of Grass*, I take it," Frannie said.

"No." Saul pulled off into a vacant lot and now drove through a gate that said YOU LOCK-IT. The headlights and a few scant overheads lit up row upon row of cheap storage buildings, and beyond that, at the end of the drive, darkness except for what Frannie took to be vehicles. Saul glanced at them. "Can I trust you—both of you?"

"Sure," Newp said instantly, but with a hint of incredulousness

"This guy," Saul said, "the one who set this fire—and I know he set this fire—he's looking for Blanks. He's combing the city."

"What for?"

"Pure potentiality, for someone like him, it's… fuel. It's power, and power we can't let fall into his hands."

Frannie asked, "Well if that's so, why would he come here and not hit us?" They had left the storage buildings behind and had rolled into a row of parked boats and trucks. Frannie watched the prows slip by in the dark, the streetlights dancing between the masts and trailers and casting fingerlike shadows on the car.

"Hold up," Newp said. "What are Blanks?"

Frannie touched his arm. "Special books, very rare, leave it at that. We have a bunch of them. And around here, *only* we do. Right?" This to her Uncle.

Saul lurched to a halt next to a boxy aluminum trailer not much smaller than his car and began to back up to it. As he maneuvered the car towards the trailer he said, "The collector can smell them. That gets him as far as

Laguna Beach, anyway."

"So how come he hasn't found them? We have lots of people come looking." She nearly said, *How come he hasn't found us.*

"That's complicated," Saul said. "Help me with the trailer. Hurry."

They left the car doors open and in a few moments, after much cursing and shouting of instructions, the rear of the car dropped as Saul lowered the trailer onto the hitch.

As they hustled back to the car, Frannie asked, "Complicated how?"

"You know how you're studying the curses, the *toykhekhe?* Well, we got other stuff like that. We have ways of blocking guys like this." They got into the car and Saul started to gingerly back up the trailer so he could aim his car back towards the road.

"Like what?"

"Like we can put a sort of a screen on the place."

"A *screen?*" Frannie asked.

"Some really hard-shelled Hebrew stuff, takes a while, but when it's done, we're in the screen. We're behind it, or the Café is. He can't smell 'em in there. He'd have arrived in town and then *bupkis*, and he'd have to start flat-footing it, work it like a detective."

They pulled back onto the road.

Newp said, "But if I were this Book Man, okay. So I'm being Mike Hammer now, right?" Mike Hammer was a book series and a TV detective show with Darren McGavin. Frannie's pop liked it. "I already know somewhere in town they got a stash of special books. I mean, Mike Hammer would take one look at Café Monstro and say, that place with the wacko sculpture, I gotta check that out."

"Not if he can't see it," Frannie realized. "Is that it? He literally would look right at it and miss it."

Saul nodded. "Can't see it, can't even hear tell about it."

"I ran into this guy." She was certain.

"What?"

"I know it." She was picturing the man whose face shifted as he stood in the gazebo in the field by the library, watching her go by and not watching. "I saw him coming out of Maxine's Books on 3rd. He ran right into me. He was… he was weird, like he was there and not there. He acted like that too."

"What did he look like, did you get a good look?" Saul was intense now. "No one has said."

"Uh… my mom thought he was handsome. We saw him for just a moment. Yeah. He had a tweed jacket, and a beard. Like a…"

"Like a professor."

"Right, right. But with a face that kept moving." She shook her head. "I'm sorry, I know that's strange."

"Go on."

"His face looked blurry, like it was in several places at once."

"I think it's a *swartz-yor*." Saul whispered.

"A bad year?"

"Don't be so literal," he said. "The Book Man is a devil. A demon."

"This is crazy," Newp said. "We were talking about saving inventory from a fire. You guys sound like you're looking for a fight with Vincent Price."

"But why would he set a fire?" Frannie asked.

"I have some idea." Saul cursed and slapped the wheel, and then a burning bookstore came into view.

CHAPTER 23

Within moments, the flickering fire filled their vision, mixing with a swirling circus of emergency lights. Frannie saw a police car, long and black, and a white station wagon with a wooden AMBULANCE sign on its door.

Maxine's Book Nook, like Café Monstro, stood back from the road. Though it was three miles from the ocean, its owner had taken great care to remind visitors of the beach vacation they were almost surely taking. A facade of cut palm trees covered the front, and the roof was thatched. Sundry license plates of bright blue and white were nailed to the palms, and a life preserver hung next to the door. An expanse of sand and cyclone fencing, scattered with starfish and shells, spread out before the entrance. And all of this was on fire. Especially the thatched roof.

Saul jumped from the car. "Maxine!" A woman in jeans and a pink and yellow blouse looked back at them from the sidewalk. Maxine was in her 60s, with short hair and glasses, her makeup smearing behind her black frames.

Frannie and Newp got out and followed Saul, and the hissing of the fire hoses drowned out all sound. Two firemen handled one enormous hose, spraying the bookstore in methodical sweeps, left to right and up and down.

Two cars with trailers screeched to a halt and their drivers – a man and a woman, both in khakis and a sweater—emerged as all converged around Maxine.

"Saul," said the man in khakis, "what's the plan?" He and the woman looked at Frannie and Newp and Saul quickly gave a they-work-for-me introduction.

"And this is Dick and Darla Cosgrove, they have the Tattered Edges off in Malibu."

"We came as soon as we heard," Darla said. "We brought two trailers."

"I don't know how it started," Maxine said, wringing her hands. "I was making a deposit at the bank and came back—" and she waved, her fingers drifting towards the fire.

"What can we get, Maxine?" Saul asked.

"They wouldn't let me near it," she said.

Frannie turned and looked at the firemen handling the hose. There was one standing next to them, wearing the same red jacket, but with stripes on the shoulders. He had a moustache the size of a street broom. "Excuse me!" she ran to him. The Chief, or so she thought of him, looked her up and down and waved her off immediately, shouting.

"We're friends of the owner," she said. "When can we go in?" She gestured for him to follow to meet the gathered store owners.

"Look, people," the guy said. "I don't know what you think—"

"The fire is basically out," Saul said, and indeed the roof was smoldering, the water working its wonders. "We're not crazy people, but if you're gonna keep spraying, we need to save the merchandise."

"We're absolutely gonna keep spraying."

"So?"

The Chief looked back at the men with the hose, then at Saul with the same skepticism as before. "What do you want to do again?"

Maxine rubbed her lips, leaving a great smudge. "The front is all a loss," she said. "But I have a cage in back. Metal walls and ceiling. For the rare stuff. IF we can get back there we can save some inventory."

"Lady," the Chief said, "don't you have insurance for that? What if this place falls down around you?"

"Insurance? These are collector books, *no*, we don't have that kind of insurance, and besides, these things… they're priceless."

"Look," Saul said. "You'd say this is pretty much out, right?"

The Chief nodded grudgingly.

"We just want to go around back," Saul said. "We take what we can get. We put it in our trailers; we can store it separate until you're ready for it." He looked from Maxine to the Chief. "If we can get in the back, we need to, before the water gets it or god forbid the fire starts again in there. There's gonna be water leaking everywhere, we gotta save her stuff."

Frannie and Newp came around the back of the building as the drivers brought the cars around. The rear wall was shingled with ugly, gray asbestos, and the closed door was aluminum.

Maxine got out of the car with a key and brought it to the knob. "Careful!" Frannie said. Was the lady completely out of it? She guessed so. "It's hot, don't touch the door."

The lady wrapped a scarf around the key and made quick work of turning the lock and kicking the door open.

They peered into the bookstore. Starlight streamed in through the ceiling and Frannie saw water dripping everywhere over charred and unrecognizable bookshelves, and the smell of burnt paper hit her and made her nearly swoon. The Chief came up behind, brusquely shoving them aside as he looked and then stepped in.

The Chief stood for a second inside. "Okay." He called back to the door. "I see a metal door over there, a big metal, I guess a vault. That it?"

"Yes," Maxine said.

"Okay, go, and try not to touch the metal."

Maxine and Saul made it to the vault—for it was a vault, right out of a bank—and Maxine got it open. "One at a time, grab an armful, and get back to the trailer," Saul called.

When Frannie entered the vault she saw columns of books stacked against the metal walls, all preserved for now. That was a blessing, she figured. She grabbed an armful of history books, Pliny the Elder staring at her, and hustled out, passing Newp as he headed in. One after the other they grabbed books and hustled back to the trailer, a large, empty space that rapidly filled with the volumes.

After what must have been thirty trips, Saul's trailer was full of rare books, and Saul clapped the trailer shut and hauled it out of the way so they could get Dick and Dale's trailers closer. They filled those, too.

It was 2AM when Saul put his arms around Maxine, and Frannie heard him say, "We'll keep them safe. I promise."

They hurried back to the car.

As Frannie opened her door, Saul tapped the metal roof and she froze. "What?"

"Look across the street. Keep talking to me and point at the trailer like we're talking about that."

Frannie turned towards the trailer hitch and studied the buildings across the street.

The building she and Newp glanced at was about two stories tall, a department store.

On the roof of the building was a shadow. In the dark, she could make out a familiar tweed jacket.

"I see him," she said.

"Get in," Saul said.

They drove in silence for several minutes until Frannie noticed that Saul failed to turn right onto Ocean Highway, but instead went left heading further north.

"What are you doing?" Frannie asked.

"I know why the fire," Saul said, his eyes flipping to the rear view. Frannie looked back. The highway stretched endlessly black behind them.

Frannie closed her eyes, then: "He wants to find out where we go back to."

"Yes," Saul said. "Like I said, I have a powerful – shall we say a powerful blessing on the café. It makes it difficult to find for those like him, those who would do it harm."

Now, far behind them, a pair of headlights swung into view. "He's behind us," Newp said.

Frannie watched the highway unfurl in front of them. "So where are we going?"

"Somewhere that he won't find what he's looking for."

They drove on for miles in darkness, only occasionally seeing another car pass in the opposite direction. There was almost no one else on the highway, and streetlights were scarce as they drove along, the beach invisible below the cliffs, the ocean shimmering in the distance forever. Still the pursuing vehicle remained.

After a while, they passed a battered sign that said Milpitas Cafe Next Right, and Saul began to slow the Studebaker. "We stop and you guys can stay out of sight," Saul said. "I think I've been a little foolish to let you come."

Frannie said, "If you'd stopped to let us out, he would've caught you."

"I don't think so," Newp said. "He wanted to follow us. but, uh, is this really a fight that we want?"

Frannie ignored this, because now they were turning right into a winding seaside road, twisting past sand and cyclone fencing. Chunks of old cement on the rough road groaned loudly beneath their wheels.

Saul steered the Studebaker around another curve and now a ghostly sight came into view – an old, wooden-fronted café that looked as much like a seaside cottage as a place of business, with a clay tile roof and flowerpots under the windows. Atop the door next to the Milpitas Café sign, crooked and dirty, was a second sign bought somewhere at a hardware store. KEEP OUT. The car ground to a halt, the trailer lurching behind them.

Saul sat for a moment behind the wheel with the café in the headlights. Then he started to roll again, driving slowly around, and Frannie watched the edges of the café glow with the headlights until they reached the back lot, which was cracked and weedy.

Frannie and Newp looked at one another. Saul turned bodily, looking back. The other two mimicked his movement, but they saw nothing. Saul began to get out, when Newp said, "Wait, what are we doing?"

Frannie thought that the only thing to indicate that Saul was in the least bit worried was the uncommon sheen of sweat on his bald head. "You two help me open up," he said. "Then I want you to run for the sea."

"You don't have a plan?" Newp press the point.

"My plan was to get him away from Cafe Monstro. Now let's move quickly. Get inside."

They crawled out of the car and Frannie said, "I'll get the sign in front."

"Right."

"What?" Newp asked.

"The place needs to look open," she said. Frannie realized that she and Saul were simpatico now, as though her uncle's mind were a wave that she could surf on, and she was annoyed that Newp, such an expert surfer, was being left behind.

Saul cursed. "The back door's no good." In the dim light Frannie could see heavy boards nailed to the frame.

They all high-tailed it around to the front rather than bust down the back. Frannie ripped down the temporary sign and tossed it into the weeds.

"Well, in the night the place might look open."

"I think he's probably fairly susceptible to illusions," Saul said, "but it's just a feeling." Saul was about to kick open the front door, when Newp stopped him.

"You don't have a key?"

"You want me to go back and look for it?"

"Hang on." Newp and pointed to a narrow window above the door of the café, and looked at Frannie, gesturing that he was going to go up.

She frowned. "You think you can fit through that?"

"Is it safe in there?" Newp asked.

"Safer than it is out here."

They made the switch in an instant, Newp lacing his fingers and Frannie lunging up to the window, to touch the long narrow frame. To her delight, she found that she could push it in. It was old and jammed with soot, and the pushing was slow.

Within moments, Frannie dropped to the floor inside with the crack of old linoleum against her tennis shoes. She took a moment for her eyes to adjust, turning to scan the inside of the café.

Someone was standing in the middle of the waiting area of the café. She let out a yelp, then at the same time that her chest was flooding with adrenaline, she recognized that it was a cardboard standup, Cary Grant from some old movie, holding up a gallon of milk.

Cary Grant in cardboard was situated before a long row of tables and chairs. Next to him was a greeter stand, and a little behind him, the lunch counter and waitress station. The room was bluish gray in the moonlight, crumbling and giving off flickers of light with aluminum and Formica that shown here in there through what must've been an inch of dust. So this was Saul's old place.

Frannie turned back to the front door, finding a deadbolt and sliding it back. She yanked the door open, and beams of light with them as Saul and Newp emerged with a pair of flashlights they had retrieved from the car. Frannie could see the car's trunk hanging open where it was still parked in the clearing before the café.

Now Saul closed the door and the three of them stood in the crumbling café.

"What now?" Frannie asked. "Do we bring in the books?"

"No, it's enough that we're here."

Frannie stepped to the window, thousands of tiny pieces of wreckage crunching under her shoes. She looked out the window at the car, the trailer, and the blackness beyond.

"You were saying something about running to the ocean? Because that seems like not such a bad idea."

"I'm with Frannie," Newp said. "Look, I'm not saying I'm a coward or anything, but we don't have anything to fight a madman with."

"I don't think you're a coward," Saul said, "but I don't think he's a mad man, because I don't think he's a man."

"Then let's run," Frannie said. "To the ocean. We can come back for the car after..."

A pair of headlights first came into view, whipping around the lot. A huge green Morris Minor pickup pulled into the decrepit lot, until it came to a halt with its beams on high and cutting across the front of the café.

"Get down!" Saul hissed. They ducked below the front window.

"We should get behind the counter," Frannie suggested, and they scurried low through broken tile and bits of plaster until they reached the other side of the counter. They took shelter with apparently nothing to protect them but shelf paper.

Frannie put her fingers on the aluminum edge of the counter and pulled herself up, looking out. Gauzy curtains hung in the front windows, the beams of light from the pickup truck showing through the window and sending clear-cut shafts of light through the café. Motes of dust shimmered in the light as the truck moved again, causing the beams to sweep across the room. Frannie whipped her head down.

Saul whispered seemingly to himself, "What is thy suit, *swartz-yor?*"

Crouched behind the counter, Frannie watched the headlight beams light the room blue and filthy overhead, illuminating a calendar that said Southern California Water Department 1952. And then the beams cut out, and the engine of the pickup truck stopped.

All was silent for a moment as Saul stood, moving into the shadow of the door to the kitchen and through. Frannie and Newp slid through the door into the kitchen behind Saul. From there they could see through a window out of the kitchen, across the counter, and out the front of the café.

The door of the Morris Minor swung open, and after a moment the Book Man emerged and stood still, facing towards the café.

Below his felt hat, Frannie could not see his face. But she could see the feather in his hat band shivering in the wind. The Book Man shut the heavy pickup door with metallic *thunk*. Then he stood there in the moonlight, his hands by his sides, staring out from under the brim of his hand. His brown hush puppies shifted a second and he kicked up a small cloud of dust.

Whispered Newp, "Hey Professor! Out a little late, aren't we?"

"What does he want?" Frannie hissed.

"Well, obviously he wants the Blanks. He thinks maybe we have them," Saul said. "And right about now, I think he is considering either he made a mistake, because blocking spell or no, this place doesn't look like a bookstore or a place where we might keep anything."

"Why did you even pick this place?" Newp asked.

"Did not tell you? My ex-wife and I used to own it."

"When?"

"Before she ran off."

"Guy has an ex-wife." Frannie mumbled. "And all this time…"

And then a loud flutter spat staccato outside and Frannie gasped, then cursed herself for gasping.

The Book Man had not moved, but his form was shifting, swiveling left and right without actually moving, and then the elbows of his jacket burst like a popped piñata. The elbow patches split open and a long spray of something white and fluttering shot out, and now as this stream dispersed in the air, Frannie could make out tiny movement, strange and differentiated, white and fluttering loud as it began to swirl around the Book Man's body.

She shifted her head a little to see across the room through an open curtain. And as the clouds merged and started to flutter around the Book Man, she could describe them no better to herself then to say that the Book Man seem to be surrounded by a fluttering cloud of origami sparrows.

Each sparrow flitted all of its own, its paper wings stuttering in the wind, each one no bigger than the size of a cigarette pack.

Frannie retreated into the shadows even more. Newp was still staring over the counter, mouth agape.

The Book Man remained still, but a section of the cloud of origami sparrows moved off and swept away from him. Then the fluttering cloud dipped and coiled across the ground, up onto the porch, skittering over the peeled wooden railing and support posts. The sound of paper from the cloud of birds echoed loudly and could be heard all the way into the kitchen.

Frannie bit her lip as the birds began to thump against the screen door and the windows. They flapped faster now against the glass, some of them rapping hard, a white blur behind the curtains. One of them whacked the glass so hard she thought that it might break. The doorknob seemed to rattle as though the sparrows were trying it as they bashed against it.

"What the hell?" Newp spat.

"No idea," Saul said. "This I haven't seen."

The cloud spread out and stretched beyond the length of the front of the cafe, slapping clumsily against the windowpanes all around the house. Then Frannie saw nothing outside at all. The whole café went even dimmer, because the sparrows had covered every window.

She heard a creak in the back and something metallic crashed loudly. Buckets hitting the floor. Saul cursed.

"What was that?"

"That was the back windows," he said, "I have buckets of tools stacked against them. They've made it in."

The sound of fluttering wings, soft and papery, filled the air in the kitchen, and now the double doors into the kitchen began to swing. Frannie heard hundreds of tiny paper beaks against the door to the kitchen, and then the doors crashed apart and the birds began to flow in. Frannie froze as the clouds moved into the front of the café, creating little tendrils of origami sparrows, snaking up-and-down and everywhere, searching.

Frannie lowered herself until she lay flat on the floor beside the refrigerator. She brought her hands to her chest as a column of paper birds fluttered down among discarded cups and pots and pans behind the counter. They moved past her feet, brushing past it by inches. Beyond the refrigerator she saw that Saul was surrounded in the corner near the kitchen door, the tendrils sneaking past him, just missing him.

Then the tendril of paper avians whipped around in front of Frannie and came back, one sparrow flitting angrily in her face, just an inch or two from her nose. She gasped, watching its little paper wings flap as it hung before her. Written—no, printed—on the wings were hundreds of lines of text.

They were made of books, she realized, and then: *he is made of books and his touch is made of paper cuts*, and then the sparrow pecked her in the eye. Frannie screamed, clamping her eyes shut and the birds set upon her. She felt them peck at her head and hands as she waved her arms and lost all reason rising up and flailing. She hauled and smashed her toes against the stainless-steel legs of the counter, *it's in my hair get it out*, and she heard Newp flailing against them as well. Frannie smashed against the refrigerator and pain shot through her as one of them sliced her forearm. Her hand fell on a towel wrapped through the handle of the refrigerator. She grabbed it.

"Aargh," Saul shouted in pain and Frannie ripped the towel from the refrigerator handle and waved it, swiping it in front of her face and all around with no real goal or thought.

Stinging in her skin. Blood in her fingers. And now a buzzing, the fluttering becoming something new and deeper. The army of paper sparrows buzzed as one and made a slicing sound she could understand.

Where… are… they? Give them to us…

Frannie swatted with the towel, and shouted, "Give *what* to you? Who the hell do you think you are?"

"Frannie," Saul said, "Get down."

"No," she said. "This *meshuge* college professor is getting on my last nerve." That was it, she told herself, *get angry and get strong.*

She held the towel over her face as she stormed past the end of the counter, paper birds flapping around after her, some pecking at her and others flipping out of her way.

"Hey!" she called as she yanked the front door of the restaurant open. Frannie stepped out onto the front porch and had to stop for a moment as she got a good look at the Book Man.

He was a double geyser of paper birds now, the swarm fluttering out of his leather elbow patches and the backs of his legs, ruffling the loose khakis he wore and lifting the flaps of his tweed.

You have brown eyes, thought Frannie, as dead as Cain's brother Abel.

The Book Man looked at her, shifting his head as the paper birds swirled around him. Frannie began shouting. "What do you want! You got no business here!" Then she added, without really considering how absurd she sounded, "You hear me?"

The face of the Book Man stuttered in her direction and she heard a whisper: *Then tell me where they are.*

"We don't know what you're talking about." Frannie spoke aloud in response, but aimed her voice up without thinking about it, because the whisper seemed to be coming from the air. "We just went for a drive and you—"

"*Gey in dre'erd!*" Saul said as he emerged behind her, a towel wrapped around his head. "Drop back to Hell and let the angels of God bury you! Let the devil thou servest run in *terror!*"

The Book Man's eyes flashed, and his mustache twitched, but Frannie could not tell if the mouth below show disbelief or amusement. In the distance, Frannie heard an engine behind the Café. She looked around and saw the Newp was gone.

"We do not have what you seek, demon!" Saul stepped off the porch and stood in the rough sand, not fifteen yards from the Book Man. "We will not help you find it! Look no more and turn to God, or to hell with you."

The bearded demon began to laugh before Saul's Studebaker smashed into him from the side and sent him flying out of sight.

Newp was behind the wheel. "How…" she whispered.

Frannie had not noticed the car coming around the café. Now the Studebaker's high beams showed the Book Man crumpled in a heap on the rocky ground about 25 feet from the nose of the car. The birds had gone erratic and began to flow in reverse, heading toward their master. The Book Man struggled for a moment to a crouch. As his head pitched forward, the Book Man held a hand to his chin, but he was unable to keep the head balanced, and it fell forward completely and hung by a sliver of neck, so that his body opened up and briefly Frannie could see inside of him.

What she saw in there flowed with paper things crawling over one another like a hive of rodents. Now he put his head back and looked up, staring at Saul and Frannie. The dead eyes were just holes now, the illusion incomplete. Paper worms flowed inside those holes.

The swarm of sparrows in the air around him gathered closer underneath him and he was borne aloft by the paper birds and hidden in a cloud. The cloud surrounded the pickup truck and then dispersed towards the back, leaving the Book Man sitting behind the wheel.

He had his hands right at ten and two on the wheel, like the best driver in the world. He turned a blank, paper-filled head towards them, and with a strange normality, turned the ignition.

The books he sought were not here. Frannie could see him realizing that. They had wasted his time.

The Morris Minor pickup rumbled to life, and the Book Man unceremoniously drove away. For a long time they watched him go, the cloud of paper birds following in the wake of his truck and reminding Frannie of cans on strings, bumping behind a married couple's car as they drove away, JUST MARRIED. She could see the red lights of the rear of his truck through the cloud of paper sparrows, and soon the taillights and the paper birds and the demon disappeared over the horizon.

CHAPTER 24

The Book Man drove with ravenous anger through the canyon, the road a flickering blur in his bright headlamps. The Blankguards were frustrating him on purpose, and as he thought about the older man, his bald head and beady, angry eyes, the Book Man fumed. He would have the Blanks. But for now he needed something to stave off this profound hunger, something close to what he wanted, if not the whole cigar, as the humans would say.

The Book Man needed stories. He stopped his Morris Minor pickup at a crossroad and sniffed the air, casting his eyes down the hill. He saw only darkness, no town, no blanket of electric lights in the distance. Only the dark. He began again to drive.

Over the next horizon the Book Man saw a distant town perched atop a hill. He chose a road headed in that direction and barreled hungrily towards it.

In the Book Man's mind, he thought of meals past, so many indistinguishable meals. The recent juicy paper and meat at the bookstore fire in the north of that province called Texas.

The melted crayons and study paper and the flesh of a girl trapped in a Nevada icebox while playing. He had heard the sound—the sound of the smell, literally, the vibrations of particles on the air, and they spoke to him of books and death and he had crossed hundreds of miles to partake in *that* feast.

And he was going to feast again on the greatest of all, the Blanks, for the Blanks were rich and stories deeper than he usually had occasion to taste. It was the stories he liked, he thought, eating the stories, eating the value and the potentiality.

He killed his headlights and drove by instinct over the asphalt with perfect precision, the tan, rubber-coated steering wheel sliding through his thick human fingers.

The stories. The girl in the icebox in Nevada, he had tasted her story, short and unimpressive but so full of frustration and tragedy in the end, not the last dull tale to be rescued by a good ending. Her lifeless flesh and begun to run with the rough coloring book paper, a book of ragamuffin dolls on an adventure – – a story of mischievous dolls crossing the countryside, their reality seeping into the rotting flesh of their reader, telling a pungent story that even now the Book Man could taste on his nearly human tongue.

Briefly the Book Man had a vision of his first meal, eaten when he was but a few moments into this reality.

Angry he had come into the world, though not angry at the monks who had opened the door. They had been fools who thought they could change matter, dust into glass, iron into gold. Their incantations had attracted him, not for their wisdom but for their obscene hopes. So many things these mortals could do and yet never quite saw.

The men, those creatures God built to squirm across the earth and strive. He seethed at their hopes even as he lusted for them, he came on in fire and drank of their potentiality. He was above them and he would remain above them and he would not be mocked.

He would have the Blankguard's trove and would make of it his seat of power. He would consume and consume and consume, until all the children of men were empty. He would feast on their empty misery.

The demon sometimes called the Book Man hungered, and now having been frustrated, he turned his pickup truck towards his next meal.

CHAPTER 25

Frannie came running out the front of the Milpitas Café to throw herself at Newp, who now sat behind the wheel of the Studebaker with a stunned look.

She slowed as she got closer and then tapped the glass.

He took a moment and then looked at her through the window. Then he rolled it down. "Hm?"

"That was amazing." She leaned on the window.

"He turned into birds."

"I didn't even see you sneak out."

"Oh. Oh!" Newp seemed to come more into his own awareness. "Yeah, uh. It seemed like the thing to do." He turned, leaning closer. Frannie felt as though she were a carhop and he were about to order a milkshake. "You just *charged* him, Fran."

"Yeah." She reached out and brushed a few strands of hair from his face.

Saul came running up. "How did you pull this off?"

"What's that?" Newp said, and Frannie felt his hair drift away from her fingers. "Oh. It's complicated."

Newp got out and Frannie drew them together to hug them both. They were both so much taller than her that her head came to about the center of Newp's chest and about Saul's neck. At once the terror of the night caught up to her in all its absurdity and she became aware that she was still dressed for dinner, in a cocktail dress and heels.

"So," Newp said as he stepped back. "What was that thing?"

Not a *man*. It *was* a thing, after all.

Saul grimaced. "Why don't you come back to the café and we'll talk about it." He looked back at the broken-down hulk behind them. "Not this place. Café Monstro."

# # #

The Book Man followed his hunger and the swarming of words ringing in his head as he drifted down yellow-lit streets. He passed a car wash where a man in shirtsleeves sprayed down his Ford while a pair of teens goofed around—that was the expression, goofed around—in the next stall, washing a '57 Chevrolet and throwing sponges at one another, the streets warm and the air cool.

He passed a bar with seven cars in its a lot, but this did not interest to him; he wanted stories, but not that flavor just now, not the near-languageless stories of sadness found in a bar. He yearned for something else.

The Book Man drifted in the Morris Minor, feeling more at ease among possible meals, but still tense. Finally a great shadow fell across his windshield, lights from the tower—a university smelling of paper and glue, the smells moving like a shockwave through the air towards him.

He pulled into the parking lot, killing his lights and rolling to a stop before the library of the University of California at Laguna Beach.

# # #

"I've never seen him. But I've heard about the Book Man," Saul said as they gathered next to the stage at the Cafe Monstro half an hour later. The whole place was dark but for a swag lamp which hung over the booth, the lights sending out shards of reflected red and yellow through the paste jewels dangling there. Kurt had been waiting when they arrived and sat with them, dangling his skinny legs off the edge.

"Did you know about the Book Man?" Frannie asked Kurt.

Kurt shrugged. "I do the art. Books are Saul's thing."

"So why do they call him the Book Man?" Newp asked.

"Because he's made of books," Frannie said. "And I get the impression he likes to *eat* them."

"He likes to eat *stories*," Saul said. "He likes to find stories and consume them, especially in fire. This much I've heard about before. But what he really hungers for, really yearns for, is in *there*." Saul jabbed a skinny finger at the beaded curtain leading into the book section. "He wants the Blanks."

Newp nodded. "Okay. So do you think we threw him off the track?"

"For now, yes," Saul said. "Frannie said she saw him at that bookstore the other day. So I think we can surmise he'd learned about the local stores and felt sure one of them held the Blanks. He learned that the merchants have a co-protection deal, so he felt certain he would follow us to the Blanks. But he had no idea that the spell I had hiding the Blanks was powerful enough to confuse him, that he wouldn't be able to tell that we were leading him on a wild goose chase. So he's good and frustrated now."

Frannie said, "Well, frustrated doesn't sound like *done*."

"Nah, I don't think he's done. I think he'll lie low and look for another opportunity."

#   #   #

The Book Man moved along the cloisters of the little university and felt a thrill when every student looked at him. He liked the sounds of the place at night, the tiredness and the eagerness, students with books, some hurrying back to dormitories and some walking slowly, girls chatting with boys as they walked, heads hunched.

He heard the giggle of a young woman with brown hair and a ponytail, in a white sweater and brown slacks. He put on a look that he had observed many times, a human, a normal person looking withdrawn and distracted. The girl who had giggled was walking with another young woman, their heads inclined towards one another conspiratorially. The Book Man let them pass him and then began to follow them up the cloisters. The one who giggled said a few more words, and then they were saying good night, and he followed her into the library at a distance, the glass doors only briefly between them.

She made her way to the elevator, and for a moment she stopped and spoke with a young man.

The Book Man waited at a rack of magazines and leafed through a copy of House Beautiful as the girl and boy chatted.

He heard the girl say, "No, I'll take them up, I'm going up anyway." So she worked here, the fluttering paper birds in his skull said.

He was lucky that way.

He shot past the young man and joined the girl on the elevator before the doors closed, and she smiled wanly, not really paying attention to him. He put his back to the beige elevator interior. The little elevator was full, she and he separated by rolling book cart, an A-frame on wheels, filled to the brim. He pulled out a pipe from his coat and caressed it.

She was thinking of someone she knew. Her heart was giddy, and her mind shone with the story she was starting and restarting in her head:

She walks into a café—no, a cafeteria—now it was a parlor, a pizza parlor, and was morning, no, night, *flicker flicker*, story shifting, and she saw the boy studying and she said words/she laughed/she bumped into him/ no that was absurd/she smiled and said nothing and sat across from him, this coolness as absurd as the pratfall she planned as an alternate.

She looked up from this litany of fantasies. "Say, are you a professor here?"

He lit a match and brought it to his pipe.

Down in the lower floors, smoke began to pour out of the elevator shaft, with the sweet smell of burning flesh.

CHAPTER 26

As Frannie and Saul pondered the Book Man and waited for his next move, the Legionnaires became obsessed with one thing: the luau.

There were bonfires all the time, Frannie knew, but the luau was something else: a night-long ritual of debauchery and song. Frannie knew almost nothing at first.

She ducked into the office at Café Monstro and found Newp, Betty and Truly deep in conversation. Frannie figured they were talking about Ed Sullivan, but she heard the word *luau* and she perked up like crazy.

Newp tried really hard to look bored. "Don't worry about it."

"Oh, come on," Betty said. "Don't be such a drip. Let's go shopping, Frannie. I'll fill you in." This sounded wild coming from someone wearing a flannel nightgown because she couldn't handle any other threads. Frannie was dying to see what shopping would be like with her.

Betty saw Frannie's glance. "Oh, honey. I know I'm a piece of work, but I can still shop."

An hour later Betty, Truly and Frannie were downtown rummaging through racks of dresses. Betty turned out to have a good eye despite her sleepwear. She was holding up a polka-dot blouse that reminded Frannie of Daisy Mae in *Lil' Abner* and said, "The thing is, Newp doesn't want you to come to the luau. If you haven't guessed."

Frannie felt the blood prickle at her cheeks. "I thought he liked me." It sounded absurd. She wanted to find a hipper way to say it, but none came. For the love of Pete, she had spent all Saturday night fighting a man made of origami sparrows with the guy.

"It's not that," Truly said, as she picked up a jeweled head cover that looked like something a flapper would wear in *The Great Gatsby*. She put it on her head, then looked sheepish as the lady behind the counter cleared her throat to let the three of them know that they were being watched. Truly smiled and put the headdress down, sliding her hands over it and caressing the jewels.

Frannie asked, "*You're* going to the luau, right?"

"Ha!" Truly laughed. "I'll be there singing, and that's the *only* reason I'm going. Listen, you may think we have a really great integrated beach here, but the truth is it's not all that comfortable for me. I kind of get the impression some of the locals don't want me to get off the bus."

"They bring girls *in* for this party," said Betty.

"They what?" She didn't follow that. "What do you mean *bring them in*?"

"I mean," Betty said, dipping her head so the ribbon in her hair seemed to be talking for her, "they will literally have a van going to the local universities and bringing girls in for this party. *College* girls." She said this last word knowingly.

"Aren't you a college girl?"

"Not as much as some of these fellas would like," Betty said. "Besides, I think they're a little put off by the flannel."

"You just keep bein' you, Bets." Truly said.

"And what?" Frannie was incredulous. "Are you saying this luau is some kind of orgy?"

"No, not an orgy," Betty answered, "But they can get kind of wild."

"And they have a van? Whose van?"

"Oh I think it's Rafe's." That was one of Hooky's Legionnaires. "Anyway, Frannie, the thing is, *that* is why Newp didn't want you to come."

Ugh. "Because he doesn't think I'll put out at this party."

Betty crinkled her eyes. "No! Well, actually I have no idea, but I think it's something sweeter. I think he wants to protect you from it all."

Frannie folded her arms. "Okay. Well, if you were me, and your two best friends were singing at a party that all of your other friends were going to be at, would you let the boy who you were *occasionally going out with* keep you from going?" She thought for a second. "So you said they're taking Rafe's van?"

Truly and Betty nodded.

"So Raphael is on this bird hunt. And Newp doesn't want me to come. So that leaves Crainiac, Go-Go and at least a couple others to hit up."

"Oh, honey," Truly said. "That's not much of a choice."

"Well, I don't know anybody else who's going to go to this shindig."

Betty ticked off on her fingers, the frilly flannel sleeve waving. "Go-Go is in his own universe. He can't talk about anything but shaping boards. And Crainiac, he's as dumb as a post."

"That's not very kind," Truly said.

"Really?"

"I suppose he could be smarter," Truly agreed.

Frannie waved that off. "Okay, but neither of them has gotten particularly hands-y when we've been surfing." The more confident guys like Rafael and T-bone had an unfortunate tendency to let their hands drop all over her "accidentally."

The girls dropped Frannie off at the beach at 1:30 in the afternoon and followed the sound of the lathe scraping across wood. She found Go-Go behind a small shed near Hooky's hut.

Go-Go looked up. "Oh, hey, Frannie. I ain't seen Newp or Hooky. Actually...I think Hooky's in his hut, but you know..."

Frannie made a face. She didn't need to picture Hooky with whatever random female he had managed to steal like the Creature from the Black Lagoon off the beach.

She put a hand on the sawhorse and sidled up next to the boy. "Go-Go, are you going to the bonfire, you know, the luau?"

"Oh... yeah, I guess."

She moved her hand closer to his. "Do you have... a date?" She kept still and tried to avoid revealing how suddenly awkward she felt. She had been surfing for six weeks and was now as strong and muscular as an Olympic skater, but it hadn't taken away her basic fear of being judged by boys who could seemingly always try something else.

Go-Go gave her a steady look. He wasn't bad looking, Go-Go. Light brown hair buzzed short, like everyone, a deep tan, soft brown eyes. "Frannie, what the hell are you up to?"

She pouted and told the truth. "Oh, Go-Go, I want to go to the luau. And there's just no one to take me."

"That's some bull right there and we both know it." Go-Go smirked. "For one thing, I've seen this bit on *I Love Lucy*. You need a date and you're going to bat your eyes and get me to take you for *some* reason that maybe is just hilarious, at least for you, but that I promise you it doesn't work out for me. For some reason, here you are talking with *me* for the first time since you came to buy a board over a month ago." He waved his hand, indicating the board. "You know, there's a whole history of board-shaping. I could fill you in on all that. You can't understand surfing without a profound understanding of the board."

"I've kinda got a lot of studying going on already. But that does sound fascinating. Anyway…"

"So if I know my Andy Hardy movies, you want something that Hooky or Newp won't give you. "

"Ugh." Frannie folded her arms. "If I wanted to be psychoanalyzed, my pop already knows lots of shrinks. Come on, Go-Go. Newp doesn't *want* me to go to the luau. And I haven't mentioned it to Hooky."

Go-Go eyed her conspiratorially, "Yeah, but Hooky *guards* you, and you know that. Anyway, Newp doesn't want you to come because it's going to be deep in chicks, is why. I'm guessing that you don't really put out, right?"

"Excuse me?"

"It's just a question. I mean, do you? I'm guessing no." He looked at her expectantly as though he figured he'd get a lot of credit for this.

"Well, if that's all you're looking for…"

"Spare me, sister. You came to me." Then he squinted into the sun. "Point is, the girls at this thing, they *do*. So that explains a lot, I hope."

Frannie felt as though she's been slapped. She looked down, realizing that her face was tight, and she could feel prickling wet beginnings of tears at the edges of her eyes.

"Why do you want to go, anyway?" Go-Go asked. "To hear the band?"

"Yeah."

Go-Go sighed as if his life were comprised of a series of inevitable but poor decisions. "Okay, for Pete's sake, okay. But if I get close to some fresh catch, you're going to have to find your own way home."

"Deal." She shook his hand and kissed him on the cheek. "You're all heart, Go-Go."

"Don't mention it, jailbait," Go-Go said.

CHAPTER 27

The Laguna Beach Library sat on Ocean Highway, sided all around with glass and the occasional support column of gravel and cement. At one in the afternoon, the library hummed with polite activity. Kids found books for the beach. A few old folks in the history section were engaged in some kind of hissing argument. Julie Chen was on duty at the reference desk and couldn't make out the argument, for which she was thankful.

She held a pencil in both hands before her and closed her eyes, listening to the sound of the ocean that grew louder and quieter as the front door opened and closed.

"Excuse me." A deep voice in front of her broke her reverie. She opened her eyes to see a professor. That was her first thought, some local professor, elbow patches, beard, unlit pipe sticking out of the pocket of his tweed jacket. He held a newspaper loosely in his hands and seemed to want to ask her about it.

"Hello," she said. "How can I help you?" She shook the hand that he offered and found it curiously rough and solid, familiar even. When she was a girl, she had spent time on the docks in San Diego where her older cousin was a stevedore unloading cargo from overseas. His hands were like that: solid.

He unrolled the paper, showing her an item. "I've been reading about an event coming up," he said. "This complaint."

She looked at the paper:

CITY COUNCIL AGENDA, and various items. One of them was a complaint to be registered by the Laguna Beach Decency League, a name which made Julie both laugh inwardly and also register the tiniest ping of fear in the back of her mind. Not that she hadn't heard of them. They had meetings all the time, and Julie often wondered who on earth went to those meetings. "Yeah, it looks like they're going to discuss a place called Café Monstro at the City Council in a couple of weeks."

He looked at her just then, tilting his head as if he hadn't quite heard her, but smiled and nodded. "Could you say that name again?"

"Café Monstro?"

"Ah," he said.

"I know! Sounds crazy." She had the strangest urge to scratch his beard.

"I'll say," he said. "So do you know where I might fight this group, this Decency League?"

"You really wanna…" she stopped. "Sure."

Julie stepped away from her desk, touching his shoulder—also rigid as an oak—and he followed her to the community bulletin board by the door. She looked back at him as she pointed out a small yellow card, typewritten.

"They have a meeting today at four on the Gull Balcony at the Franc Pavilion. That's a summer hotel," she added hopefully.

"A summer hotel?"

"You're not from around here." She touched his shoulder again, shocked by those blue eyes. She wanted to fall up into them, somehow. "We have a handful of hotels that cater to the summer tourists. Franc Pavilion, The Riviera, The Sea-Air. Um. Where are *you* staying?"

The strangest sensation of warmth throbbed from his shoulder and made her shiver. How strange.

"With a friend," he said.

"Oh, and are you a… Lecturer?"

The man smiled. "Sometimes."

He reached out a hand and wrapped his fingers over her shoulder, as intense heat that traveled through her body. "Perhaps I'll be in to see you again."

She was lost in thought when she realized he had left, disappearing into the blazing sun.

CHAPTER 28

The only movement to speak of at two o'clock on a Sunday was Truly and Betty swaying onstage. Frannie did Saul a favor and tended to the last *goy* church luncheoners finishing their coffee.

Frannie thought the song they the girls were singing, *Saginaw Michigan*, was a neat choice, not properly a folk song itself, but more a pop country ballad that Newp had arranged to sound like something straight off of a Weavers record. Frannie poured the patrons another cup and gave the whole café a quick once over before allowing yourself to stop and listen. Truly and Betty, high and low, twisted their way around these folk songs and cast a spell on Frannie and anyone who chanced to hear them.

"Newp!" Came the voice of Saul from his office. "Telephone."

"Cool," Newp said and scurried off as Saul joined Frannie in the center of the café to listen to the singers.

Saul jabbed his thumb over his shoulder. "Your boyfriend gets more calls in this place than I do."

Frannie at sixteen was already old enough not to be baited that easily. "That's because he's running a business here."

"Boy, can you be harsh."

"They sound great, don't they?" She nodded at Betty and Truly. Betty was her usual strange dream, pigtailed blond hair hanging over her flannel sleepwear. Truly wore a gorgeous short cocktail dress. They were as mismatched as humanly possible and made a perfect sound together.

"They do indeed."

Newp came running up behind them. "Hey!"

"What?"

"It was the Sullivan show again. They're sending a scout to the luau." He turned and yelled this at the stage as the girls took a break between songs. "Hey!"

Truly was affixing a harmonica to a holder and looked up. "What are you yelling about?"

"The Sullivan show is sending a scout to listen to the show at the luau."

Frannie laughed. "Who was this again?"

Newp look to her as if he had momentarily forgotten how to form words. Frannie rolled her eyes and then threw him a lifeline. "By the way,

I'm gonna be there, whether you're going to be there with one of your college chippies or not." He didn't have a response to this and looked away.

"Well..."

"Oh, go on about the scout," Frannie said. Truly and Betty dropped off the stage to join them.

"Well," Newp said, "they want to listen to the show, but more it's a way of promoting the appearance on Labor Day. See, the press here will be interested in the fact that Sullivan is interested."

"Isn't that sort of inventing news?" Frannie asked.

"Making," Saul said. "That's why they call it *making* news."

Betty frowned. "I'm not sure it is."

"Anyway, this is fantastic for us." Newp put his hands up as if to frame Truly and Betty. "I'm telling you, you two are going to be world-famous. By the time we're done everyone will be wearing flannel nightgowns around the city."

Saul looked up just then, because he had heard something that Frannie had heard as well: a tiny jingling bell.

Frannie slapped her forehead. "Hey, so, I just remembered we have to get the remainders ready."

The way the book business worked, Saul had a line of credit with new book dealers, but had to send back the books that didn't sell if he wanted to get the next ones. This was a lot of work, and everyone was aware of it. It was a good excuse to scurry off.

"Absolutely," Saul said as they headed back to the book section, barely noticed by the still-chattering folk group.

Through the beaded curtain, Frannie found Saul standing with his fists balled out his sides, looking at a little black jingling bell above the black shelf.

"What is it?"

He didn't respond.

Frannie looked at the bell. "It didn't actually ring out loud, did it?"

"No."

"Can you tell me something—why is it that I can hear it?"

Saul waved a hand. Not interested in this. "You know the answer to that. You've become one of us. The magic is choosing you."

"So what does the ringing mean?"

"It means," Saul said, "that he's near."

CHAPTER 29

At four o'clock, Callie stretched her legs under a metal table on a terrace behind the Franc Pavilion, listening to Dolores Cleveland drone on. She waited, taking a sip of her iced tea and adjusting her hat to shade her eyes from the sun.

"… and of course we've got to get Jeff to do the special hot dogs," Dolores said.

Dolores was talking about a cookout that was coming up that did not interest Callie at all. They had all heard about Jeff's special hot dogs, which were, Dolores explained helpfully, coated in caramelized brown sugar. Dolores waited for Callie and the other two women, Phoebe and Margaret, to indicate their excitement.

Finally Callie said, "Can we talk about the city meeting?" She sounded more impatient than she intended to.

"Of course." Dolores was secretary but the meetings were an informal affair.

"Because I want to talk about this Café Monstro. I asked them to take down that—that cross," Callie said.

"You went there?" Dolores asked, looking at the other two.

"Yes, I did. To see if they could see reason."

"I've been there," offered Margaret. "My son Donny goes in there. It's just a café."

"A café with filthy art and dirty books."

"They don't have dirty books, Callie." Margaret waved her hand and snorted. "What dirty books did you find in there?"

"I wasn't *looking* for dirty books." Callie wanted to say *but it feels dirty*. "They keep their books in the back like they're selling illegal drugs."

Phoebe nodded. "They probably *are* selling drugs." She was on Callie's side.

"Does that old Saul look to you like a drug dealer?" Margaret chuckled. She was not taking this seriously enough and it made Callie's brain buzz with irritation.

"How would we know what a drug dealer looks like?" Callie asked. "Anyway, I told him that if he didn't take the more offensive pieces down that we would address it at the city meeting, and that he could very well lose his license to operate."

"Oh, Callie. Did you really say that?" Dolores patted the air in front of her. "Come on."

"Can we *do* that?" Margaret asked.

"Easily." Callie pointed at Margaret. "Your husband is Deputy Chief of Police. He can issue a public morals citation if any one of us makes a complaint. And I absolutely will."

"Easy, tiger."

"I think we should leave them alone," said Dolores. "I mean, what harm can one cafe do?"

"But it *does* harm," Callie hissed. "Monsters being crucified. Art twisting scripture. It's a message of disrespect, and all of those young people, all of them barely dressed and bumping against one another and it's—it does harm. You know it does. And just because that—" and here she dropped her voice—"that man who runs the place doesn't understand Christian values, doesn't have respect for what made this country great…"

"Oh, God," Margaret rolled her eyes. "Are you seriously going in front of the city council and hint that Jews can't be trusted? This is Southern California. You'll be laughed out of the room."

"Don't *oh God* me, Margaret Chatsworth," Callie said. "You just wait until your son comes home with some terrible… *VD* that he gets there." The man at the next table near the railing looked up at this with curiosity, or perhaps amusement.

"Ugh," Phoebe said. "Please, do we have to talk about VD?"

"I know all about that," Margaret laughed. "I loved *The Lost Weekend*."

"I *lived* The Lost Weekend," Dolores giggled.

"Next Wednesday," Callie said. "Whether you take it seriously or not."

Callie lingered after the rest of them left and the man at the railing nodded at her, tilting his coffee cup her way. Callie smiled. He was attractive in a very professional way. He reminded her of a lecturer she had known in Santa Cruz—but she couldn't recall just which right now—and she knew by looking at him that she would be deeply disappointed if his voice didn't sound exactly like that one, whoever that had been. It was an unreasonable expectation, but there it was. We expect people who look alike to be alike.

The man folded his newspaper and rose to gaze out to sea while turning slightly towards her, barely our yard away. She thought what he was doing was "cheating out," a theater term she'd learned in high school, where an actor in a play looks in one direction but actually is presenting himself for an audience in another direction.

"Beautiful," the man said, tilting his hatted head at the sea. He was speaking to Callie.

"Are you not from around here?" she asked. She felt her mouth go dry. Of course he wasn't from around here; this was a hotel. Absently she toyed with one of her sandals with her other foot as she turned more towards him, smoothing her white skirt along the length of her long legs.

"I'm traveling. I'm sorry. I'm not trying to be mysterious." He turned fully towards her and extended his hand. "I'm Ted. Ted Bookman. I'm a collector."

She took his large hand and gasped out loud as she felt it, and tried to cover this by clearing her throat, making an absurd sound. His hands were—she tried to work her mind around it. She felt as though she could cut herself on the palm of his hand. She felt her body flood with warmth.

"What do you collect?" She rose to stand next to him.

"It might sound strange, but I collect books."

"You have the right name for it," she answered, and to her delight his eyes crinkled as he met her smile. "I'm Callie, Callie Stevens." She felt so foolish.

"Mrs. Stevens. Pleased to meet you."

"Oh it's Miss… Well, it *is* Mrs., but I'm…"

"A widow?" Smooth.

"Yes."

"I'm sorry."

"Thank you." *Please say more things.*

He gestured towards the empty table. "So you were having a meeting?"

"Oh, yes. Sort of community organization."

"I see. A community leader, no less."

"Are you… I don't know what the word is. Collecting? Hunting? Today."

"Hunting," he echoed. "I like that. It makes looking through stacks of old books seem so much more exciting."

"I'm sure it can be," Callie said. She was watching how his grey eyes glistened as they reflected the ocean.

"So what is there to hunt in this town?"

"Um…."

"I mean, bookstores—any interesting collections?"

"Well, there was one downtown, but they just had a fire."

He frowned. "I hope they didn't lose anything valuable."

"Oh, I wouldn't know, but they mostly sold new stuff."

Now he seemed to be studying her eyes and she couldn't look away. "Anything else?"

"Well, there's…" Callie paused. Did she really want to send someone to that awful place that she was plotting to have shut down at the first opportunity? Surely that was unseemly. Nevertheless: "There's always Café Monstro."

He seemed to start. "Could you say that one more time?" The man cocked his head, the feathers in his hat jiggling in the air.

"Oh, I *know*," she touched his sleeve. "It seems absurd, but it really is called Café Monstro."

"I see. Where is this?"

"They serve coffee– it's a café, you know. But I must tell you, they have all their books in the back. The place has rather a bad reputation. It may not do for you."

"Who can say?" He shrugged. "Where was this again?"

"Oh, it's on Ocean Highway," she noticed he was staring intensely, hanging on her words. She added, "across from the Hotel Riviera."

"Across from the Hotel Riviera," he repeated, nodding. When he smiled he showed perfect teeth and his moustache moved. Unlike most professor types she knew, who got out of the army and went right to pot, he had taken care of himself, with a massive chest and a lean stomach. He reminded her of an adventurer in a novel or spy in an Alfred Hitchcock movie. Not someone Cary Grant would play, but someone that Cary would probably have to kill or be killed by at the end.

"And they have books, you say?"

"Oh, yes. Actually they have a collection of rare books. In a section in the back. It's very beatnik, beaded curtains and all that."

"This place sounds like an opium den." He smiled and she laughed appreciatively. *Take me take me take me.*

"Would you care to accompany me to this place?" As if the idea has been there all along. "I could probably use a guide."

I would go anywhere with you, she did not say out loud. The wind picked up and she touched her own hat to keep it from flying away. The roar of the ocean seemed far off as the waves sparkled and reflected in his gray eyes.

"Oh, I'm sorry," he said, folding his arms as she realized she hadn't actually answered him out loud. "I should know better. How forward and uncouth of me."

"No! Not at all." She had other errands, but now they had flown clean out of her head. "Of course! Of course. When?"

"I have absolutely nothing else to do." He spread his wide hands as though indicating an empty table. "We could go now, as far as I'm concerned. I could buy you a coffee for your trouble."

She indicated his empty cup. "You must drink an awful lot of coffee."

"A weakness," he said. "If you'd like to go, we could take my—well, it's a truck. I'm afraid it's awful, but it's useful for carrying a lot of what I pick up. It may be a little too rough for you."

"A little too rough?" She repeated. "No, a truck sounds fine."

She followed him off the terrace and through the lobby of the Franc Pavilion to a clean but battered Morris Minor pickup in the parking lot. She was forming a story about this man, now, the rugged intellectual, combing the highways and byways in his adventure-ready, trusted old truck.

When he opened the door and she slid in, he even took the initiative in fastening the seatbelt for her. As his arm fastened the belt around her, his forearm brushed against her hip bone and she felt an electric tremor travel through her body.

Then the strange Mr. Bookman went around and slid into the other side. As the pickup rumbled to life, he turned to her.

He smiled again. "Show me this place across from the Hotel Riviera."

The woman had no way of knowing, but not once had the Book Man heard the name of the café when she had said and repeated it, nor could he hear the address or even the street when she said them. When she said the name of the restaurant, all he heard was *skrrsksskrrsks,* static, like someone taking a coin and scratching the words out of his mind just as they came in. That was the Blankguard's doing.

They drove onto Ocean Highway as she pointed the way to go, looking up at him. He had learned so many theatrical tricks—the transfer of heat through his fingertips, the modulation of his voice to align with subconscious proclivities among the humans. He had wandered the earth destroying futures since what men called the Middle Ages, and he was a skilled hunter.

"The *skrssks* is right up there on the right, at *skrrsks*," she said, the number once again scratched right out of his mind. He drove along the highway, restaurants and hotels on either side.

"I think you said there was a hotel," The Book Man said. The paper screamed hungrily inside him, lusting, for he knew even in his blindness that the place was near. "You mentioned there was a hotel across from it?"

"Oh yes." Callie enthusiastically lifted her slender legs up onto the bench seat and leaned against him to point. "That's the Hotel Riviera, on the left."

"Ah." The Book Man looked up a bit to the left and saw a great white swoop of arches and a glassed-in swimming area, and a large carport for guests to unload their baggage.

Now would be the moment. As the Book Man drew near he kept his eyes on the hotel, hearing a certain blockage in his brain. And then when he knew he would be directly across from the place he sought, he turned his head.

And saw the Café.

Café Monstro: squat and black and guarded by a statue of Kronos, the old father and child-eater.

CHAPTER 30

The Book Man brought the Morris Minor to a stop at the edge of the parking lot. It was as though the café snapped in and out of his vision, trying to static itself over. He idled at the entrance of the lot, half in and half out of the street, when the woman spoke. "Well?"

"You know," he said, adopting his most calm and normal-sounding voice, "I think I want to park on the street." He shrugged and spun the vehicle around to find a parking spot in front of the Riviera Hotel. He looked again at the café and was mildly surprised that it was still there. So the spell was limited—and he had beaten it. He could feel the woman staring at him and so he smiled at her, remembering to crinkle his eyes because he had observed that cleverer mortals would not accept a smile without the crinkle. So many *rules*.

"Why would you want to park way over across the street?"

"Oh, I… thought we might want to visit the Riviera afterwards." The woman flushed crimson and the Book Man got out of the truck.

He had them now.

Callie was chattering mindlessly behind him, and if he'd known less about the rules of her society, if he had spent less time among them, he may well have snapped her neck without a thought. But he let her prattle as they crossed the street and into the parking lot.

He heard whispers from inside the building, whispers of the stories waiting to be consumed in the Blanks.

He nodded in greeting at the curious statue of Kronos as he walked right past it and up to the glass door. The woman was coming up behind him and when she reached him, he bowed with a flourish. "After you."

"Of course," Callie said, prepping her hair for a moment in her reflection in the glass. She cleared her throat and he took a moment to realize she was waiting for him to get the door. He had a vestigial fear the door may resist him, so he pretended not to notice, and she gave a minor harrumph of irritation, apparently assured he had forgotten all manners, and opened the door for herself. The bell above gave a jingle and he strode inside smoothly.

Darkness inside compared to the blazing light of the seaside highway, but his eyes—which were illusions anyway—needed no time to adjust. He took in the room as they stood in the entry next to a stand that said

PLEASE WAIT TO BE SEATED. On the stage in the back, two young women were singing a few bars of music and stopping, talking with a young man holding a clipboard. A series of statues stood in two or three available spaces between tables and he took in the first, an interesting sacrilege that gave off an aura of a sad man whom he immediately identified as the light-haired and thin person reading near the bar on the right.

He heard a clacking of beads and looked to the far corner to see a strung curtain through which two mortals now emerged, walking towards him at a steady gait. Of course it was the girl and the old man that he had seen at the fire. So there was no doubt.

Well. What do we do now?

The Book Man stood still, putting on a smile and not bothering to bring it all the way to his eyes. He raised his hand in a nonchalant gesture that he believed said *hi*.

The man with the girl stopped, and the Book Man was sure his name was "Saul" just as he was sure that the girl's name was "Frannie." He could read that much, as they stood side-by-side about a meter from him. The raised hand had been the only mode of communication between them so far.

Saul cleared his throat and was the first to speak. What would be is opening gambit? He appeared to choose a strategy and addressed the woman. "Callie, what brings you in?"

Callie laughed a little sheepishly. "I know, I know, it's as though I can't… well I *am* welcome, aren't I? After all, I'm fighting to *keep this place open!*"

Saul seemed unsure where to begin with this last bit. "Hey, you're always welcome. You hungry?" He moved his gaze to the Book Man. "And who's your friend?"

"This is Ted," Callie said, gripping the Book Man's arm with her small, bony hands. "Ted Bookman. Isn't that the most amazing thing? He collects…"

"I collect books." The Book Man looked for a moment at the girl. "I'd love to see yours. I hear you have quite a collection."

The girl Frannie seemed about to say something and his paper innards flooded with expectation at the heat and anger pouring off of her. Yes, she was righteous now, on her way to becoming some sort of shaman, whether she knew it or not. He watched her stow her anger and consider her words carefully. "Saul was telling me we need to close the book section for a few days." She shrugged. "Sorry."

"Oh, that's silly." Callie practically stomped her foot, jerking her knee a tiny bit. I just saw you come from back there. And anyway…" Here she adopted a faintly conspiratorial tone is she leaned towards him. "He's a collector, Saul, not a cop, you know?"

Saul smirked. "Seriously, Callie, what do you think we have back there?"

"I know *I'd* like to see!" The Book Man smiled wide, this time with his eyes and beard as well. He also added a hearty laugh. He made eye contact with Saul and read a great deal there, not actual thoughts but a clear communication. *You won't try anything foolish now. That much is clear. There are people around.* But that was not at all true. Because if the Book Man saw the Blanks he was ready to–

Saul nodded. "Well, then-- this way."

Frannie looked perplexed for a moment and then they all began to walk towards the beaded curtains, the Book Man's shoes cracking on the tiles. He touched his hat in a gesture of hello at a child eating a hotdog with a pair of young parents, the only patrons left in the café at this time of day. The family looked his way and went about their business.

They walked past the statue of a werewolf dispensing Holy Communion and passed the stage, where the Book Man recognized the young man as the boy who had hit him with a car at the Milpitas Café.

"Newp," Saul said, a slight edge in his voice, and the young man turned. They were nearing the beaded curtain and the Book Man was finding it hard to pay attention to anything else. The whispering grew stronger. The boy looked at him and recognized him instantly. What a delightful charade they were all putting on.

"Say." Saul stopped next to the curtain and turned, indicating what he thought to be a bird cage, with a gray sheet hanging over it. "You're an antiques man. I'll bet you'll enjoy this item."

"I would like to see the books." A throb was beginning in the Book Man's head, they were near, he knew it—or was the throb coming from...

"No, I insist," Saul said, and he pulled the sheet down.

The Book Man froze. On a small pedestal of iron stood a metal square about two hands wide and tall, and all through it were numbers.

"Excellent," he said, glancing. "Now I..."

Nine numbers up, nine across, nine rows, nine columns, did they resolve—

Never mind that now, the Blanks—

Saul had a cigarette in his mouth and pulled out a lighter. "This acrostic is something I picked up overseas. You know, I'm not even sure if it's correct?"

"I'm sure it's correct," the Book Man said, trying not to look at it. His head swam and the numbers stared back, enlarging in his vision and he had to know—Row 1, fine, Row 1 was complete, one through nine were there. "I'm..."

Saul flicked the lighter at the pedestal and the numbers caught fire, blazing with whatever phosphorous substance was painted on them. The acrostic blazed.

"Whoa!" Frannie and Callie exclaimed.

The Book Man threw up his arm and staggered back.

"Ted!" Callie tried to catch him, and he stumbled backwards past her, tripping over her as his arms flailed and the numbers sang, begging him to assure their resolution, *Row 2, was that—*

The Book Man fell, smashing his arm against a table edge and rolling.

Suddenly the girl Frannie was on her knees, close to his ear. He realized something was wrong at the same time she pointed it out to him, even as he could not look away from the numbers and could not look at them, as his brain threatened to shut itself off.

Frannie whispered: "Your arm is torn. You'd better get out of here before your girlfriend sees it."

And it was true. He brought the human arm on his right side around and saw that the table edge had ripped it from palm to elbow, the incision open and crawling with paper worms that squirmed beneath. He sat up quickly and pulled his sleeve down.

"Gosh, I'm awfully sorry," Saul said. "Are you all right?"

"Of course," the Book Man said, turning away and rising. Still the heat of the flaming numbers burned at his back. "Of course." This was all wrong. They would have more tricks. He needed to get his bearings. He must summon the patience of the prosecutor of Job.

"I'm suddenly… darling Callie, I need a… let's come back."

She nodded, looking concerned and clearly thrilled to be able to serve him.

He allowed the woman to lead him out. He had no need to hurry. The Book Man stopped at the door and turned back.

"It's no problem." He spoke clearly and distinctly as he adjusted his jacket and held his arms so that she would not see the damage. "We'll try again later."

CHAPTER 31

"What the Hell did you do?" Frannie paced in front of Saul's filing cabinet as her uncle took a place in his creaky old reclining chair, his desk overflowing with orders for food and liquor. The guy had actually come in the café!

"I used an acrostic," he said. "I was hoping it would work." He rose and went past her to open the filing cabinet. He rummaged around and found a small wooden box. "Here."

Saul turned back to her, holding a bronze Amulet about the size of a clam. "Take a look."

Frannie stared at the box. "What is this? The same as that metal sculpture?"

"It's for you."

Frannie saw the glint on the metal amulet, turning it over in her hand.

There were nine rows, nine columns, with a jumble of tiny numbers in them. Heavier lines on the amulet separated the big block of numbers into nine smaller blocks.

"I don't get it?"

"I don't either." Newp came in bearing a pitcher of water and eyed the amulet. "You scared him off with a crossword puzzle?"

"It's not the same, but it does the same," Saul said. "It's an acrostic puzzle. Solved, but you'd have to study it to make sure. The acrostic is an ancient form of magic to hold the demons at bay. This is a simple one, nine boxes, each line equals the same number. I'm not very good at them, but I've seen sixteen-box acrostics, even bigger."

"This totally freaked the Book Man out. Why would this have power against a demon?"

"Is just the way. They see it and it can slow them up. The forces of evil are often obsessive and one of the ways it comes out is in the need to count things. So they see a set of numbers like this and are compelled to make sure all of it's correct and equal. Did you ever meet someone who had to have things *just so*, their shoes tied a certain way, cans stacked a certain way?"

Newp spoke. "I do. Betty. She won't wear anything that's not soft."

Frannie was thinking of Natalie, a girl from school, nice enough, but she wouldn't eat any food that touched any other food.

"Well demons are kind of like that," Saul said. "So I want you to keep this near you. For protection."

Frannie put it in her back pocket and Newp said, "You got another one o' those?"

"You just stay out of trouble." Saul held up his hands. "He wasn't supposed to be able to find this place."

"What do you mean? *Anyone* can find this place. You have ads and parking. It's a café."

"For us it's easy. For him, not so easy. I made sure."

"How?"

"It's a very useful spell from the *Luria* that renders invisible a place such as this to *Kitzoynim* such as them."

"*Sprit of impurity?* You called him a *swartz-yor*, too." Frannie was thinking of the tentacles of paper sparrows back on the cliffs.

"Demons. Same thing." Saul waggled his fingers. "Can I ask you a question?"

"Shoot."

"You got acrostics amulets and mystic books and spells comin' out your ears. How did you become a guardian of these things?"

He sighed. "You really want to hear an old man talk about—"

Newp sat on the edge of the desk. "I know I do."

"Saul, come on."

"I came to it late. South China Sea, 1945. I was 22 when I came across my first Blank."

"How?"

"That's a long story, but suffice it to say it hit me in the head; it washed up in a wave and hit me. It was in a casket—a wine box." He gestured with his head in the direction of the cafe, and Frannie followed this in her head to the stairs up to the apartment where he kept the box into which they had banished the ghost. "We call them dybbuk boxes, because typically they're used to capture wayward spirits."

"That's not such a long story."

"Maybe it's not. But once I had one Blank I was compelled to find more. After the war, I was a manager at that club in the Catskills. Do you remember all that?"

"Oy." Frannie had spent two summers when she was ten and eleven vacationing at a resort in the Catskills. She had a sudden flood of memories of canoeing and bizarre Indian rituals and her parents dressing way too well for dinner every night. But that wasn't what Saul was referring to. She had faint, distant memories of her first several years in the United States, sleeping in the spare room of the cramped apartment where her family stayed with her uncle in precisely the time he was referring to.

"So I'm managing this place and one day this fellow, this audience member, turns up dead in the club. Just keels over between sets of the Flora-dora Girls. Turns out he drank poison—actually poisoned his own drink.

So we call his home and his son has just died in a car accident. Horrible thing. I found out that no one had come around to telling the guy yet. But the old guy had left a note."

"The father had left a note?" Newp asked.

"Yeah, it said: *I shouldn't have looked.*" Saul stretched out his hands, looking at his fingers for a moment. "In his suitcase I found a set of books, blank books just like the one that I got in the war. And this guy had *seven*. I remember I opened one and felt that hot flash and closed it. Because I knew what it was. Anyway. This guy read one and took his own life. And he should have *guarded* it."

"Have you read one?" Frannie asked.

"No. I don't read them. You shouldn't either."

"Why not?" But Frannie had some idea that the answer may not be satisfactory, but it was definitely going to be the right answer. Because she had not looked, and she had a feeling that she shouldn't.

"They're not *for* us," Saul concluded. "We're the guards."

"When you say we," Frannie said softly, "You're including me?"

"Frannie, the Blanks call to you. I can't explain how. But when they do, people like us are called to protect them." Saul shifted in his chair. "After those first seven, they started coming faster, and now I found that others, other people, would seek them. Just wander into the club like they were being pulled by an invisible leash. I didn't even have a *bookstore* then, just a suitcase. People would find me and ask to see one of these books, not even knowing why."

"But if the Blanks are dangerous for us, are they dangerous for everyone else?"

Saul appeared to think for a little bit. "You would think so. But it always turns out to be no. For those who are called, the Blanks show a possible future that is within reach, and a past that leads to it. That's the amazing thing!" He shouted. "I mean, take for instance a person's life, like your life or mine. So many things happen along the way. You're what, how old again?"

"Sixteen."

"Sixteen, times three-hundred-and-sixty-five days, and all of those days, stuff happens. But the Blanks take all that mess and serve up a... a story. A thread that might begin when you didn't even know what it was. A narrative. And if you get to see your story and know it, you can do it right." He waggled his head. "At least that's the way I figure it. All these books but none of them is an instruction manual."

Something struck Frannie then. "But... does that mean nothing great will happen to me?"

"Oh, honey, why would you assume that?" Saul smiled with kindness, shaking his head. "First of all, being a keeper is a profoundly great thing. But second, no, geez, just because the Blanks tell some people's stories don't mean you ain't got a story to tell. Nah. Get that out of your head."

"I gotta admit," Newp said. "I've been here as long as you've been open and I've never been... as you say, called by them."

"And it doesn't mean anything except that you don't need a book to pull you in some direction you're missing," Saul said. "Which all told is a good thing. At least for now. You're a kid, you have plenty of time to get off track."

"So are there others, others like you?" Frannie restated it. "Like us?"

"There are others," Saul said. "Scattered around. Not so many. We never had a reunion or anything. But yeah, there's others." He drifted for a second and Frannie could tell he was trying to decide whether to launch into another story or to wrap it up. "Anyways, one of them sent me on the path to take the books and learn to protect them."

"Are all of these guards Jews?"

"No. We got all kinds."

"Okay. So what are you thinking?"

"We need to *get into* Book Man. We need to find out how to send him away."

"Send him away?" Frannie asked. "Is that what you do with someone like this?"

"As opposed to what, kill them? You don't kill the Book Man. No, we saw him. He's not a live person."

Frannie thought about the Book Man's torn arm. "He's got a human body. Human skin."

"Yeah, he does."

"But he's full of paper. That's what it seemed like, right? Like he's full of paper birds. So do you think that skin is his?"

"I think the skin is probably stolen. And the birds are probably... I don't know. Self-generating, probably." Saul shrugged. "They come in and take over a body. Destroy the body in the process. I don't think the guy who owned the original skin the Book Man wears is going to be able to use it again."

Frannie tapped her lip. "And if we tear this guy up, what's to keep him from jumping into another body?"

"Listen to you, talking like an *abba*."

"What's an abba?"

Saw smiled. "A learned user of the powers. I don't know. I know general demons but each one is different. Even if we destroy the body, we will need to know how to make sure he stays destroyed. That's a lot of stuff we need to know."

"So what's next?"

"To stop a swartz-yor, first you need the most important thing. We need to know what he's really called. We need to know his *name.*"

Frannie nodded. "So: the question isn't *what* is the Book Man. It's *who* is he?"

Saul and Newp hit the books, but the answer came to Frannie at home, in a sepia-toned black and white memory that had been whispering to her for weeks.

CHAPTER 32

The next day, Frannie burst into the back of the Cafe and said the word, "golem."

Saul and Newp looked up from their study—papers strewn everywhere, while Saul had to peer up from behind a tower of books. "What?"

"It's so obvious," Frannie said. "If you want to learn something spiritual you have to *use* something spiritual, right?"

"golem." Saul repeated the word as though the blood had drained from it.

"Yes. Let's haul out all this bitchin' Hebrew knowledge and make ourselves a golem."

"Like the Golem of Prague?" Saul scoffed.

Newp looked up. "What's the Golem of Prague?"

"It's a movie," Frannie said. "Actually a fable, but yeah, I thought of it because of the movie."

"Where did you see this?" Saul asked.

"My pop showed it to his grad students last year and I saw it with them."

Saul cleared his throat. He made a teepee with his fingers and addressed his story to Newp. "In *The Golem,* the honorable and learned Rebbe Loew of Prague realizes that a great misfortune will befall the Bohemian Jews. What the misfortune was, who can recall? But what he does is fashion a living man of clay to do his bidding."

Newp frowned. "How does making a man of clay stop a great misfortune?"

"It's a movie."

"A fable." Frannie smiled.

"Right, because that's so much better." Saul waved. "So the rebbe makes the man of clay and then goes to the court of the Emperor to put on a show, basically, to do tricks and impress the Emperor, in hopes that the Emperor will aid the Jews. And do you remember what... I can't believe I'm even discussing this, but Frannie, do you remember what happened?"

"Well, he made some mistakes."

"The golem ran wild! He created even more problems! Now there was an eight-foot-tall clay man knocking down walls; he threw the Emperor's messenger from a tower, for heaven's sake."

"Now, that guy deserved it," Frannie said. The messenger was a jerk in the movie she saw.

"Even so."

Newp said, "So he's like Frankenstein?"

Frannie waved her arms with excitement. "A golem is a messenger of God, a walking piece of the power of God. You have oodles of research in front of you, but I'll go ahead and use the word, the golem is magic. He would have the answers you seek. You see? We could ask him to tell us the name of the demon we call the Book Man. That's why a golem. Forget the messenger and the emperor and all that. We should do it because we need answers and a golem is a direct line to God."

"And how do you know that?" Saul demanded.

"I…" She caught herself. Oh, what the Hell. "I saw the golem. He came to me during the accident."

"So, a concussion told you." Saul ran his fingers over his bald head. "He's—it's too risky."

"So don't make him so big." Frannie shrugged, putting her hand at about the level of the top of Saul's stack of books. "Make him, you know, manageable."

Saul put his hand on hers, tilting his head to study the height of the stack. "Like about a foot and a half."

"Like the Little Gingerbread Man," Newp offered.

Saul peered at his niece. "You just *see* this."

"He talked about *Emet*, about truth. Yes. I do."

Saul seemed to be thinking. "Well… Kurt has the clay."

"But how's it done?" Newp asked. "You know how to make a clay man?"

"The sculpting is easy. Bringing it to life, not so much." He started pacing, a new energy taking hold of him. He stuck his head out the door of the office. "Maybe we're all *meshuge*. Kurt!"

"Yeah?" Kurt called from his studio in the back.

"Get about four pounds of clay." Saul turned back to Frannie. "You're onto something."

You're onto something. She felt like she had waited her life to hear someone say something like this to her.

Frannie was not a religious girl. Her parents were intellectuals, played a lot of jazz, never went to Temple. But she knew a religious activity would be called for here. She threw herself completely unto the creation of the golem.

On the day of the beginning of the ritual, Frannie rose and kissed her parents. "We're making a golem today," she said to her mom.

Her pop didn't look up from his paper when he said, "Be sure he doesn't kill the king's messenger."

On her way out to the car that waited for her at the curb, Newp's engine idling, Frannie heard the laughing chatter of her friends with whom she'd begun the summer.

Carol from down the block threw her a glance from across the street but really barely noticed her as Frannie put her surfboard into the back of

Newp's car. When she got in, Newp nodded towards it. "What's up with the board?"

"We're about to start a long process, Saul says, so – oh, come on, I want to get some waves. I need it, it helps me focus."

They stopped at the beach and paddled our, even as Frannie knew that Kurt would be gathering up the clay and beginning to fashion the crude little body along the lines that they had described—basically Frannie drew a picture of the golem from the movie and said, "make him like that."

Frannie's own body felt unformed this morning—she was a paddling clay gangly thing, spindly but muscular legs and arms, almost no breasts to speak of, but here came the swell, and as she brought her feet under her she felt whole, completed by the wave.

"Pipe, Frannie," Newp called as a vast rolling tube came into being; she aimed for the pipe and hit it just right—she felt drums suspended in the air and in her mind, the chittering of the water hard against the underside of the board came in a drumming rhythm. Shoot the curl.

As she came in, they passed Raph, one of Hooky's lieutenants, and he muttered, "Not bad." Shooting the curl, lots of people talked it, but Frannie was doing it regularly now. That wasn't true of anyone else. Word was getting out.

"Not bad?" she repeated, hauling the board on her shoulder. "That mean I get to go to the luau?"

She looked at Newp and he made a face like he was embarrassed that she was putting him on the spot. "Frannie, come on, it's…"

"Never mind. I shot the curl. The rest is bullshit." They hit the café next.

"The instructions for making a golem come from *Sefir Yazzir*," Saul said, "in the second-century Book of Creation." Saul sat cross-legged in a little chalk circle in the attic of the café, wearing white robes. Frannie had no idea where he would have procured white robes, but she couldn't suppress her giggle when she first saw her uncle dressed like a wizard. "Put these on," Saul said.

Frannie ducked out to put on her own robes and came back feeling like an idiot. Like Gandalf in the *Lord of the Rings* books, which had come out when she was a baby and which her parents left around the house through most of her childhood.

When Saul saw his niece, he gestured for her to stand with Newp to Saul's right at one side of the circle, and now Frannie noticed a little bench on the opposite edge of the circle, about eight feet away on the bench lay a little sheet-covered effigy of a man, about the height of a Chatty Cathy doll. They had fashioned it from clay and baked it in a furnace out back the night before.

"You do the honors, for you have learned the *Luria*," Saul said, and handed her a knife.

She pulled the sheet down to the effigy's shoulders and beheld it.

Spectacularly, Kurt had given it exactly the bowl cut, little eyes and flat, thin mouth of the one in the movie. She carved a word in the clay man's forehead: *EMET*. Truth.

"Chant with me," said Saul. The three took hands and she followed Saul's lead.

The words coming out of Saul's mouth formed a word bridge of sorts—starting with a simple chant, just a recitation of the Hebrew alphabet, but this was combined with each of the letters of the name of God—the Tetragrammaton, YHWH, YOD, HEI, VAV, HEI— each letter of the Tetragrammaton combined with each letter of the alphabet, so that Saul worked his way through the alphabet and the Tetragrammaton like so:

Alef YOD, Alef HEI, Alef VAV, Alef HEI,

Beit YOD, Beit HEI, Beit VAV, Beit HEI

… and on, all through the alphabet and starting again, so that soon the words entranced her even as she said them.

For hours, chanting.

Saul broke away from his place at the circle and moved to the sheet-covered man. He held forward his hands, palms up.

"I use the words of the creator and wield the might that reflects Him and His secrets, I summon life with a sacred word, Adam, the man from golem, the man from Mud, the life from Clay. So be it, let him rest, and let him rise."

There was silence and Saul turned back and shrugged. "Okay."

"Okay?" Frannie stared. "What do we do now?"

"Now? Now we go for dinner." Saul walked past her, patting her shoulder as he went. "I've been standing here for hours and I could eat a horse."

Frannie's heart sank as they walked down the stairs. "But—I didn't see anything."

"It's a little clay man." Saul nodded at Kurt, who was hanging a new painting, and gave him the thumbs up. "Like a doll. Same thing."

"But don't you want to know if the spell worked?"

"Not as much as I'd like a corned beef on rye, Frannie. Newp! Make that happen." Saul was already pouring a beer from the tap. "Frannie, get yourself a soda."

Get herself a soda? What was this all about if they were already done and nothing had happened? She and Newp pulled up chairs and ate with Uncle Saul, who seemed determined to ignore her clear disappointment. Finally Saul said, "What?"

"It didn't work, did it?"

Saul shrugged.

And then they heard the pitter patter of little feet.

CHAPTER 33

"What putrid nonsense are you convincing yourselves of now?"

The voice boomed from somewhere in the room—though it didn't exactly *boom*; it sounded distant, ghostly; to Frannie it sounded like an announcer on a radio, reading something that excited him and everyone, but far away, like it was supposed to boom and in some distant land did boom.

Also it had an accent, so that the sentence came out VAAAATT PYOOTREED NUNSENSE AH YOU CONVEHNZING YOURSELF UFF NOWWW!

"What the Hell was that?" Frannie looked around.

Saul put down his sandwich. "Oh, boy."

The clicking sound of clay feet drew nearer, and then an eighteen-inch man of clay jumped up on a chair at the end of the booth where Frannie and

Saul sat. The creature stood in the chair and leaned forward to put his hands on the edge of the table. He turned his baked-clay visage towards them. And puffed.

He was smoking, the golem was. His face was cruel and gaunt and blockish, with two wild horn-like shocks of clay hair on either side of his otherwise bald head that reminded Frannie of a mad scientists' mane. In his mouth was a little clay cigar, proportionate with its smoker, and smoke poured out of the golem's mouth around the cigar in a regular, impossible stream.

Frannie was flummoxed. "Where did he get a cigar? Did you make the doll a cigar?"

"I have no idea, and no."

"You ASK the wrong QUESTIONS!" shrieked the little smoking doll. "You are like children who behold Einstein's theorem, you are a GOAT biting onto a Studebaker. You are TRAPPED," and here the clay man rolled his head as forcefully as he rolled the r in *trapped*, "*trapped* in the slimy, small, inconseQUENTIAL mind and you think yourselves GIFTED because on occasion you manage to summon the impenetrably dim wit to ask WHYYYY."

Frannie blinked at the doll and its thick, almost luxurious accent (*SLIIIMY, SMULLL, INCONSEQVENTIULL.*) "Maybe he made the cigar out of attitude."

The golem raised himself up and crawled out onto the table top, little clay arms and legs struggling as the smoke poured more furiously out of the corners of his mouth. Finally the creature sat on the tabletop next to jug of wine, leaning back on its two little hands, its legs stretched straight out before it. It puffed the cigar and looked at them. Had little black hole eyes. *"Zo,"* it said.

Newt finally said, "You have got to be kidding."

"I tell you, Christian," the golem answered him, "peer into the swirling gyre of meaninglessness that is existence, and then tell me who is kidding."

Saul cleared his throat. "Hey, baldy, you got a stopper for that mouth?"

"The only stop is the end, the abyss, final and oozing in its nearness but never its completion." The golem puffed.

"Great." Saul looked at Frannie. "I think we conjured my late Uncle Theodore."

"You must have had a very sad childhood," Frannie said.

"It had its moments."

"Do you really think it's a reincarnation?" Newp asked. "How could that happen?"

"No, I don't think that," Saul grimaced.

"Right, because that would be far-fetched." Frannie changed the subject. "Okay, so we got a golem. You are a golem, right? We didn't make a demon instead?"

"I am not a demon or an angel or the reincarnation of Saul Cohn's Uncle Theodore; I am just plain folks."

"But do you know the ways of—"

"YES, yes," the clay man waved his tiny clay hand. "Of course. I am a servant. For it is ever the dominion of the wise to be in service of the hopelessly limited."

Saul grimaced. "Hey! "

"Yes!" the clay man said. "Speak, de-MAUND, I'll answer."

"Shakespeare," Frannie said. "That was a bit from *Macbeth*..."

"Yes, yes, you're a girl who reads," Saul signed. "All right, golem. Ugh. That sounds terrible. What would you like us to call you?"

"Whatever your heart desires, for it is in our desires that we experience our deepest and most educational deh-LOO-zeeyuns."

Frannie blinked slowly. "I think Adam? Name of the first man. So there you go, Adam."

"Hang on, that's a *nebekh* name for a golem." Saul waved his hand. "That's terrible."

"You're an expert in naming homunculi now?"

"You should be so expert. Nah, that's tempting the evil eye... what about a diminutive, Addy."

"What about Truth," Frannie said. "*Emet*. Or Emmett, two m's and two t's."

"Mm," Saul nodded. "Emmett I can go with."

Frannie turned back to the golem. "We dub thee Emmett."

"I accept your designation."

"Great."

"It will stand as a reminder of the hopelessness of mortality."

Saul dabbed his mouth with a napkin. "Outstanding. Okay, Emmett, the reason you're here other than to share your sparkling personality with us is to identify a demon for us."

"You cannot identify this demon yourself?" The creature removed the cigar (to Frannie's amazement) and blew out smoke. But it had no ability to curl its lips, so the smoke just drifted out in a puff.

"That's right," Saul answered. "But we need to know in order that we may dispose of him properly."

"Mm," the golem shifted and looked to Frannie as though it were trying to tilt its head in consideration, except that its neck did not move. "I will have to see him."

"The demon?" Saul asked.

"No, the Archduke of Austria," Emmet said. "Of course the demon."

"Well, it's not like we have him locked in the basement: he's out there somewhere."

"You let him escape."

"Right," Saul said.

"Hey!" Frannie protested. "We fought him. But..."

Saul held up a hand, *save it*. "Emmett, if we describe the demon to you, can you identify him?"

"Yes."

"And help us catch and destroy him?"

Another plume of smoke. Where was the smoke even coming from? "I can tell you how he can be bested. But only the Heavens say whether you will succeed. In a meaningless existence all things are possible."

Frannie took that for all in all. "Great. So this demon is called the Book Man."

"We call him that," Saul said. "And lots of people do. He may even call himself that."

"Possible," Emmett said, "but obviously not an old name."

"The Book Man looks like a professor, a human with a jacket with patches and a beard."

"This human guise tells me nothing."

"He's found a woman to travel around and do stuff for him."

"Secondary possession." The golem raised his arms as though he expected to clap them together but could not. "Go on."

Saul said, "And the son of a bitch is full of paper."

"Paper?"

"Little paper birds," Frannie said. "They move and squirm around inside him."

"These birds can come out and travel abroad?"

"Yes."

"And they seem folded?" the clay man asked. "Like Japanese *origami*?"

Frannie laughed at this because it seemed absurd to imagine that a clay man would know his way around Japanese arts and crafts, but then he was a reflection of the eternal, after all.

The golem continued. "Is Japanese writing on this paper that comprises these birds?"

"No," Saul said. "We've gotten a look or two at the paper birds and the writing is not Japanese. Also not English, not Hebrew. I don't recognize it."

The golem moved his body slightly to tilt his head towards the table. "Write me some words."

Saul took a napkin and wrote a few words. 'I didn't look at it that long." He walked around to the end of the table and showed the napkin to the golem.

The golem leaned farther back and stopped pouring out smoke for a second, a stoppage that Frannie interpreted as a gasp. The little clay man slid off the end of the table and started crossing the floor, mumbling. Frannie, Saul and Newp followed as the golem entered the book section.

"Why does the golem even know?" Newp asked.

"Because he's magic," Frannie said.

"Like hocus pocus magic?"

"Like God and the *sheydim* and the Garden of Eden magic."

In the book room they found the golem propped impossibly on the high bookshelf, and Frannie was sorry she had missed seeing him climb the shelves to sit next to the Blanks.

"If he picked up a Blank, your demon, to read it, he would see a personal message," the golem said. "Und so I can show you what he would see."

"You can do that?" Frannie asked.

A blur then, and the golem had a blank book in his hands and turned it around to show its pages to Frannie and the rest.

She saw the pages and then all went black.

CHAPTER 34

Frannie floated in no physical space at all, in blackness that stretched endlessly, and then in the distance, stars came into view and burst. From the stars flowed ribbons of light so dense that she wanted to touch them, but they were huge and infinitely far away.

And before the ribbons of light hung the golem in space, vast, and she could only see a portion of him, a spot of leg perhaps, and at the same time was aware that all of him was there and endless. A ribbon of light wavered and flowed towards Frannie and for a moment there was only a flow of spots, images too numerous to see—and then she was aware of the golem opening his vast hand.

The image the hand showed her as it opened was shining with gold and silver and swirled with doves.

There was a Watcher in the old days when Y-H-W-H set his soldiers to watch over the earth. This was after the Garden of Eden, after Adam and Eve, after Cain and Abel, but still before the Great Flood. The Watchers stood in the mountains and walked the roads and guarded men from the attacks of monsters and the Great Enemy.

The monsters, though. Even Y-H-W-H knew what the monsters really were, for does not Genesis tell us these were the offspring of the Watchers themselves, who lusted in their hearts for the daughters of men, *thence on earth all monsters sprung*?

And there was one Watcher in those days who had a great affection for the woman he loved, even though she was a mortal and far below his order. And his sons were two, one weak and nearly human but the apple of his eye, the other a great beast, and crafty.

And it was the mortal son that this Watcher taught the secrets of the gods, of words on paper and the hidden meanings that might be stored and shared. He shared the mysteries of writing, a great thing, a boon to mankind. This Watcher was the one who gave men writing.

The name of this Watcher was Penamue.

And then came the War in Heaven and the great flood, and death and loss to Penamue and the other Watchers and their sons, even the monsters.

The Watcher floats there, as Frances Cohn floats, beholding his story. The Watcher Penamue floats in eternity, a creature of Logos, of Word and

Light. He has fallen after the war but in the sea of eternity he hears the stories of man, stories told by mortals, those his dead sons cannot tell, stories that his friends cannot share, that his dead wife cannot see. He hungers. He stretches endlessly in the stars and the thin membranes of his mind warp with that hunger.

He will have his revenge on God through man, and he will eat their stories.

# # #

"So his name is Penamue?" Frannie sat at a stool at the bar, still shaken. The door began to clink at the front as the dinner crowd began to emerge.

Saul watched the patrons coming in from the other side of the bar. "Yeah. Penamue. Okay. You go do dinner. I'm gonna do some research. Now that we know his name, we can plan a ritual to get rid of him."

Newp was putting on his apron. "How do we even know where he'll be?"

"We'll find him. We have to capture him, and then we take him out of the game."

"When?" Newp grabbed a pencil and pad and handed another set to Frannie.

"The night of the luau," Frannie suggested. At their curious expression she continued, "It's perfect. It'll be light in here. Very few diners. We can even close. Everyone will be on the beach. That's the time."

"Yes," Saul nodded, seeing it. "Yeah. We destroy him on the night of the luau. That's six days. Okay. Next four hours, you need to learn some *Luria*."

Frannie felt herself hop to attention. Yeah, pop, that was the stuff. "That was the book you got the hiding spell from."

"Six days, the time of creation. We purify and you learn the curses for calling and banishment. The words are easy," he said. "Words are just the focus. It's the heart of it. The knowing that goes on in your mind. So let's start learning. And then we have to figure out where the Hell he is."

CHAPTER 35

Callie stood on her balcony at one o'clock in the morning and swayed to the sounds of the radio coming from her bedroom. She had only of the vaguest memory of the gentleman driving her home after the café.

Those rude people!

Something had happened at the café, but it was hazy now. Wasn't that *strange*? She felt tipsy and tired but thrilled to feel the cool air.

The gentleman had fallen and risen at the café, she remembered that, taking her arm for support. She remembered the thrill of her own pulse as he touched her, suddenly weak and needy, and then he had still been the one to drive her home.

I insist, he had said. *I wouldn't have it any other way.*

She had no memory of him leaving, just a feeling of him at her door promising to return. And then he was gone.

Then Callie had drifted through the evening, starting the radio and listening to a baseball game. She lay on the couch the way her father used to and listened to the Oakland A's playing, drifting with the hypnotic staticky roar of the crowd, the monotonous drone of the deejay narrating the game.

She awoke sometime after midnight and now stood on the balcony, swaying as Dinah Washington sang "A Foggy Day," a husky woman's voice wrapped in a gauze of static that gave the song a faraway sound.

The song receded a bit, a piano tinkling, and she heard a truck approaching. She heard the distant wheels on the street and the sound mixed with the swaying of palm fronds. She swayed in her nightgown to the piano and the sound of the arriving truck. And then that strange blue vehicle was there in front of her house. She did not see it arrive. Like there were gaps in her time, like she was dreaming awake.

She saw his shape in the driver seat.

She *was* dreaming; she must be. For then a cloud of white spots came fluttering like butterflies out of the truck. A wave of churning white glowing bits like paper came in a wave, and as they fluttered closer, she saw that they were birds, tiny origami birds, flying around one another and switching places and flowing up to her balcony to swirl all around her.

And then there *he* was borne on the wave of tiny birds with his arms raised. He floated and surfed up the milk arch of paper birds and down onto the balcony, and she stepped back, leaning against the glass of her French doors, the radio fuzzy and

From this moment on, you are for me, dear!

Her knees were weak, and he was with her in a wave of origami birds, and for a moment the wings of the birds had words on them that she could see when they swooped and hovered near her eyes. She read them as one came into view and fell away to be replaced by another, and another, snatches of words in each.

His hands on her hips and the birds flying with the words:

You've got the arms to hold me tight

She thrilled as one of the birds cut her, sweetly and painfully and he ran his fingertips of her sides, and his touch was rough and sharp. The birds flew and swirled and sliced even as she melted with his kiss. She was fluttering herself as he spoke your name and asked her questions.

Who is the owner of the café?

The lips to kiss me

His name is Saul Cohn

And the girl, she heard him ask as he kissed her neck and the birds sliced her legs and blood flowed on her nightgown

His niece

Frannie is her name. She lives nearby

She had no idea, was she speaking aloud or just thinking, or did the answers come in her blood, flowing into his fingers?

She thought of the University where the girl's father worked, and the street where the family lived, though she had not been there, had not met them once, and a slice of jealousy came to her that he would be interested in the girl, and then that feeling was gone with his lips and the blood seeping between them.

And she felt alive, her head bursting with need, his lips on her shoulders, the white birds flying toward them. She panted as his hands ran down her legs and the bird sliced up her back.

Lost in the rush, lost in the fuzzy sound of the radio, and then she staggered, falling, the glass of the French doors giving way.

Oh

She struggled to waken, *what the hell?,* she looked at her bleeding hands as she struggled to crawl through the bedroom and grab the comforter of her bed, and he was

She looked back and he was following.

She reached for the telephone but found the radio.

Picked up the radio—oh her eyes, she couldn't see, she had to blink--

From this happy day, no more blues song!

Got the arms to hold me but the lips to kiss me good night!

She tried to hurl the radio, weakly tossing it, and saw it bounce as it reached the end of its cord. She reached for the telephone again and he was standing there and staring, the birds flying about the room, blotches of white against her green curtains. She lifted the phone and her back was--

Was she coming apart? *Oh God.* And then the birds flowed through her eyes and mouth and sliced and sliced.

And no one saw the creature, no one looked as he went about his dark ministrations, how he slid like a snake of white paper out of the bearded body, how he worked and lifted the naked woman and slid the skin from her, how he dumped her skinless corpse in a closet and then searched the closet for something suitable to wear.

He chose a cream dress and a pillbox hat and strolled out into the night, and got into his truck—or *her* truck, now—and rolled away.

CHAPTER 36

It was 5:45 on Sunday morning when Mom stood at the bottom of the stairs with her smallest suitcase in her hand and looked at Frannie as though they might never see one another again. "Are you sure you don't want to come with us?" Mom was in clothes fit for flying, a gray suit with white piping and perfect white gloves. Behind her was a stack of suitcases too big for her to comfortably hold. Frannie was reminded of Northanger Abbey, where Austen spoke of the baggage "carrying down" for hours on end in preparation for a visit to the country.

No more trips to the country for the Cohns. There used to be those summer mountain visits, but now Saul wasn't there anymore, and besides, it wasn't what her parents—or anyone else—seemed to want. Now her folks, and really everyone, wanted to cross the Pacific to see the new frontier: to go Hawaiian.

"She's right, Fran," Pop said, dropping his own modest pair of suitcases next to her mother's. "We could get you a ticket this morning."

"Here's your other one," Uncle Saul spoke from behind Frannie and she got out of his way as he lugged down a military-style duffel bag and tossed it onto the pile. Frannie noticed Saul and Pop exchange a brief look that meant nothing to her.

"Mom, Pop," she sang. "I have work."

"She has work." Pop shrugged at her mom then looked back at Frannie. "Saul would let you off work. How many times will we be going to Hawaii?" His eyes looked huge and liquid and Frannie's heart melted for him.

"We discussed this," Frannie said. "Look, I won't even be on my own. I'll be upstairs at the café in the apartment." This was true. For the month and a half that they would be gone, Frannie had arranged to spend that time working for Saul and living in the apartment upstairs. Actually the living room up there was the very place where they'd raised the golem and where she'd already spent so many hours learning, but Frannie didn't mention this. "I'll be doing good."

"I know." Her pop hugged her as she came down to the bottom of the stair and she leaned against him, smelling tobacco. "It's just that, you know, you used to come with us, and I feel like maybe you won't ever again…"

"No, come on."

"... and that's what I feel, and it makes me feel sad. That's all." He looked down. It must have been very painful for him to say this, because he was German, and Germans just didn't do that. He was a marvel, she thought.

"Hey." Saul clapped his hand on Pop's shoulder. "You ain't gone yet. We gotta drive you so save it."

Pop let Frannie go but nodded as though he were accepting a grave defeat. "You'll take care of her?"

"Absolutely," Saul said. Frannie had no idea what was in the answer; whether it meant what it sounded like or if Saul's mind was already on capturing a demon and Frannie and he were just moving parts of the machine at the center of the plan.

"Okay, you weeping willows," Mom cooed. "Let's go or we'll never make the flight."

"You still got three hours." Saul consulted his watch. "You don't wanna be bored."

A knock at the door and they all started, shocked that anyone would knock before the sun came up. Mom looked back at Pop as she walked to the door. "Did you call a cab or something?

"Not at all."

Mom stood tiptoe to look through the peephole, then dropped back, her brow furrowed. "My God, it's Callie Stevens."

"What?" Frannie pushed past mom and looked. There in the porch light

in a jacket and shirt, looking like she were making an Avon call, stood Callie. Frannie looked back at Saul. Last time they'd seen Callie it had been as a traveling escort of the Book Man. And now she was here. "You know her?"

"Everyone knows Callie," Mom said. "She's on every committee in town."

Frannie's backpack gave a thump against the wall. That was Emmett the golem, signaling his awareness. Frannie pictured the golem for a moment, his mouth taped to stop the incessant pouring of smoke, and wished that she could take him out of the pack and have him go out and talk to Callie. But the parentals would definitely not be copacetic with a little clay man walking around.

"It's barely 6 a.m.," Pop said.

"Wait," Saul said, but Mom was already opening the door.

Mom put her hands on her hips. Just folks. "Callie!"

"Mrs. Cohn." Frannie saw Callie step forward, so petite and yet aggressive, energetic. Callie's eyes swept the group and she lingered for a second on Saul and Frannie. She returned her gaze to Mom. "I hope you don't think me intrusive."

Mom shrugged. "It's a little early, but we were just—" she waved her hands at the stacked baggage.

"Oh," Callie said, tilting her head as she looked at the bags. "You are going away." She seemed to process this some more, so absently that Frannie had a notion that Callie was a little drunk. She wondered how many times Callie did this, embarrassing herself around town, with all parties probably choosing not to remember. "Well, I have something to discuss with you."

"Of course," Mom said. "But—"

"About your daughter." A glance her way. No, not drunk. Studied and careful which made her slow to speak, but not drunk.

"What?" Frannie demanded.

"Of course it's understandable," Callie said. "Young people want freedom and opportunity. But I felt it was my duty to inform you that this young lady has been associating with a... a dishonorable element. Yes." She swallowed, nodding. "A very dishonorable element."

Frannie wasted a good few seconds trying to work out which dishonorable element Callie might be referring to before Saul said, "You mean me, right? The café?"

"You know very well that the Town Council has grave misgivings about the goings-on in that establishment. Obscene sculpture. Sacrilege of every kind."

"Come on, Callie," Saul said. "We *just saw you.*"

"Evil books," she chirped. "And I know that we—*you* know that we need to confiscate them."

Saul looked at Frannie's Pop and mom and said, "This is crazy."

Pop waved his pipe. "I agree; this is insane. Are you hearing yourself, Mrs..."

"Stevens," Callie said.

Pop continued, "Are you aware of how crazy this sounds? Disturbing a family at this hour?"

Saul smoothly took Frannie's backpack and held it casually in under his arm and a little in front of him as he spoke. "Look, I don't know what you think you're talking about, but we don't owe you anything."

Callie wobbled violently and her nostrils flared as the backpack drew near her. "It's not a matter of owing," she said, looking intently at the pack and then back at Saul. "It's for the community's own good. They're illegal. Obscene."

Pop's soft laugh filled the foyer. "Well, that sounds like something you can discuss at Saul's place of work. If you don't mind my asking, how did you even know that Saul would be here?"

Callie started, annoyed by the question. Saul peered past her and said, "Is your friend with you?" He threw Frannie a look and Frannie made out the truck parked in the street—that Morris Miner she'd seen the Book Man drive off in. So he was around here *somewhere*. She couldn't see anyone in the driver's seat.

"A friend?" Pop said. "You mean she has someone hiding out there?"

"We're leaving, Mrs. Stevens," Mom said. "I'm sorry, but we don't have time to listen or try to understand, and I hope you understand—we were having a nice goodbye and we have to catch a flight. So really, we must do this another time."

Frannie heard a jingle and saw that Saul's number-cross medallion had dropped to the back of his hand as he held the backpack. "Let's go," Saul said as they started to move through the door.

Frannie shrank back from him as he glared at Callie and pushed by. Callie stammered and stepped away as Mom and Pop hustled the baggage out of the door.

Saul moved past her and Frannie noticed that he was *pushing* the backpack in a way, making sure she saw him clutching it. "Come see me at the Café. Okay? Come see me and we'll talk business. But lady, coming here like this was crazy."

Callie stood on the front porch as they got in the car and left her behind. Frannie mouthed the only words she could think of through the window. "You're crazy."

But she knew better. As they rolled down the street Frannie watched Callie take a few steps toward them and then turn back towards the truck. Then they turned out of the neighborhood and left Callie behind.

"That was *meshuge*." Frannie looked forward, setting into the back seat of Pop's car.

"There's something wrong with that woman," Pop said.

"Saul." Mom turned to look back from her place in the front. "Is there anything to this town council stuff she was saying?"

"Who knows?" Saul responded next to Frannie. "The Ladies' Decency something or other doesn't like the art. I don't know. There might be a hearing."

"We'll be there," Pop says.

"You'll be in Hawaii, if it happens in the next couple of weeks," Saul reminded them.

"Okay," Pop agreed, both hands on the wheel. He caught Frannie's eyes in the rear-view mirror. "*You* should be there, though, Frances. People need to know this community leader is not so good, that she's the one who's crazy and harassing people."

In Saul's arm, the backpack he still held rustled and Frannie watched him unzip the opening. Emmett the golem popped his head up out of the opening as Saul pushed the pack down into the floorboards. The golem's eyes blazed with rage as he looked from Saul to Frannie, his mouth still taped to prevent the constant expulsion of smoke.

"I agree, it was strange," Saul said as he took a notepad from his shirt pocket and wrote in pencil:

NOT CALLIE.

AFRAID OF GOLEM IN PACK.

IT WAS HIM.

Frannie looked back. They were being followed at a distance by a gray Morris Minor.

The truck followed them all the way out to the highway, in fact all the way to the Orange County Airport. With every mile they chattered about her parents' trip, about how Frannie was going to have to maintain the house if she went back there, about how mom expected her to serve her uncle well. This struck Frannie as a hilarious phrasing, like something from an old story where the hero is being sent to serve a warrior relative. And in a sense that was the case. And all along the way, the Morris Minor followed at a distance, and only Frannie and Saul noticed it. The Book Man was clever—at times Frannie felt certain he had disappeared, and then the truck would reappear miles later.

Forty-five minutes later, Frannie was hugging her father at the gate. He held his duffel bag in his arms and awkwardly hugged her with his free arm, patting her on the back. Frannie tried not to search the terminal with her eyes but did and saw nothing, sensed nothing. Even the Morris Minor had been gone by the time they had parked.

"I won't ask you again to come with us."

Frannie leaned her head against her pop's chest. "Good."

"Your uncle is a good man," Pop said. "Different from us, he left so early to come here, so long before us. I think you were meant to help them, and you should. But it doesn't mean I have to always feel good about it."

"Okay, pop."

Frannie watched the plane take off through the giant windows in the terminal. Then she and Saul let out a deep sigh.

Saul rocked on his heels as the plane pulled away. "Well that's something. Come on."

"Where to?"

Saul was walking very fast. "I thought we'd go drag racing." Frannie stared.

"That's where we'll catch him," Saul continued. "I gotta make a phone call." He dashed to find a phone booth near the exit.

Stewardesses who looked like Cinderella in blue streamed into the Orange County terminal. Frannie felt tiny and insignificant as they rushed around her, with their blonde hair and steel blue eyes sparkling colorfully as they streaked past, a stampede of graceful blue gazelles. By the time the rush of them had passed, Saul emerged and tapped her arm. Time to go.

In the parking lot of the airport the 8 AM sun was streaking across the tops of cars and blinding them. Pop's car was parked a few rows from the exit out to the highway. As they found the car, Saul said, "Here's the thing. There's an unusual landing strip on this airport. It's called the Santa Ana. And everyone will be gathering there even now."

In the car, Saul dropped the canvas backpack between them. Emmett popped out, raising his arms up, which Frannie understood instantly to be as close to *untape my mouth* as possible. She undid the tape. "I'm sorry we had to do that."

"The indignity we suffer is a reminder of the best in consequence in which we—"

"Don't make me tape you up again."

It was the beginning of the morning rush in earnest now as they weaved through the parking lot, dodging travelers in business suits and more flight crew. Frannie was scanning for the Morris Minor as they neared the exit to the highway. "Come on, you mother."

And then it was there: they passed the gray Morris Minor where it was parked facing out. It came alive and immediately whipped around out of its spot and they pulled onto the highway together.

"Callie's driving." Meaning *it*-as-Callie. Frannie could see the woman's pillbox hat in silhouette.

They lurched left and turned down a feeder road and the Morris Minor lumbered after them. They passed a sign: Santa Ana Flats.

Frannie absently patted the golem on the head as she turned to look out the rearview mirror. The area they were pulling into was full of people and she took them in:

On either side of the airport runway, people were parking cars and setting up for races. She saw kids in blue jeans and T-shirts, a sea of baseball caps. Young and middle-aged people working under the hoods of cars. They passed a souped-up Lincoln. A kid in a chipped, mechanic-style fedora, the kind Jughead wore in the Archie comics, looked up at them. The Santa Ana runway stretched for two miles into the morning sun, and on this and every Sunday morning was nothing like a runway at all.

"What does he want?"

"I'm betting he wants this." Saul reached into the backpack next to the golem and lifted out a single Blank.

"Are you kidding me; you brought a Blank?" "It's bait, baby girl. He knew the golem was there, but he still wants the Blank, because I'm sure he smelled that, too." Now the truck rumbled onto the runway itself as Saul sped up. "I like this car. You know, I was with your pop when he bought it, it looks *square,* like the kids say, but it's got an eight-cylinder engine and *come on you yemakh*!" He turned to Frannie. "Put on your seatbelt."

"What?" Frannie looked down at the straps lying limp next to her legs.

"Put it on."

"But—"

"Oy, Frannie."

"Okay, all right." Frannie have never worn a seatbelt in her life. Why would she? It wasn't like she did any regular drag racing herself, and in fact most of the cars she was around didn't even have the things. She struggled with the weird clasp on the end of the canvas belt on either hip, and finally managed to click them together at her navel. "What for?"

Her words were cut short by a loud *crunch* and she gasped as seatbelt bit into her hips. Emmett the golem shouted something in German, and she saw him smack into the air conditioning console and fall down at her feet.

She looked back to see Callie close behind and backing off. She had bashed them from behind and suddenly she was accelerating again with a roar from the truck.

"You want it?" Saul cried. "Come and get it." He looked at Frannie. "Gimme the Blank and get the box."

"You brought the Dybbuk box *too*?" Frannie opened the sack with one hand as she picked up Emmett and placed him in the seat next to her before hauling out the shoe-sized wooden box that Saul had used on the beach. She had a vision of the ghost that had hated Hooky so, and wondered if she was still in here somewhere.

The Morris Minor had pulled up alongside them as they raced now past the crowds. Frannie looked ahead—they had a curious audience among the people setting up. They were drag racing, a sedan and an old Morris Minor truck, alone on the runway as they approached the empty bleachers and press box halfway down.

Just about three feet from Frannie, Callie's body drove the truck, staring back at them from beneath that absurd pillbox hat, white-gloved hands wrapped around the leather steering wheel. Saul motioned to Callie to roll down her *(its?)* window. When the demon in Callie's body obliged and the glass in the car next to them lowered, Saul hollered over the roar of the engine.

"Hey, this what you want?" Saul waived the blank book. "It's from my own collection, but you probably sensed it back there at the house. I'll race you for it, how's that? Demons like games, right?"

Callie broke left and smashed into them as they tore down the runway.

Saul struggled to keep the car on the road. "Okay, then." He accelerated and then whipped right, bashing back. The two vehicles crunched together as they hurtled forward. No there was a strange hissing sound over the engines and Callie opened her mouth in something like surprise.

"We are visited once more by Penamue," the golem intoned. "VAAT AN HONNORRR."

In the car next to them, what Frannie had taken for surprise in Callie's open mouth had moved past surprise into something else. Her head split open at the cheeks and the top half folded back, and a cloud of origami birds burst forth. The birds closed the gap between the cars instantly. Frannie rolled up the window as one of them got in. It flitted at her hair and she smashed it against the dash with her foot, smearing it into one of the air conditioning grills. Paper birds clattered against the windows and windshield and Frannie heard them slicing over the roof.

Saul turned on the windshield wipers and little paper birds got rolled under the rubber blades. "He sure can hold a lot of them."

"The transformation of matter is but a trivial thing," the golem responded, though it sounded like *Zeh trahnsformehshunn uff mahtter iss...* "to the wielders of the powers of the Tetragrammaton."

Frannie was able to tear her eyes away from the strange image of waves of paper birds crushed by the windshield wipers. "*Tetragrammaton? The power of God? That thing isn't God.*"

"But he was *of* God, and was *next to* God, and so he still holds some of the power of God," Emmett said. "As do we all. And as far as he might be from God, this is no farther than you are from God in any sense that matters, if one could but look at the distance from the vantagepoint of God."

"So can I do the bird thing?" Frannie asked. The truck was rolling on right next to them, barely visible as a dark outline in the cloud of paper birds. "Because that would be a cool power. But I'd make puppies. Waves of little paper puppies."

"I certainly hope not."

"Or giraffes, because that's easier to make with origami."

"The focus on paper has to do with the focus of the Angel," Emmett said. "He was dedicated to letters."

The truck bashed into them and the birds scattered. For a moment, Frannie found herself just two panes of glass and about eight inches from the half-head of Callie, which kept pouring out origami like a Mount Vesuvius of paper crafts.

Then a horn sounded.

A high horn letting out a yodeling tune, a charge tune, and another car came into view, whipping out from behind them to create a great shadow on the other side of the demon's truck. The birds scattered for a moment as the demon slowed to assess this newcomer. As the birds cleared, Frannie saw the driver of the new car give a little wave. "Hooky!" Frannie cried.

Hooky's car dropped back and broke hard and he plowed into the rear of the demon's truck, clipping the rear bumper. The truck slipped forward and bashed the back of Saul's Studebaker, and Saul fought to keep the vehicle straight.

Now the birds started coming thicker again on the windshield, tiny beaks beating on the glass. For the first time Frannie saw it: a crack had formed.

She felt something strange at her feet and looked down to see a paper bird coming up under the dash, then another. They flew up around her legs and she swatted at them. "I think they're coming up through the engine block," she said.

Saul batted a couple off his cheek, one of them drawing blood. He pounded the horn three times. BLLEEEET. BLEEEEET. BLEEEEET. "Now, you sonofabitch."

A fantastic lurch then, as metal crunched behind them and the truck flew past, grinding against them as it went. Saul yanked the wheel hard towards the passing truck and hit it hard, and for a moment Frannie got a good look at the blinking eyes of Callie, staring at the road as origami poured out of the enormous hole in her face. The demon holding Callie's body hostage steered furiously, and then Hooky hit it again—

And it was spinning, balletic in its flying form as it stopped spinning on its wheel and flipped, tumbling off to the right. Callie's car rolled and Saul hit his own breaks and the Studebaker screeched to a halt. He spun off the road as the birds dropped to the ground, powerless for a moment.

They approached a truck that lay on its back, a wave of origami birds flying into it like an unholy breath. Saul looked at Frannie and then grabbed the box and handed her the Blank. "Now we're gonna take him."

Bursting open the car door, Frannie heard Hooky running up behind her. She looked and saw that for once he was wearing shoes. "Hi, Angel," he said to her.

"Hey, Penamue!" Saul howled as they got closer to the overturned truck. "You want this?"

The truck's wheels were still rolling, Callie's body with its ruined face half out of the window. She was crawling, moving oddly, as though she had multiple elbows and could find purchase in the concrete with all of them. It looked like a snake moving inside of a human body, although Frannie knew what she was looking at was the effect of thousands of tiny bits of paper, causing the body to reach, and flow, and reach, and flow, staring at them with eyes that no longer held the illusion of humanity, but now squirmed with paper.

Police sirens, then. The crowds two miles up the runway were running, and she saw a station wagon ambulance hurtling towards them.

"Quickly." Saul set the box near Callie, who was still crawling, slowly, now quite out of the car.

"Here it is," Frannie said. "The blank." Frannie got around in front of Callie and held the book there. The split face moved, shifting, as though some central repository of thought still resided there. The head moved side to side, the golden hair falling lazily over the paper eyes that churned like dry noodles.

Frannie held the Blank next to the dybbuk box. "There is a trade."

"Say the words," Saul said.

Frannie nodded, breathed. "I command you." She waited for the demon to stop and tilt its broken head before she went on. "So many stories, Penamue, so many lives. This is what you live for, yes? The best collection. The best of all human tales. But Penamue, you are weak now. You need a place to rest. And I can give it to you."

The birds circled around them, clattering against one another as the wounded body of Callie struggled. Frannie heard a thought run through them all: why not take this one? That was interesting. As though part of the demon's consciousness spread out in the birds, and so detached itself that it was capable of independent thought, even argument.

"No time," Frannie said. "The skin you're in is damaged. And I'd destroy you before you had the chance to get into mine. You know this is your only choice." She held the box before her.

I command you, Penamue,

by the Lord Elohim,

by the might of the Tetragrammaton,

by the numbers 6, 12, 9 by 13, 36, 43,

I command you,

take your reward of refuge and your repose and your rest!

She was shouting now. "It is more than you deserve but we are merciful, and all things serve God. Rest!"

"Or take this," Hooky said. Frannie looked up as she heard a click. Hooky was holding a hose with a strange nozzle on the end, a pilot light like you'd see in a furnace. The hose ran back to his car. It was a flamethrower, military style, and where he'd gotten it, she had no clue. "Where…"

"Army surplus," Hooky said. The broken Callie head stared, and Hooky said, "the box or burn, buddy."

The ambulance drew closer, its siren wailing. Frannie held the box closer, cracking its lid. "Now!"

The birds hissed and seemed to be arguing amongst themselves and then all at once they drew their decision to retreat. They stopped circling around the humans and formed a thick, almost liquid line, a milky snake of paper and chittering sound, flitting and flowing into the box.

All of them—and then, silence.

Saul clasped the box. He closed and turned hidden locks on the wood itself, and then they sat there as the ambulance roared up. Men ran out, shouting at the three live people and the one body and the overturned vehicle.

Frannie threw herself into Hooky's arms and kissed him before he could respond, and then lay her head on his chest, the beads of perspiration wetting her lips.

They had captured the demon called the Book Man.

And now, in a roar, the police were coming.

CHAPTER 37

Frannie's trip to the Laguna Beach Police Station afforded her an opportunity to be glad that her parents had gone to Hawaii. She stood in the corner of the station next to a metal bench not far from the open glass front, awash in light. Saul sat silently on the bench while Hooky amused himself by reading the Most Wanted signs posted near the water fountain. Across from them, next to a little window that reminded her of a bank teller's vestibule, three police officers quietly conferred, occasionally looking back at them. She'd never been in a police station and found the whole thing kind of a drag, with linoleum floors and the kind of cheap wood paneling you saw in travel trailers. But the cops seemed bored and happy and that had to be better than what she saw on TV, where people in her position were always suddenly being punched in the stomach by grumpy officers in long coats.

Finally a young uniformed cop with slick dark hair—he looked a lot like the trumpet player she'd helped with a Blank that said he'd do a lot of fake surfing for some reason—came up and told the three of them to each follow a cop deeper into the bowels of the station.

She followed the young one down the hallway, her stomach knotting. It felt like *being in trouble* and though she liked to make trouble and liked to argue, she'd spent a lifetime around people who coddled her constant arguments, and only rarely did she get the horns. When she got in trouble, she felt like she was six years old again and caught painting the walls with jelly.

Down the hallway to a small room, duller still, no windows, white walls. She took a seat at the single table and realized that the room was boring because the focus was supposed to be on one person: her.

After a moment of the cop standing awkwardly with his thumbs looped in his belt, Barney-Fife-like, a woman who looked more like a teacher came in. She seemed to be in her 30s, hair up, glasses, cream blouse. "Frannie, I'm Sheila," she said.

"Um," she started. "Hi, hello, ma'am."

Sheila smoothed her skirt and said, "I'm here to observe this interview."

"Okay," Frannie said. Now she *really* felt like she was in trouble. And she should; there was an overturned car and a dead person—a dead *skin* anyway—back there on a drag racing strip.

Just tell them she came out of nowhere; tell them the truth except the demon part. Saul's advice.

"Frannie," the woman repeated her name, "I want you to know you're safe here."

Now the spell was broken because that was square city. "Of course," she said, remembering the coolness her mom taught her. "Of course. I was just dropping off my parents at the airport."

The cop had produced a notepad and nodded. "You said they were leaving you alone for the summer?"

"I mean, it's nearly July, so it's hardly the whole summer." Too harsh. "I mean I wouldn't call it that. I'm staying with my uncle, helping him at his café."

"Okay. Why don't you tell us what happened out there this morning?"

"You mean—the crash?"

"Please," the cop said.

"There was a car following us all morning, that lady's car. I guess it's a truck, a little truck, you know?" She looked from one to the other. Now they were listening, and she put a mental clamp on herself: *be nice, be elegant, get it smooth.* "She chased us, close behind. Saul turned onto the Santa Ana strip."

"The drag strip. Do you know why he chose that?"

"I don't. She was real close. We were just going. And we tried to outrun her. And she bashed us and then Hooky—"

"The other fella?"

"Yes. When she bashed into us, she bounced away, and Hooky came up next to us—"

"Between you and the lady?"

"Yeah."

"Okay."

"And they bashed at him again and then flipped."

"They?"

"What?"

"You said they bashed at Hooky, was there more than one person in the little truck?"

Yes, a woman and a demon. But only one pink suit. "No, sorry, it—it was just the lady. She spun out of control. Flipped away. It was awful." She didn't need to fake that; it *was* awful, except that she had felt exhilaration and relief when it happened.

Now the woman spoke from where she was leaning against the wall. "And did you know the woman who was… found? The one driving the truck?"

Frannie nodded, sighing. "Yeah. Her name was Callie. She's been in the café."

"She had a problem with your Uncle?"

"She's like with the city council or something. She doesn't like the café because it caters to people she doesn't hang with."

The cop slumped. "Who was driving that truck, Frannie?"

"Callie was."

"Yeah, I... see, the problem with that is that Callie is dead."

"Well, she flipped over..." Frannie didn't have anything better. Here came the hard part.

"She was dead already." The cop opened his hand plaintively. "Had to be, see? She was – did you see her?"

Frannie bit her lip. "She was crawling..."

"The lady we got into an ambulance, she's not even recognizable. You know what I'm referring to?"

"She was dying."

"She's a *skin,*" the cop practically whispered, as though this were too obscene to talk about.

"A what?" She widened her eyes. Now she was six again and what jelly? What wall?

The woman said, gently, "Frannie, that woman was so badly injured that it... it just can't have been her driving."

"Look," said the cop. "I understand what you're saying, but sometimes we go through somethin' rough and we don't see what's really happening. So this is very important." The cop looked at the woman and then leaned forward. "Did you see anyone running away? Did you see the real driver?"

# # #

"Who was in the other car?"

Saul leaned back, interlacing his fingers. "I never got a good look. They chased us, they bashed us."

"And you were just leaving the airport?" The cop had salt and pepper hair and was still trim, his face pockmarked by ages-old acne.

"I dropped off my brother, yeah, and his wife. We're coming out and the Morris Minor starts chasing us—I tried to lose it and it bashes us, just wham."

"Why did you turn onto the, ah..." the cop looked at his notes.

"The Santa Ana strip?"

"You know this spot?"

Saul shrugged. "I run a café for kids. Yeah, I know it. They race there. I turned onto it because I figured if someone was chasing us that was better than a busy street."

"That's very heroic of you."

Saul said nothing. No point in being a wisenheimer.

#   #   #

"So where did the other car come from?"

"I was supposed to meet up with Saul after he dropped off his brother," Hooky said. "We were supposed to drive to La Jolla with his niece, get supplies for the café."

"That needs two cars?" Hooky's cop was paunchy, also middle-aged, deep blue eyes.

"Sometimes we need both trunks, both back seats. So yeah, I was gonna meet him at the airport."

"And did you observe the Morris Minor pursuing his car?"

"Yes, sir," Hooky said. "They zipped right past me and Saul turned onto the Santa Ana Strip. I followed them."

"You don't have to 'sir' me," the cop said, laughing. "I work for a living. So did you see who was driving the truck?"

"No," Hooky said. He smiled.

The cop shrugged. "See anyone running away after it flipped over?"

"Oh, no," Hooky said. "I mean, there was dust everywhere. Everywhere. And that lady—jeez, what was left of that lady—came flying out." He winced.

"Mm," the cop agreed with the wince. "So what do you do for a living, Mr. Carmichael?"

"Right now?"

"Right now."

"I help out Saul from time to time. I give surf lessons some."

"So you're a bum."

"Right now?"

"Yeah."

"Yeah, I'm a bum."

The cop took out a cigarette and asked as he lit it, "So overseas, what?"

"I flew."

"No kiddin'." The cop raised his eyebrows.

"Absolutely, Sergeant. You?"

"Pacific, infantry."

"Hell of a thing."

"No shit." The cop looked at his hands and then out a window that wasn't there. "It's just—*this* is a Hell of a thing right here. There's something we're missing. It's all weird, you know? And I gotta say if I could lock you up I *would*, because I *know* there's more going on. And I'm curious what that is."

"I don't know what else to tell you, Sergeant." Hooky said.

# # #

Across the desert, just west of the Santa Ana Strip, an observer might see a box that had been left behind at the edge of the strip. The box moved along now at a steady pace, making its way deeper into the desert. A little clay man bore the box on his back. He was running, loping, his arms raised over its head.

Emmett the golem stopped behind a large stone and looked to the heavens to judge the direction back towards the unimpressive hovel his master Saul called his place of business.

The indignity of his burden stung his pride, but he was used to the indignities that life among the mortals brought. He turned east and kept running, moving steadily towards the ocean.

He could hear voices inside the box, sometimes whispering, sometimes catching a powerful wind of energy and shouting at him. He ignored them.

Set us free, they demanded. Of course he would do no such thing. He reached a highway.

Now, this would be a trial, the golem realized as he judged the impossible distance between two curbs and the passing of cars, one every second or so, and two rows of them. Too many cars. He foresaw the smashing of the box, crushed with him underneath it. He spent some time using his gifted golem brain to work out the likelihood that he could pass safely.

He decided he would wait for sundown and hide behind a tumbleweed.

A police car passed, paying no heed to the tendril of black smoke coming from the golem's mouth, which in the wind was hardly visible.

The car was speeding to the police station with news.

"Okay," the cop said to Saul as he came back in. "You're free to go."

"That's it?" Saul rose as the cop bade him.

"Toot suite, my friend," the cop said.

They entered the hallway where Frannie waited. Saul patted her shoulder and asked the cop, "So, what…"

"They went to Callie Stevens' house." The cop leaned in, trying to keep this away from Frannie. "You know how we got her skin at your wreck? Well, they found the rest of her. And get this: they found another skin."

Saul grimaced. "I got no comment."

"Yeah, getoutahere."

# # #

Just outside the police station, Saul turned to Hooky. "We need to get our box back."

"And put back the Blank, too," Frannie said, tapping his coat where he still held the Blank that he'd used to bait the demon. "I hate for them to be separated."

"Oh, they'll be separated for a while yet," Saul said as they reached his car and Hooky lingered before going back to his own.

"What do you mean?" Frannie looked at him.

"The blank here, it's the only one I know of on the west coast. The rest are safe for now. A precaution while we make sure the demon's secure."

"Where?" she demanded.

Saul smiled. "The whole rest of the collection went with your pop in a duffel bag."

CHAPTER 38

Five hours before one ritual, Frannie was determined to see another one through.

The night of the luau began at the Riviera just as the sun was dipping beyond the sea. Upstairs in the apartment over the café, Frannie put on a flower print and took a moment to assess her own reflection in a long mirror that leaned against the wall as though left there accidentally.

Still Frannie, all right, still essentially breastless and hipless, though she noticed as she swiveled that her legs were thick and muscular, her shoulders were broad and well-defined, and even her non-breasts stuck out a bit more thanks to the definition surfing had brought to her pectoral muscles. She heard the padding of Emmett's little feet behind her and said, "Well?"

Emmett had made it back to the café hauling the dybbuk box by four in the morning and now he divided his time between guarding the box and wandering the upstairs rooms of the café. "The prophets tell us that all is vanity."

"They sure do, Em," Frannie said, turning sideways to check out the line of her dress. "So am I vain enough or not?"

"You are as vain as you might be expected to be," said the golem, as he crawled up and sat on the vanity dresser, black smoke pouring from his mouth and mercifully floating up and away immediately. For some reason Emmett's smoke never lingered.

Uncle Saul called up from below. "Frannie!"

She lifted her head. "Yes?"

"Date's here."

"Vanity," intoned the golem as Frannie touched up her lipstick.

"See ya at witching hour, ya mook." She patted the golem on the head and left him sitting there on the edge of her dresser.

Penamue, the Book Man, was locked up. She felt a tingle of anticipation at the thought of the circle they would draw to banish him. She had never banished a demon before, but she was certain it would not be the last.

Stopped for a moment at the door. Smelled the sea air wafting from beyond the Riviera and down to the beach, mixing with the motor oil from the highway at dusk just as the first signs of Hawaiian music filtered over and mixed with the roar of cars. She went back and shut her window, struck for a moment that she didn't want Emmett to get cold, realizing immediately that this was absurd.

It was 7 o'clock. At midnight she would be doing her duty to God and Uncle Saul and even her father. Her pop was no religious man, but he was part of her story, nonetheless. She pulled the door to the stairs open and started down. Her uncle stood smiling at the bottom, wearing a suit even. And then he moved aside and there was Newp.

"Newp!" she called, clomping down the stairs. She wanted to explain her inelegance, wanted to say, *I'm sorry, I borrowed these heels from your sister which is hilarious really because she never wears them herself because of her slippers you know?* But wait. "I thought it was going to be…"

"Go-Go couldn't make it," Newp said as she reached the bottom step. Behind him, the café was ablaze with flaring red glass candle holders, and he seemed to glow in a yellow-and-red halo of chunky glass. "Did I hear this right; did you actually hire him as a chaperone?" Newp laughed, dressed absurdly in Bermuda shorts and a white shirt with jacket and tie. And sandals.

She folded her arms. So she was going with Newp. She couldn't add it up. He didn't want to go. And she'd practically written him off. And he had wanted to stop her from coming. And Bermuda shorts. "Newp, what in God's name are you wearing?"

"It's a gas, you know?" he looked down at his getup. "I guess. I don't know. I'm sorry."

"No, it's fine." Newp was staring at her and she tried to stand up straighter.

He went on as he pulled a loose thread from his Bermuda shorts. "T-bone told me you needed a date, though, because, and I'm quoting on this, you wanted to make someone jealous." He looked up. "That sound right?"

You know darn well that that's right, she wanted to say. But she was struck by the round sadness in his eyes and she couldn't bring herself to say it. "T-bone says all kinds of jazz. So what's the plan?"

The plan was straight across the street to the Riviera. Newp put his arm in hers and they walked out past surfers scarfing early-evening sandwiches and cherry cokes and into the evening, which was salty and cool.

Into the courtyard of the Riviera, where Frannie saw a mix of families grilling hot dogs and couples in evening dress headed up wooden stairs to the restaurant, which Frannie knew boasted outdoor seating that hung right out over the beach, so that the whole ocean flickered at you as you ate. On quiet evenings through the summer, the place would empty out, and the beach people could wander over and occupy the best seats.

She'd been in there, but every time she went, she found herself less disappointed than *unfinished* in a way, as though such a place was too pretty to just hang out in; she wanted someone to be impressed with.

Newp had reserved a spot and it was a killer, right at the edge, so that when they approached the table, the silhouette of the flowers against the reflection of the sun on the water froze her for a moment.

When they sat Frannie heard a roar of chattering and cameras over near the bar. She couldn't make anything out but the backs of a lot of suits and dresses. A waiter came by and lit a tiki torch near their table and Frannie nodded at the crowd. "Who's the star?"

The waiter shrugged. Like he didn't get into these things. Newp said, "I think it's George Burns. He and Gracie are on vacation, I think they have the President's Suite." George Burns had a TV show where he *knew* it was a show. He could talk to the audience about how he was going to manipulate which way the story went. Mind-blowing stuff.

For a moment she caught a glimpse of the TV star, a slim man with light brown hair and a dinner jacket, telling jokes to the crowd in a cigar haze. "We're lucky we got the seat we did," she said. "Newp, you outdid yourself."

"I'll get us some drinks. We could eat if you like, but…"

"Oh, but there's a whole pig roasting at the luau." She reached out to pat his hand as he lifted the menu. She stared out at the waves. Frannie heard the sound of guitars and marimba coming from down the beach, out by Hooky's Roost. She had to turn to look back in the direction of the hut, and she could see tiki torches and people gathering around the fire pit. "Wow," she said. "It looks like the whole getup is on Hooky's front door."

"It is," Newp said. "The fire pit is twelve feet from Hooky's hut. The king is holding court."

"Don't you need to be setting up for your concert?"

"Pssh." He waved. But he did look a little stressed, and she felt sorry she'd mentioned it. "Betty and Truly are as rehearsed as they can get, and I've already checked the juice. We have time."

"Oh."

"You're worth it, you know," he said. "I don't know why you'd think you weren't, but you are."

She could think of no response as she looked out at the great chief of the waves.

He rescued her by saying, "So."

"Yes?" Frannie leaned forward, and the waiter came back and she gripped the coke like a buoy. Why was she even nervous? "What is it, Newp?"

"You had some excitement yesterday." He seemed to be trying to sound amazed, excited, but he sounded forced.

"Yes! We caught the bastard thing. Oh, Uncle Saul was brilliant."

"Hooky, too, I hear."

"Well, yes." She nodded. "Saul called Hooky because he was trained in combat, and had Hooky do a – he called it a pincer move, with Saul's car."

"Yeah," Newp said. "That's amazing."

She pursed her lips. "Newp, for crying out loud. What do you want me to say? That Saul should have called you? That you should have been there for the trap?"

"Frannie—first off, yes. I was at the roadside café, right? So yes, I would think I would be someone you could call."

"He," she said.

"What?"

"He; it was Saul who called Hooky, I didn't have any idea this was going to happen. Not yesterday morning, and what, you were going to come to drop off my folks at the airport? Come on." She touched his arm. "Come on! Bring a boy I'm dating to send my parents away? It was right place, right time. Or wrong, you know."

"Really?" he looked out at the water.

"Yeah." But yes, she thought, of course Hooky is the type for the job, the hero type, the muscles, the scowling hero we all know and want. Right now he's about to give some girl a special night.

"Well, I just…" he stopped. "You know, this thing you're into with your Uncle. It's an important thing. I get that. So I want to help, okay, I want to be someone you can rely on. I want to be there."

"Oh, Newp."

"I just thought—I don't know. I thought that we were adventuring, like the Hardy Boys and Nancy Drew. You read those, right?"

"Yeah."

"There's Frank who she likes and Joe who she's a great pal with," Newp sipped his beer. "And I thought I was Frank. But I guess I was Joe."

"Newp, no one is Joe."

"Nah, I'm Joe."

"You can feel as sorry for yourself as you like, you big baby, but I'm not going to say you're Joe." She dabbed her mouth. "Keep this up and you'll be Nancy's annoying girlfriend."

"Yeah, okay." He pulled out his wallet. "You ready to hit the concert?"

"Absolutely."

"Good, because my sister and Truly are gonna knock 'em dead."

CHAPTER 39

As the luau crackled with fire and heat, Saul and Kurt enjoyed the quiet of an utterly empty restaurant.

The dybbuk box sat upstairs and the tomes Saul had been studying were stacked now on the bar next to the tequila and shot glasses, waiting for the ritual that would banish the contents of the box forever. Now all was quiet. They had closed the café after they last dinner party left, satisfied that most of their usual patrons would be at the beach. This turned out to be true; all evening less than three people came to the door, peering in and seeing the place deserted.

Kurt lit a roll-your-own and slapped a deck of cards on the bar. "So how come you didn't go to the luau the kids are having?"

"You answered your question already," Saul said, waving off Kurt's offer of an extra cigarette.

For a second Saul had a perfect memory, Kurt, leaning against the railing of a steamer he and a bunch of dancing girls had taken down to British Honduras to do a winter tour. Kurt was sketching, painfully contorting himself to see the foxhole of the ship while using the railing as a table for his sketchpad.

Goin' to see my brother at the plantation, he'd mumbled. *It's a long story.*

The story had grown and grown.

"You wanted to go?" Saul said, taking some cards.

"I get enough damn noise here. I stay with the art." He exhaled a lot of smoke. "It's all I need."

"To the art," said Saul.

"To the art." Glasses clinked.

"You know, it occurs to me that we're not gonna have any more trouble from the Decency League." He shook his head. "The way things go."

"Wouldn't think so. Good for you not saying that at the police station, though."

They laughed and Saul took one of Kurt's smokes after all.

CHAPTER 40

Curve now with the smoke from Saul's cigarette, up the stairs, towards the box.

In a darker place, in a wider place, the being called Penamue stood on a beach next to rocks rich with glowing things.

Fascinating. He had not made this world. It did not emanate from his own consciousness, or at least most of it did not. It was a world seeping from the mind of the other being in this box that was all his current world, and he was intrigued by the shining and dark vista that her angry consciousness built.

Waves swelled in the black ocean and he became aware of the ghost, in the image where she focused her consciousness as surely as her consciousness flowed through this entire experience he was seeing.

He saw her rise from the surf, her back to the shore where he stood, white-skinned in her black dress, the black waves flowing around her calves as she stood, arms at her sides, long hair undulating as if under its own will.

Then she looked back at Penamue— he suspected that she did not see his true form at all, and he wondered what form he appeared in. Then she looked away and out to sea again. A great black swell built and burst forth in a hard, onyx curl, a long tube of black liquid that rolled and finally ebbed, and after a moment she shuddered. He could feel her shudder as the waves broke around her.

A shadow emerged on the waves, a personage both there and not there, clearly a vision of this ghost. Penamue recognized the vision as the surfing man who had taken part in his capture. She kept the vision before her, a shadow that floated on the waves on a surfboard of translucent gray, bobbing and riding, circling away and back. The shadow rider there craned its head towards her, listening. Penamue was fascinated by the urgency with which she created all of this around her.

He did not know this lost ghost, but he knew a consciousness he could manipulate when he saw one.

And he seized the moment, saying, *so he is the one you are angry at.*

She answered: *He was good. We were good to him.*

But when the time came for him to help you, said the demon to the ghost, *he did not, did he?*

No! And the whole world shook, great geysers of black water and foam whipping around the shadow-surfer who floated and stared at her.

Penamue read her thoughts and said: *And when you sought his attention again, in the best way you knew, making many sacrifices—*

He let her continue with her mind and he studied her, the agitation so plain to see. He burrowed into her, seeing it all, seeing her trek across the oceans, seeing the mortals that she dragged under and led into the waves.

He did nothing!

And worse! He betrayed you, he and his friends, they came to you and tempted you with peace and they put you in this captive world, and are you at peace?

The ghost turned to the shadow surfer who reached the edge of the water and stopped, a glistening shadow of the mortal she loved.

We can be at peace, she implored the shadow surfer.

But this is not he! proclaimed Penamue, *This is a dream. Do you not surmise that you have created this yourself? What is it you feel, Sang-ook, the always good?*

Love!

Love for the one who is out there, not this shadow! Look at it and tell me if your soul is at peace!

The ghost faltered and then the shadow surfer began to shimmer in and out of view.

He is still out there, Penamue whispered, *and should he now know your love? Should he not feel your loving RAGE? You could be out on the waves with him, now, he waits, just beyond this word. As people say, love is as strong as what?*

What, the ghost turned, *what do they say?*

Love is as strong as death. Sang-ook, as you were called, call forth your own soul's power, that power that is greatest of all, that force that hastened you across this human sphere.

Penamue floated closer to her, and now flowed past her, a fluttering wave of birds, circling the shimmering shadow surfer. The birds perched on the shadow's shoulders and dipped through the waves around him, and the shadow surfer put up its hands, then faltered and slipped into the black waves.

Penamue knelt, taking a mound of the black sand in his papery fist. *Let go and reach to the edges of this world—feel its false boundaries, for they cannot hold your strength, your will, your desire!*

Cliff!

The whole world began to slide and flash, lightning crackling cross the sky. The ghost's eyes grew wide, her hair flowing like a whipping wave of snakes.

Yes! Shake this world and feel it fall, reach out and show these fools your rage, and let us go and take this love of yours!

Love! Love is as strong as death!

Stronger! Love can peel back these waves and this false sky!

She roared and the waves curled back towards the horizon like a tsunami about to break, the black sand bare and dancing with gasping white fish.

Shake this sand and send it back!

The sand began to churn, little holes and cracks growing and the grains disappearing in waves below the ghost's feet, and as they churned away Penamue looked down and saw a foundation of *wood*.

Shake! Shake the sky! Shake the world!

And the sky cracked and began to splinter in chunks of plaster and wood, and as the chunks rained down Penamue read in the pieces of wood the engravings of mortals, the pitiful spells.

This is fakery, a dream, no great reward. You can leave it. Burst this accursed illusion with the love that draws you to the man you deserve!

Sang-ook spread her arms and flew as the whole world roared with her. Penamue looked up with great satisfaction as the sky split asunder.

Saul was about to uncork the bottle when he heard a crash that shook the foundation of the café.

Kurt looked up. "What the Hell?"

Saul put down the bottle as the sound of shattering glass and the howling of wind echoed down.

Running up the stairs, cursing himself and his faith, knowing already that he would fail.

He reached the upstairs room, throwing open his niece's door, then the next one.

The door was embedded with chunks of wood. Flurries of paper birds whipped around the room and cut Saul's flesh. He could see the dybbuk box on the floor in pieces, exploded, the table the box had sat on overturned. The wind whipped where the window had been burst. Beyond the flurry he saw the ghost at the window.

The birds spoke for the ghost and the demon. *I should kill you, shaman. But there are more delicious hurts than death.* The ghost and the waves of tiny birds lifted off and crashed through the window, sending shattered glass to the street below. The birds went fast, flowing over the sill, tearing curtains as they went. Saul ran to the window and saw the birds and the ghost soaring across the parking lot, across the highway, aiming for the beach and the sounds of celebration.

CHAPTER 41

Frannie took in the sight of Hooky's Court just as they reached the edge of the torchlight. Heat reached her in a wave and rippled through her body and she gripped Newp's hand and trembled.

The fire pit, a great black area of hot coals and sand, stretched twelve feet long and six feet across. Tiki torches dotted the beach all around, the smell of the lamp oil as sharp as the orange flames above the wicker poles, and the air itself was thick with *exotica* music, basically wild imitation-Hawaiian jazz on phonograph records. The music was fast and wild, animal, and everywhere bodies shimmied and shook, girls in everything from bikinis to cocktail dresses twisted *like they did last summer* and every summer forever.

Every summer must be full of youth, wild at dance.

Watching the boys in slacks and shorts and everything in between, some in loafers—*loafers in the sand!*—and some barefoot like as Tom Sawyer, Frannie tugged Newp's sleeve.

"Oh, Newp," she said, meaning it, "It's just the most."

"Hey, Angel!" called Hooky, loud and lean, and she saw him twisting under torchlight with two Va Va Voom girls, his big straw hat coming clean off his head every time he bobbed, the chin strap the only thing keeping it from sailing off and catching fire.

Frannie let go Newp's hand and waved high and wide. Then Truly and Betty emerged from the shack—apparently Hooky had volunteered it to act as the dressing room— and took the stage.

The singers wore sequins, Truly in a number that shimmied and showed off muscular legs, and Betty in a flannel nightgown, yes, but owing to what must have been a sense of humor that allowed Betty to be patient with herself, she had sequins on the flannel. So all was right with Betty's world, but she sparkled too. They formed up near one of two mike stands and looked out expectantly.

Newp started running to the stage and Crainiac ran up and grabbed Frannie and spun her around, hanging on her shoulder. He waved, clowning for someone, and said a little too loudly SMILE, FRANNIE! She saw a Channel 4 News reporter (judging by the number on his microphone) complete with sport coat and hat, standing in front of a camera held aloft by a cameraman.

Frannie and Crainiac danced some for the cameras and Frannie maneuvered them close to the stage so that she could toss her shoes by the edge.

Newp bounded up between them and grabbed a microphone from the other stand, then dropped to the back of the stage to grab a guitar near the amps. When he returned, he planted the mike again and shouted. "Hey Laguna Beach! Say hey!" A whoop rose from the crowd in response.

Frannie felt and then saw Hooky beside her, and he put his giant hand on her shoulder. Frannie realized as she and Hooky listened that Newp was a natural.

"Everybody, tonight is something special," Newp continued. "It's July Fourth weekend and we're gonna have some joyful Independent Noise."

"Yeah!" The crowd answered, and the Hawaiian music cut out as someone pulled the plug on the record player.

"And let me tell you, tomorrow night there will be fireworks, but tonight we got fireworks of our own, man. Before the suits descend—" and here he pointed at the TV camera—"and I know you're watching! Before the highfalutin fellas from the City and the Hollywood royalty get to this beach, it's just us. Us Laguna Folk, and we got some folk fireworks for you." Newp raised his voice, holding his hand out towards the girls. "Some folk-fire. Some folk-works. Say *hey!*"

"Hey!" Hooky's voice boomed above the rest.

"So here tonight from your very own Café Monstro, you know the one,

I give you The Fencers!"

Then Truly and Betty started in harmony, kicking it off with what Truly had told Frannie was an old murder ballad, *Tom Dooley.* As they sang, the gang on the beach all swayed, hanging on one another as the hypnotic words flowed. In the middle of the song—

Hang down your head, Tom DOOLEY—

Hang down your head, and CRY—

Frannie turned around, Hooky's arm around her shoulders as they watched the band. *Poor boy, you're bound to die.*

The stars shone on the waves, the moon so bright that it cut a long white runway across the ocean, a waterway for her heart to launch a plane of spirit and dip a wing at the parentals in Maui.

Next they sang a calypso-styled number, "Bay of Mexico," and Frannie and Hooky danced and swayed. On and on the band played—"Good Night, Irene," next, and couples crept hands on onto another.

Sometimes I live in town.

Over the sound of the waves the harmonies of Newp, Betty and Truly droned on: *kisses sweeter than wine.*

"Hail, Hookele!" came the voice of T-Bone, and Hooky turned away from Frannie as a group of Legionnaires dropped to their knees in the sand and waved their arms in bowing salutes like Arabs in a Popeye cartoon.

"Hail, Hookele, Chief of the Feast!"

"All right, Legion," Hooky called, clapping his hands together. Frannie watched him go to work. He was a master of men, was Hooky. She backed all the way to the water to watch them while the surf sucked at the sand below her feet. She watched him, his arms held out in magnificent gestures, the yellow lights of the stage behind him, Truly, Betty and Newp still singing.

It was time for the feast, and Hooky directed the Legion like General Eisenhower himself, showing them where to dig around the fire pit. They used shovels to dig trenches and move coals out of the way, and soon two boys, one on either side, pulled on great ropes, hauling up out of the coals an enormous mound of what looked like a stretcher, all covered over in silver paper

Soon the foil was stripped away and the smell of deliciously pulled pork wafted through the air, a whole pig on a bed of apples, pears, oranges, pineapples, mangos, guava and kiwi. The smell mixed with the flying sparks and waved along with the orange fingers of the tiki torches, sickening sweet and gorgeous as Hooky, that wondrous man on the sand.

She knew as she watched him that nothing could ever be as good as this night nor as luxurious as this July 3, 1958, no sound as gorgeous as the cackled fir and the laughter of sun burnt surfers and the folk music of the Fencers. It couldn't possibly be. Frannie stood and turned her back to the scene, and ached deep for her future without this. It was bound to come as sure as 1959.

She felt a tap on her shoulder and turned to see Newp with a plate of glistening luau pork and fruit. "Frannie, I brought you some."

"Thanks. But nah."

"I thought you ate pork."

"It's… I don't know. I don't eat it tonight." She hadn't even noticed the music end. Frannie took the plate and looked back towards the stage where Truly and Betty now stood, hounded by new fans. "Newp, you should be with the girls!"

"Well, we couldn't forget about you," he said.

The exotica-faux-Hawaiian records started again and after a moment Hooky pointed. "Hey! I see a ray!" Frannie turned to see a white, glistening manta ray leap and dive offshore, and as it slipped away Newp called, "Hey, let's look for some more manta rays." Then someone shouted words that she would curse until the day she died.

CHAPTER 42

"Night surf!"

Night surfing is a rarity even in Laguna Beach. The surfer must go through all the usual motions—paddling out beyond the breakers, waiting for a wave, then paddling to meet it before trying to ride atop the wave as it comes back—but at night, every step is rife with added risk. Shadows that might be visible in day to warn the surfer of a sudden drop off or underwater danger, a reef or a wrecked boat, disappear. The waves are choppier and harder and other surfers are near invisible, their chattering voices lost amid louder winds and waves. Collisions happen, legs break, eyes are gouged out by board fins. Night surfing is alive with risk, and this is what those who practice it lust for.

In her two months surfing, Frannie was a risk-taker, but not generally a night surfer.

But the moment the concert was over, Frannie joined the shouts of "Night suuuuurfff!" She hugged Betty and Truly- who'd done such a beautiful job that the sounds of the music still echoed in her ears—and she grabbed Newp and Hooky both and dragged them towards the water.

She wanted both of them. They were a mess on land, or at least she was for them, crazy with jealousy and butterflies, halting and nervous, riveted with love and hurt. But not on the waves. She held their hands and ran in her dress to answer the call of the ocean. There was no strange emotion out there, out there you only thought about the art, mind focused only on the board and the body and the balance.

The three of them ran and grabbed tiki torches as they went, and then others followed, all of Hooky's Legion and even more from up and down the state, a whooping army of night surfers charging out to sea. Frannie saw dinner jackets flung and boards brandished, churning up and down and flickering, board and tiki, tiki and board.

Fifty yards out the army of surfers rested on their boards and watched the horizon for shimmering deep-blue waves. Frannie floated and dangled her feet, Hooky on her right and Newp on her left, dark silhouettes of lean muscle. She could see the shaggy hair on Newp's head and Hooky's cowlick, as if they were construction paper cutouts, Hooky's seashell bracelet practically glowing against the water.

"Hey, Frannie, look," Hooky called, pointing out.

"Surf's up." Frannie breathed and started to paddle as the two silhouettes let her go first. She dipped her hands and pushed, watching a long rolling swell coming in. The other two started paddling behind her and moving apart, splitting like machines, Hooky going way left and Newp headed for the south end of the wave. Frannie took center and paddled for all she was worth.

It hadn't broken yet, but boy it was swelling. She was lost now, her brain shut off except for a thousand calculations, looking for the right time, the right feel of upsurge against her body, and then she realized it *still* hadn't broken and she wasn't even going to try to get on top because she was going to shoot the damn thing.

The front of the swell pushed her up and she caught a glimpse of yachts in the distance, waiting for July 4, and then the wave broke ahead of her and here it came.

A wall of glistening night wave and she heard Hooky call "Shoot it, Frannie!"

She pitched forward, slipping the nose of the board right into the curl just as the wall started building, the bottom of the curl lifting her, the chittering sound of the water against the underside of the board slamming like a machine. The wall thrust up next to her so high and flat she could hang a poster on it. No shudder or shake, distant voices disappearing, just her and the wave and the sliding board, the wall glistening slick and she stuck out her hand and touched it, the water ripping out around her fingers as she flew down the night pipe, flying until she ducked under the dying curl, racing and crunching her body as the pipeline narrowed, her feet perfect and the roar a faraway echo.

She burst through the north end of the pipe still on her feet and time smacked back, she rode and reached the breakers and dropped to her feet, grabbing her board. She ran towards Newp, who was wading towards her.

Newp grabbed her and spun her around in the water. "Jesus, you're a natural."

Then Hooky got here and damn if that bastard didn't literally tousle her hair like she was the son of the Rifleman.

Then she put her arms around her men, lost to the world and the other surfers, lost to all.

After a moment she looked back out to sea and said, "Let's go again."

She heard a whisper in her brain, really more a vibration in the hair on the back of her neck as she started to paddle out. She thought of the little golem in her room and the thought made her laugh. She knew that soon she'd need to go ashore and participate in the planned exorcism of the box.

She paddled out and pivoted, turning with a rising swell. Probably had an hour to go and she'd make use of it. She found a wave, not too big this time, and got to her feet.

Something yanked on her feet and she fell forward, smacking her hip against her board.

What the Hell? And then a pair of arms, white and bony, reached from the waves and grabbed Frannie's hands, pulling her towards the board so fast that her teeth banged together as she smacked her chin on the board and she went in the water and she felt a panicked urge to swim and she kicked and swam.

And flipped her legs under her to stop because someone's head was half-in the water, black hair and burning eyes, and then it sank below the waves.

She started to shake, treading water.

How the Hell did you get out?

She started to shout and then the white hand burst from the water and grabbed her by the neck, yanking her under the waves.

Newp felt giddy and alive as he hopped up on the board and rose the wave, eyes searching for obstacles and Frannie and Hooky.

He had kissed Frannie. Kissed Frannie! That crazy kid was impossible for him to describe or understand, but she strode into everyone's life and turned it upside down. Stop thinking, stop, surf, feet and board, and he could taste her mouth and feel her hands.

Newp saw for a moment Hooky's head and body silhouetted against the sky about twenty yards off, the crazy beachcomber king.

A sound like the grinding of corn or beans sounded off towards the shore, and he looked back.

Newp saw a white cloud shooting across the water and pegged it instantly. He could see the cloud coming against the waves, tiny beating wings in one long column, and then as he started to fall at the ebb of the wave, the birds were upon him. They struck him hard and he fell, feeling them slice his chest and arm as he flew back off the board and into the water.

Newp dove, swimming for broke under the water, kicking against the tiny birds as they flew through the water, and he opened his eyes and saw them all around. A long line of origami moving through the waves like a great barracuda of countless tiny winged pieces, glowing under its own light.

One of them came plowing through the water and struck his forehead and he felt it churning, biting, the cut singing with salty pain, another plunging at his neck, rhythmic and brutal, *thrum thrum thrum*.

He would not open his mouth, he could not, that was what it wanted, he realized, an easy way in, it wanted to dive into his mouth and down his toward and rip his flesh from the inside, and no, he would not open his mouth.

Newp's chest went tight and the air in his mouth burned rancid and he yearned to open his mouth; he fought, swatting slowly at the birds under water, He felt them between his toes, felt them slicing his belly, the burns warm and agonizing, and they sliced at the drawstring of his shorts.

Newp screamed.

\# \# \#

Frannie flailed under the water, her wrists locked in the bony hands of the ghost. The water was cold and clear; she could see perfectly, for she was bathed in the glow of the angry dead woman, whose own legs kicked and steadied her. The girl's eyes were wide, dark circles, her mouth open and black. She stared, almost unseeing, and Frannie got the impression that if she watched her for another second, the ghost's mouth might widen and sprout enormous teeth and she would tear Frannie apart.

Her hair flowed like an oil slick, trailing the light died in the green-black distance. Motes of dust swirled between Frannie and the ghost, sparkling with the eerie incandescence.

Frannie kicked and tried to rise and the ghost held Frannie's hands with an impossibly tight grasp.

Come on. Get free.

And the ghost held—she started to scream, and the ghost only stared and held her. It intended to let Frannie tire and drown.

I feel sorry. I do, Frannie thought. *You were innocent and you loved a man and you were hurt and you were killed. But I don't deserve to die. It's not right!*

Then a voice in her mind, in the water, in the black circle eyes: *what does right have to do with anything?*

Come on! She fought. She couldn't breather. *Don't panic.* She kicked.

The ghost held. The air in her lungs grew toxic. *Don't panic.*

Please!

The ghost grinned.

Frannie fought and rolled back and closed her eyes and the Blanks filled her vision, the stories hidden there and then she rolled forward in the water and said:

Ver dershtikt, ver dershokhtn

A regular curse, a curse anyone might use, but the words were bodies and she was filling them with *Hod*, with glory—

Ver dershtikt, ver dershokhtn, get strangled and get stabbed,

Ver dervorgn, get choked, and she saw the ghost looking at her, wonder creeping into those angry eyes,

Ver tsezest!

Explode!

Water filled her mouth as she screamed the words. She heard her voice burbling, the jumble of numbers on her chest burning against her, the last bit of air in her lungs bursting forth in bubbles.

The Hebrew words flowed. She felt herself encased in warmth, she felt power seep through her body as she locked eyes with the ghost.

"*Ver dershtikt, ver dershokhtn, ver dervorgn, ver tsezest, get strangled, get stabbed, get choked, explode!*"

And the ghost began to scream.

I banish you! By the power of the wise one, by the Holy of the Holies, I banish you! Be gone, angry and misbegotten thing!

And the ghost faltered, the motes of dust suddenly visible through her. The ghost didn't so much loosen her grip as lose her solidity.

Frannie kicked and broke loose.

"Seek peace, ya crazy lady," Frannie screamed as she rose in the water, hitting the surface and gasping for air. She opened her eyes and saw a wall of wave coming and dove.

She went deep, looking for the ghost again, but saw no glow, no motes of dust in the brilliant shimmer. Frannie bobbed under the water and saw nothing of the ghost, then swam back up to the surface as the wave passed, to look around.

"Newp!" she called. "Hooky!"

She heard a splash and a scream.

Newp's scream underwater brought a gush of water into his mouth. And as the tiny birds flashed in the water, one of them flitted before his eyes, glowing and with tiny words he could not read. The water undulated and thrummed with the beating wings, and he swore he heard a voice.

You are their friend, aren't you? You will make a vessel to be proud of. Perhaps I will even return your thoughts, embedded somewhere in the minutest part of your sin, perhaps I will even ride the waves with your friends. And when I find the Blanks, we will enjoy them together.

Newp fought, stuck underwater, screaming *no more,* he clamped his eyes shut and felt cuts along his back

GOD NO

Then—light.

There was light blazing beyond his closed eyelids. He felt the birds suddenly lurch, scattering, ceasing their biting, and he forced his eyes open. The birds were moving away from his face and body and he saw fire.

A flare, underwater, a signal flare burned and spewed, as a figure attacked the birds and came closer. Newp saw the muscled form of Hooky, lit up in a red glow beneath the waves, as he stabbed at the wave of birds. He set some to flame, and as they broke off and scattered, Hooky grabbed Newp by the shoulders, digging in his fingers and dragging him up.

They struck the surface and Newp gasped for air, spreading out his arms and lifting himself aloft.

Hooky and Newp spun around, calling in all directions as Hooky waved the flare. "Frannie! Where are you?"

Newp coughed and Hooky threw him a glance as they treaded water. "You okay?"

"I think so." They started to swim for shore, body surfing, letting the waves help until they hit the beach.

# # #

Not far away, Frannie fell in the sand, exhausted. She rose on her elbows as she heard them come ashore. "Guys!" They found her in the edge of the surf, crawling and exhausted. Now that she had seen them, she regained her strength. She rose and ran to them, whooping as she threw her skinny arms around them.

"I got your ghost, boy," Frannie said to Hooky. "That lady didn't want to share you. But I don't know, I think I just rattled her. She got away."

Newp nodded. "Bookman did too. But look at this damage." He held out his arms and showed her the paper cuts all along his skin.

Frannie winced. "Ooh, do those hurt?"

"Like crazy." But Newp gestured at Hooky and laughed. "Hooky licked the birds, though."

Hooky's flare was dying but still casting a red glow on their faces. They looked down the beach and Frannie realized they were half a mile up from the luau. She pointed out the hut, where tiki torches still burned as surfers still went in and out of the water.

"That thing *knows* us now," Newp said.

"Yep," Hooky said. Then he clapped Newp on the back. "Come on, let's get you some iodine."

"Kids!" came the voice of Saul, who appeared at the top of the cliff, running down a stairway with what looked like blanket in his arms. "They got loose!"

Frannie laughed out loud. "We noticed! Your dybbuk box must be a lemon; I'd take that thing back."

As Saul reached them on the beach, he dropped the blanket he was carrying. It unrolled, and Emmett the golem stood, smoking and looking annoyed—his only look, really.

Frannie crouched down in the sand and gave the golem a peck on the cheek.

"Ugh. We lost our boards," Newp said.

"You are not safe!" the golem intoned.

"Tell us something we don't know," Frannie said.

Hooky laughed, folding his arms, a god-man against the night sea behind him. "Boy, he never lets up, huh?"

And then there was no time to scream as a great column of milky white paper birds burst from the water, split into two and clapped itself around Hooky. Just time enough for Frannie to give a short cry as the birds yanked Hooky high and shrinking into the distance, disappearing into the endless distance of waves and night.

CHAPTER 43

"Hooky was short for Hookele," said Newp. "Big Chief."

The night after the luau, Newp stood surrounded by torches in front of Hooky's hut, and in the distance fireworks began to wind into the air and burst, the first hints of the July 4th celebration. Hooky's Legion gathered in silence, each with their boards, standing like sentries. He saw "hot curl" boards with their bottoms shaved on either side, Hawaiian-style boards with no fins, new boards with two fins, even an experimental quad-fin that Go-Go had fashioned, given up on and sold for a song to Crainiac.

Newp went on. "I've been surfing here at Laguna for two years and Hooky was here already. He built that hut with his hands from old lumber and license plates, and he was chief from the start.

"He had a name: Cliff Carmichael. But he left that name in Korea, he said, and I only learned it when I found an old picture of today that he kept on the little dressing table next to his bunk. He was here when we all got out first finned board; he was here to test the first press-treated composites. He showed us how to survive on clams and fish and the bread we earned from the day trippers. Well, not me." Newp smirked. "Some of us had jobs."

Some of the Legion chuckled and Newp nodded. Frannie was not among the gathered. "He was ageless, and he was our Chief.

"Hooky told stories when he got to feeling like it. He told us he got the tiki mask over his bed from a Hawaiian tribe and his curved knife from a trip to Africa where the natives put a curse on him for disturbing a sacred ritual when he walked in on it, and how he had the curse lifted by seeking the help of a gypsy woman in a camp outside Rome.

"And you know what? I don't know if any of that is true at all. I don't know if Hooky even ever went to Hawaii or to Rome or if he could find any given country in Africa. I have no idea.

"I know he was wounded far from home and that he came back and threw his dog tags in the sea and now the sea has taken him.

Newp paused, looking own. Then: "Tonight, we ride for Hooky."

He stamped his foot. *"Hookele. Hookele."*

The surfers returned the chant: *Hookele. Hookele.* One by one the Legionnaires began to move (*Hookele!*) and take up their boards, moving slowly and then faster towards the water as they changed.

Hookele. Hookele.

Twenty torches and forty surfers paddled out, scanning the horizon for waves to catch for their fallen Chief.

One Legionnaire was not among them. Frannie sat inside Hooky's hut, listening to Newp's speech as she sat huddled against the corner of the bunk where Hooky had slept every night, a black blanket wrapped around her. She heard the chant *Hookele* and whispered it and fell silent. She heard the chant recede into the waves, punctuated by the firing of July 4th rockets up and down the shore.

"I brought you something," came a voice. Frannie looked towards the door as Saul stuck his head in, his bald head framed now against a portrait Hooky had hung of Gracie Allen, whom Hooky said he taught a lesson to in 1954, when Gracie was already 59 years old and still the star of a TV show that he'd never watched because Hooky never owned a TV.

Frannie fluffed the blanket and said, "What is it?" She couldn't look at Saul. Did she blame him for Hooky's death? Because he should have known the box might not hold? She could not decide. It didn't matter now. She barely had the energy to blame or to raise her head.

Saul came through the clacking beaded curtain and let it fall behind him. He was holding a black ashtray out, his other hand in his khaki pocket. She didn't respond—vaguely aware that she made a distant, puzzled look—and he said, "This has nothing to do with Hooky, really. It has to do with you."

"With me?"

He came closer and she could see flecks of light glint on the back ashtray. "May I sit?"

"Free country."

"That it is." He sat on the edge of the bunk and laid the ashtray on the mattress next to her blanket where she could read the words embossed around the edges. SHLOSSMANN'S RESORT & CASINO. In the center of the black glass was a silver diamond, still lustrous even though it had to be twenty years old.

"You think I'm so overwrought I'm gonna take up cigarettes."

"You do and I'll disinherit you."

"Yeah? What were you gonna leave me, the golem?"

Saul tapped the ashtray. "When you and your folks came to stay with me, you were—gosh, you could crawl, I guess. Maybe walk. You were a tiny thing. So smart. And you loved these things."

"Ashtrays?" She tugged the blanket but looked up at him.

"Well." Saul scratched his head. "The room you and your folks in was really tiny. Really. I mean, you were there because your pop had run out of money, you know."

"Uncle Saul…"

"I'm not saying this to shame anyone. He was broke and he had to put his doctorate on hold while he worked. Anyway, you spent a lot of time in the tiny room and the tiny den in my apartment.

"You would steal the ashtrays. You collected them. I had no idea why. Then once I saw you hold one up to the light—I mean, people were running around the house with their cigarette ashes out to *here* because you had all the ashtrays in a pile in your room! You were holding the ashtray up to the light and I could see you, this little black-haired beauty with the glint of the sun through the window, shining in the diamond in the center of the ashtray. Your mom came in and she was—ah, livid. You had spilled ashes all over yourself."

Saul picked up the ashtray, turned it over. "Your mom whisked you up and she looked at me with *rage*, and I knew why. I know why. I mean, none of us likes to see our children covered in ashes. But your eyes were on the sun and the diamond." He looked at her. "I see you look at the ocean like that, you stand and bask in the light, in the glint."

She didn't have a response to that. "I'm not going to disrespect that story, Saul, but…"

"Hooky came here to be away from his pain. Not to run from, but I think, but just… to heal, and maybe he would be healing forever. Or maybe he'd have gone from here. I don't know. But when you walked into my café, I knew you were here for a purpose."

"I'm not saying I—I'm not saying anything."

"You are not Hooky." Saul looked her in the eyes. "Your path is not the same, your life is not tied to his, and it is not gone when he is gone." Saul rose and went back to the beaded curtain, and she heard again the fireworks in the air. He opened the curtain and stood holding it, indicating the outside. "Come look."

"I don't want to."

"Come on, it won't kill you and you can go right back."

Frannie sighed, then moved off the bed, the blanket wrapped around her. She stood in front of her uncle and followed his gaze. Across the beach, she saw the torches dancing in the water, silhouettes of the surfers barely visible.

It looked like a sea of stars.

"Look at that crew," Saul said. "We all honor our dead the best way we know how. And that way there, I didn't want you to miss seeing it. It's beautiful, and you'd regret it if you didn't look."

It *was* beautiful. She watched the torches dancing on the waves, wondering which one was Newp. "Newp makes a hell of a speech," she mumbled.

"Yes he does," Saul said. "Anyway, they honor their dead their way. Yours is still waiting."

She rolled her eyes. "I know what you think it is. You think we need to saddle up and go after Book Man, but Uncle Saul, I have no idea how you'd do that, and I… I just…"

"What? You think you can't? Frannie, you learned those incantations better than I did, better than I've ever seen. And you're so damn smart. Yeah, you can."

Frannie thought for a long time. Then she looked down. No, she couldn't.

Saul squeezed her shoulders and said, "May God comfort you among the mourners of Zion and Jerusalem," and kissed her head before he moved out silently.

She watched the torches for a long time before she returned to the oblivion of mourning.

CHAPTER 44

Mark and Sally Cohn left the poolside bar at the Hilton Hawaiian Village and held hands like teenagers. Sally held to her floppy hat as the nearby beach at Waikiki sent a wind that rustled the palm trees, making them sway like hula dancers.

"Frannie's up to something if she wanted to miss this," Sally said.

"Her uncle will watch her," Marc replied, and this made Sally laugh harder than anything.

"Watch her," Sally snorted. "Your brother is likely to have her making beer runs for him."

"*Mazik*," Marc said. "Don't be crazy."

"You watch, he'll take her to a nightclub."

"We should be so lucky," Marc said. "Have you seen the kids on the beach? At least a comedy club would have everyone in clothes."

"Marc, we should call her." They stepped onto the path heading to the pride of the resort: the dome.

"It looks like a city on the moon in a magazine," Marc said. The four-hundred-foot wide geodesic dome, flickering with countless interlocking metal panels, was the premier showroom and concert hall of the Island of Oahu. Just this night they were going to see the bandleader Desi Arnaz himself, who was in town for a limited engagement of Cuban music.

Marc waved his hand and rubbed Sally's shoulder. "Ah, we'll call them tomorrow. Maybe. It costs a fortune."

"Do you think Lucy will be there?" Sally was asking about the band-leader's famous comedian wife, whom Sally adored. She ran her fingers along Marc's arm as they walked. Sally wore a gorgeous light wool dress patterned with pink piping and a pillbox hat. She had not looked so lovely in twenty years and Marc was compelled to say so, many times. "I love Lucy."

Marc laughed as the walkway grew crowded with other vacationers headed for the dome; all the men dressed the same in suits and suits and suits, black ties, no variation, while the women explored as many colors as humanly possible.

A man with no hat and scant hair raised his hand when he saw them coming and called their names. The man's wife, a sturdy but beautiful former dancer, embraced Marc and took Sally's arm. The man was Dave

Fontenot, a movie producer who Marc knew through the university.

"I got your tickets to the show," Dave said.

"Is Lucy going to be there?" Sally asked.

Dave shrugged. "She doesn't travel as much, so I doubt it. But the band is something else."

They entered the dome underneath a great shining arch, and for a moment Marc's eye was caught by the ocean beyond the grass around the done, beyond the walkways and even a small highway. His attention was drawn clear across the beach to the edge of the water.

He saw a lone surfer on the beach.

The surfer was barely visible, standing amongst seaweed just at the edge of the water, tall and lean, and something struck Marc, a tiny distant bell clanging.

He had had this feeling before, spotting people up to no good, and it had served him well. A German, he had seen the soldiers standing in the street corners conversing and looking his way as he and Sally and the baby came home from Temple one Saturday afternoon. Something was changing fast. He booked his train out the next day.

But the clanging was distant, the surfer alone and far off, and the bell, to be sure, was rusty. Marc shivered and joined again the chattering of his party. He listened to Dave Fontenot regale them with tales of Hollywood as they entered the dome and found their seats.

Desi Arnaz, the bandleader known the world over for his hot salsa sound, led the band in a concert that lasted hours, the first set alone lasting an hour. Marc and Sally danced to the bongo rhythm many times.

At half past ten he returned to his table and found a porter waiting for him. "Mr. Cohn, you should come." The porter, a young Polynesian man, looked grave.

"What is it?" Sally arrived at the table a moment later.

"I'm afraid something has happened to—in your room."

Back to the suite then.

Yes: something had happened to and in the room.

As Marc stepped in, he felt the wind instantly and he knew the sliding doors had been destroyed. The first thing he saw was glass, a great expanse of shards lying all over the carpet and bed.

Somewhere there's music… the radio played, tinkling and ghostly as Marc surveyed the twisted aluminum shards of the torn-down blinds.

And he knew before he saw that the bag his brother had given him was gone.

CHAPTER 45

On Monday, some ladies Frannie didn't know visited Café Monstro for tomato sandwiches and a brief talk with Saul. The matter of the hearing against the Café had been championed by Callie and was to be postponed indefinitely, and there was a likelihood that the matter would be dropped. Just as Saul had predicted.

Frannie, who had dragged herself from Hooky's tent to work out of a sense of loyalty that drove her even more than misery, overheard the gist of this conversation and felt a moment's uplift, but the fact that her uncle's good fortune owed to the Book Man clouded over her feelings. She bused, talked, and wound her way forward to the office, where Newp was on the phone as the golem sat on the edge of the desk.

Newp hung up the phone. He looked ashen and opened his mouth, then made no words.

"Newp, what's the…"

"They're killing us."

"What?"

"All hope is misplaced where time moves forward," said the golem, a trail of smoke coming out of his mouth, like a weird little decoration immolating itself from inside.

"Shut up, you," Frannie told the golem. "Newp, you're freaking me out." She pulled up a chair across from Newp.

"That was Ed Sullivan's office."

"About the Labor Day show?" Frannie tried to trace the concern on his face.

Newp nodded, the little shark tooth on his chest rising and falling beneath his open cotton shirt. "They saw some of the TV coverage."

"That's great," Frannie said. "Everybody loved that show." And they had, and again a good feeling came over her, immediately to be overswept by pain and loss.

"Yeah," Newp said. "People did dig it. But the producer said that they thought it was great, but that they have to, you know, they have to cancel. They're canceling us," he repeated.

"What?" Frannie stared. "What? Why?"

"Understand, the lady sounded—I don't know. Embarrassed."

Frannie felt a tiny tinkling of anger because whatever was going to come next was going to be some primo bullshit. "What was the reason?"

Newp shook his head. "They… they said that they don't think we present the kind of image the show's viewers are comfortable with."

"Oh my god," Frannie fumed. "Because of your freaking cutoffs below your jacket? Because of the beatnik thing?"

"Frannie, no."

"Because the girls were in cocktail dresses, at least you could have worn pants."

"That's not it."

Truly spoke from the door, her voice high-pitched and smooth. "They don't want a mixed band." She and Betty stared at Newp. "That's it, isn't it?"

Newp seemed to try to decide how to answer as he met the eyes of all of them in the room, even the golem. "That's right."

"That can't be," Frannie said, her throat catching. "They wouldn't do that to you, to all of you."

"Oh, yes," Truly said, "yes, they would. I didn't even have the conversation and I could probably recite it for you."

"That's absurd," said Betty, twisting the flannel at her neck. "Can—can I call them back for you?"

Frannie rose and threw her arms around Truly. Did it really work like that? Someone could see a dark face and say it doesn't belong on TV?

"Vanity," said the golem, and Frannie burst into tears and ran from the room. She ran and didn't stop until she'd reached the beach, her apron fluttering behind her in the sand. The roar of the waves blasted out all feeling and thought as she paddled out. She had flashes of thought and the waves blasted the thoughts, Hooky dying and the wave she caught slammed around her, the sound of the board on the wave sending the memory flying into fragments.

They were nothing but potentiality, Saul had said. Hooky was a potential something and then not, the Ed Sullivan Show appearance was a part of the potential of Newp and Betty and Truly, and then not. But so much potentiality is hard to predict—*you had potential in Germany when you were a baby*, Saul had said, *but who would predict that you would be here, riding the surf in California.*

It wasn't the end. But some potential was worse than others and some just lay there daring you to despise it.

Frannie came in on her second good wave and was about to paddle out again when she saw Saul waving from the cliff. She felt sullen and dull again as she walked to meet him. He had a slip of paper in his hand. He hurried to meet her and thrust it into her hands with a dark expression.

FROM: HONOLULU.

Frannie read out loud, then looked up.

# # #

Saul tapped a map on his desk. "Book Man crossed the Pacific. I had no idea he'd do that."

"Oceans are as nothing to the will of the Sons of God," spoke Emmett before Frannie smacked the little creature on the back of the head.

"He got *all* the Blanks?" Frannie asked dully. "Are my parents…"

"They wrote us a telegram, so *they're* okay," Saul said. "Look, if Penamue got all the Blanks—and that's pure potentiality between those pages, barrels of human paths—there's no telling what he could do."

Frannie rubbed her face. "I need to talk to them."

"We can call." Saul nodded. "Frannie, I'm sorry. I never should have sent them with my brother."

"No," Frannie corrected him. She saw it clearly. "If you hadn't, Penamue would have gotten the Blanks days ago."

The room at the hotel rang and rang. Frannie put her hands on her hips, still in her bathing suit. She stared at the map, at 2500 miles of blue between herself and the demon that had killed Hooky and now taken the prize that she had been pledged to protect. "Saul," she asked. "Do we have the tools to stop him? Not stick him in a box. Really stop him?"

Saul looked at her, then Newp and Emmett. "Yes."

She swiveled her head, considering. Then: "We need to go. He got potential from those books? Well, we have lots more. I am nothing but potential, you always say. So this is it. Newp, you in?"

"Absolutely," he said.

"Truly?" Frannie looked out the door of the office. Betty and Truly looked from the bar. "We know where he is. We're gonna kick the tail of the thing that killed Hooky. You in?"

"I got nothin' here," Truly said.

"Good. Betty, you stay, please. Hold down the fort." She turned back to the rest as they all gathered. "The rest of you. We bring whatever Saul says. We leave tonight if possible." Frannie felt something, felt the power of decisions. It was a hot and worthy feeling.

"It's time to go Hawaiian."

CHAPTER 46

White birds filled the sky around the Hawaiian Village Hotel at five o'clock in the morning as Marc and Sally entered the lobby with what was left of their bags.

"Marc, look," Sally said, tugging his arm and pointing outside the lobby, across the green to the dome. Marc dropped the suitcases and looked through the glass windows.

"Birds." He shrugged. The birds came in a great wave, rising up and circling the dome as Marc and Sally stepped outside. What struck Marc as strange weren't the birds then, but the abundance of people who were out on the lawn. They had come in bathrobes and shirtsleeves, wandering the yard of the hotel, staring at the swarm of white birds.

The white birds circled the whole of the hotel tower, the sound of buzzing faint but clear.

"What the Hell?" Dave Fontenot looked up as he found them, wearing slacks and a white undershirt. Then as if he needed to explain himself, he said, "Couldn't sleep. Hey, you guys are dressed."

"We're leaving," Marc said. "We had an incident." He did not explain that his brother's duffel bag of magic books had been stolen. It was all too absurd.

"Marc," Dave asked, almost plaintive. "What the hell are those things?"

"They're birds—" and he looked up and saw them more closely. He was about to reach for some explanation so absurd it wasn't even worth saying out loud. Then he spotted the lonely surfer again—this time standing at the entrance of the silvery dome.

The birds in the sky were tiny, he realized, and their incessant circling was intensifying, pulling their great mass towards the dome. And Marc felt the pull as well. And so did everyone else.

The lone surfer stood stock still at the double glass door entrance of the geodesic dome, and then the birds began to form a funnel. They swirled and swept in a great arc around him, forming a greater and greater white column over the dome.

Dave walked past Marc, faster. "Wait, Dave," Marc said. But Dave was moving fast and already gone.

Marc took Sally forcefully by the upper arm. "Did you hear that?"

Sally was ashen. "Yes."

Amidst the bizarre buzzing and flapping of the half-mile wide circle of tiny white birds, Marc had heard what he could describe as a whisper, as though it were just beyond his ear:

Come, it said. *Come and see the future.*

The travelers around Marc and Sally began to march. He began to march towards the dome and the lonely surfer as well.

But he caught himself because he was thinking about it already, he could see himself responding to the whisper and it gave him the extra distance to stop and turn to Sally. "Are we going?"

It was a crazy question. The lonely surfer was barely visible now, the flock of birds a great white cloud forming all over and around the dome, flitting fast past him.

More people passed Marc and Sally, some of them repeating the whisper out loud. "See the future... come and see the future."

"Mr. Cohn," called a porter who emerged from the hotel. Marc looked back at the porter and saw the young man stop to take in with astonishment that growing pilgrimage of hotel guests streaming towards the dome. He seemed to forget what he was going to say.

"Yes?"

"Oh." The porter tore himself away and looked back at Marc. "Yes.

The phones are out, but there's a return telegram for you." He handed it over and Marc scanned it with Sally.

TO: MOM AND POP

FROM: FRANNIE

HANG TIGHT AND HANG TEN STOP WE ARE COMING STOP PS DON'T LISTEN TO THE BIRDS STOP THEY WILL EAT YOU STOP

Marc looked up to thank the porter, but the you man was already briskly walking towards the dome. The droning whispers grew more incessant. "Do you feel it?" she said.

"I do." And they turned away their heads and walked for the lobby. All the way, the incessant compulsion of the whispering swarm of birds dragged at his body, seemed to want to turn his knees and feet back. "We have to find a room where we can't hear it."

Marc opened the lobby door and Desi Arnaz nearly ran over him, sprinting in the thrall of the birds, on the way to hear more of the whisper of the future.

At the moment that Marc and Sally Cohn were watching Desi run like a madman towards what had to be his certain doom, Frannie, Newp, Saul and Truly were lifting off the runway at Orange County bound for Honolulu.

Newp wore a tie, because Frannie told him it was required for flying and anyway a man should travel with dignity.

As they took off, Frannie opened the backpack that held Emmett and saw the little clay man look angrily at her, because his mouth was taped to prevent the constant stream of smoke. It was an indignity he would no doubt complain about at length and with great eloquence later.

The benefit of living in a bookstore was that they had no shortage of books to read on the flight. But Frannie was going to tell them which ones.

A stewardess came by dressed in berry blue. Saul made a show of saying they were his church youth group and not to serve these kids any alcohol, and the stewardess winked dramatically and brought them all cherry cokes with lime. This done, Frannie turned to everyone. "What do you know about Hawaii?"

Saul leaned back with his ball-capped head. "Pearl Harbor; I know that. It's a protectorate. Basically I know what I read in the papers."

"I have never seen you touch a paper," said Truly, who leaned over to ask Frannie. "Does your uncle even get a newspaper?"

Newp took one of the Hawaii books that Frannie was passing out. "I saw Kurt tear up a paper for a papier-mâché Dracula crucifix. But I think he bought that in town."

Saul smirked. "Everyone's a wisenheimer."

"Yeah, show some respect for your elders or tape your mouth and stick you in a backpack," Frannie said.

"What are you handing out?" Saul took out a pair of glasses and looked at the book he had received.

"Books; I suggest we divide this up. First just some basics on the islands."

"It's more than one?" Newp said.

"Yeah, it's an archipelago," Frannie answered.

"A what?"

"A series of islands, we call that an archipelago."

Newp nodded. "So what you're saying is that before you started hanging out with all us beach bums, you were a major egghead."

"I'm a student. And weren't you going to college in the Fall?"

"Six weeks," Truly said. "He leaves in six weeks."

"Six weeks til you go to college?" Saul winced. "Jeez. I gotta find a manager. Truly, you want to manage a café?"

"I gotta go to school too, old man. And by the way, I *know* what an archipelago is, so it's eggheads versus the male element."

Frannie cleared her throat, addressing each of them in the row. "Okay. Everybody. Like I was saying. First, Hawaiian subjects. Then we review what we know about Penamue, or Book Man, and what tools we can use to stop him. Then we formulate a plan."

"Hey, Commander," Saul said. "How much time do we devote to this?"

Frannie sipped her coke. "We got 13 hours on this plane. So I figure one or two hours for each subject."

"Ugh," Newp said. "You want us to study?"

"I want you to learn."

Truly and Newp visibly shrank. Saul waved his hand. "You can cut your plan down by half. You've forgotten a couple of things."

"What's that?"

"First, you'll need *sleep*. When you get there, it'll be six in the morning in Honolulu. And we're gonna be busy. So I don't recommend an all-night cram session."

Frannie looked at the others and drummed her fingers, already devoting a portion of her mind to reciting Hebrew curses. "What was the other thing?"

"These broads," Saul said, as a line of female hula dancers in grass skirts congregated in the front of the plane, chatting with one another. "I talked to one of them. Halfway through the flight, not long before lights-out, they get up and do a show, a whole Hawaiian thing. I mean, we don't want to miss that, and even if we did, I don't think you can read through it."

"It's research," Newp said, eying the hula girls.

Truly rolled her eyes. "Yeah, Frannie, Newp wants to research the dancing girls."

Frannie allowed herself to laugh. "Okay. So we work our butts off 'til the floor show. Then it's lights out. Okay?"

"Aye aye." Saul saluted.

They got busy. A couple of hours in, they were interrupted by coke refills, bathroom breaks, and Frannie traded seats with Newp. She sat next to her uncle and the sound of whispered incantations filled the aisle.

Seven hours in came the hula show and by then Frannie's head was so full of anagrams and number spells and recitations that she saw Hebrew in the strings of the grass skirts flowing from the hips of the dancers.

After that, sleep and dreams of Hooky and Penamue, and all the potential in the world.

CHAPTER 47

The airport in Honolulu at six a.m. was a madhouse. Frannie got the sense as they stepped down the rolling staircase onto the tarmac that the ceremonial lei that the local women placed on her shoulders ("Aloha," of course) was the last thing the lady wanted to be doing and the last predictable thing that would happen.

As they made it into the terminal, their party ran into throngs of travelers. Lines backed up at courtesy counters, the lines doubling back and devolving into a mess of shouting, agitated people, some in traveling clothes and some wearing whatever they had worn to the beach that day.

When the gang entered the smoking lounge—the only place they could hear one another talk—the TV bolted to the wall showed them why.

"Look at that," Saul whispered.

On the screen, apparently filmed by helicopter, a bizarre drama was playing out at the Hawaiian Village Hotel and Resort, according to the subtitle on the screen. "That's Mom and Pop's hotel," Frannie said.

She moved closer to the TV set and gasped as a section of the great white roof of the dome fluttered and swirled and settled back, the first time she'd realized that was not the roof at all, but a covering unnatural. "It's him. Those are origami birds, thousands of them."

"*Hundreds* of thousands," Truly corrected. "That dome is fifty feet high and a hundred feet wide. I read that just last night."

Crowds of people appeared on the TV screen, wandering around the grounds of the hotel and the dome.

"These crowds you can see," said the news reporter, "seem to be—well, they seem to be waiting. But we have not been able to get a visible interview with any of them."

The video image cut and everyone who wasn't caught up in the procession into the dome seemed to have the same sense as the reporter—that they should leave. The highways headed to the airport was backed up and locked with cars, buses, motorcycles. You were either caught up in the call of the dome or you were getting the heck out.

"Wait here, gang," Saul said, and he slipped away.

They waited in the smoking lounge, Newp bumming a cig off one of the businessmen there, Frannie waving smoke from her face as she watched the same reporter on TV with the same report, over and over. They paced the lounge as the cacophony of the ticket lines unrolled outside the lounge glass.

Finally Saul returned with four coke bottles and handed them out. "Grab the bags."

"You went for soft drinks?"

"No, these are just a mitzvah," Saul said. "Look at her busting my chops. No, we're going."

"You got a car?" Newp asked.

"Ain't no cars," Saul said. "Not anywhere. But it wouldn't help. I got us something better."

Within minutes they were running across a different section of the tarmac where two men, one older and Japanese, and one younger and dark skinned, with the words Island Dee-Lites on the tail.

Frannie paused, not sure how to approach the whirling blades which seemed so low they might behead them all. "Like this!" Saul said. "Hunch over!" and they all ran ducking until they reached the chopper and the young man threw open the door and began taking their bags.

"This is Joey Tokyo," Saul said.

"That's not my name, you racist bastard." The older man laughed. He shook everyone's hand. "Jue Tanaka. This is my partner Chad."

Chad, the younger man, nodded. He was impossibly handsome, Frannie noticed even in the madness. Very fit. Behind him, she spotted a pair of surfboards strapped at the inside bulkhead—she assumed the inside wall of a helicopter was called a bulkhead—and pegged him for a fellow wave-worshipper.

"Joey Tokyo and I were in the Navy," Saul explained once they all got aboard. The chopper had the room of a big car, more or less; two bench seats behind the pilot and copilot's chairs.

Newp started to ask, "They had..." and stopped himself.

"Yeah," Joe or Jue looked back from the copilot seat. "They had Japanese in the US Navy."

"I'll bet that was fun," said Truly.

The older man smiled. "Everything has its moments. Chad, take us up." After a moment they were lifting off the ground and Frannie felt her stomach lurch.

Joe shouted "Aloha!" as the Honolulu airport began to zip away from them.

CHAPTER 48

For a moment, just as the flight began, Frannie could only stare out the windshield as the chopper lifted over the mountains and began to follow the shape of the island of Oahu. She saw sailboats and divers leaping off of cliffs, and more palm trees than she had ever imagined possible. But then she saw the freeway choked with vehicles and snapped out of her Mutual of Omaha reverie. "How long until we get there?" she shouted over the roar of the engines.

"About twelve minutes, miss," the surfer pilot said. She detected an American southern drawl. Army brat, probably.

Frannie grabbed for her backpack and tore it open. "Mind if I smoke?"

The boy shrugged. "Don't bother me none."

She lifted Emmett out of the backpack and the little golem squirmed until she sat him between her and the surfboard on the wall. "Nice board, by the way," she called.

"Yeah, it's a classic."

Saul saw the golem on the bench seat. "Are you crazy?"

"Look," Frannie insisted. "He's our link to the great beyond, okay? This thing is bigger than we thought, and we need him."

She yanked a lever under a large side window and cranked it open, starting a loud whistle of air. Then she tore the tape off the golem's mouth and smoke poured out at once.

"What the Hell?" Joe turned and waved at the smoke in alarm. "Chad, fans."

"You set off a flare?" Chad yelled.

"No, it's a smoke machine," Saul called. "For a party. Sorry, we got it under control." Indeed, the smoke pouring from the golem had lessened now.

"Sorry!" Frannie yelled.

Fans kicked on in throughout the chipper and after a moment most of the smoke from the golem's mouth had been sucked out.

"Oh, the indignities of God's creatures."

"Yeah, yeah," Frannie said. "Look, Emmett, here's the situation."

The strong German accent came back high and craggy. "The former servant of God now fancies himself a king of the Sons of Adam," he said.

"What do you mean, sons of Adam?"

"Us," Frannie said. "He means us."

"Who ya'll talking to?" Chad called back. He looked straight at Frannie, who shifted and was pretty sure that he could not see the clay man beside her. Still, what was it going to look like?

"We're making notes in a tape recorder," she said, but Chad had already seen the golem after all.

"Are you talking to a doll?"

"Well—" and she was ready to go into a whole spiel about how she wasn't some crazy person with a doll fetish, but she Chad had already turned away, apparently not troubled, and she needed to talk to the golem. She turned to Emmett. "Book Man has taken over the dome at this big hotel."

The golem understood. "Penamue has absorbed the potentiality of the blank books and now seeks to fatten himself on the futures of the people."

"How do you see this?" she asked.

"I have felt it since we arrived on this island," Emmett said.

"So what happens when people go inside the dome?"

"He will take from then everything that is possible. He will leave them lives of only… grey. No change. No forward motion. No hope. No potentiality."

"If we get near him, can we trap him in a dybbuk box, like before?"

"The truth is always the truth and man is always supreme over the fallen," Emmett said. "But the plans of men are hopeless either way."

"Um, if I ignore the general pessimistic caveat that you ended that with, can I get a yes or no, can we trap him in a box with an incantation?"

"I cannot see why not," the golem said. "But you must break his willingness to escape. You must remind him that you are the demons' rulers and not vice versa."

"That little gray man," Truly said, "has never met a straight answer in his life."

"The answer that is certain is the one that is wrong," the golem said.

Newp nodded. "He gets a lot more fun if you pretend everything he says starts with 'Confucius say.'"

"Oy. Good enough," Frannie said.

Soon the white dome rose in the distance, fluttering with its blanket of origami birds.

"Uh-oh," Chad said.

"What?" Saul shouted. "What uh-oh?"

"The heliport at the Hawaiian Village Resort is closed."

"Closed? It's a heliport, you just touch down."

"No, I mean—" Chad tapped the windshield in front of them. "We can't get in there."

Frannie and the rest peered forward. "All I see is a sea of people."

"Exactly," Chad called. He looked at his partner. "What do you want to do, Joe? Go back? Maybe go to the next resort?"

"No!" Frannie insisted. "We need to get to the Hilton Village." She taped Emmett's mouth again and continued, "We need to get there, and we'll never get there from a road from another resort."

"Well, miss, I'd like to know what you suggest," Chad said.

Frannie looked out the window at the busy grounds, and then her eyes drifted past the surfboards out to sea. Hm. Then she made up her mind.

"Take us two hundred yards out. Me and Newp can get out there."

"What?" Newp asked.

"Now, look," Chad continued. "You can't just swim in; we'll head south and come back when it's clear."

"*You* look," Frannie said. Saul was silent, watching her with something like marvel as she told Chad, "we have a plan. To save those people from something awful. And all I need from *you* right now is an open door and… well, and these two bitchin' surfboards."

Joe and Chad both looked to Saul.

Saul shrugged. "*I* trust her."

Minutes later the doors were open and Frannie and Newp had moved to the edge, each holding one of the surfboards borrowed from the helicopter's pilots. Frannie took the shorter one but it wasn't shorter by much—each board was over ten feet long, monstrous to lug around inside a helicopter. Heavy too. "What is this, balsa wood?" she asked Chad.

"It's *oa* wood," he said.

"There's no fins," Newp said, looking up and down his board.

"You use your back foot for a fin," Chad said. "Look, if you can't use this kind of board, this idea isn't going to…"

"People were using these for thousands of years," Frannie said. "Anything else?"

"Yeah," Chad called over the noise. "Coral. You watch it, because if you wipe out fifty yards from shore, you'll shred that pretty dress and the skin of your back right off."

"So don't fall."

Chad nodded. "Don't fall. Absolutely god damn right."

Frannie exhaled, blinked, looking at the rolling waves heading into the beach at Waikiki. It would be deep where they jumped. Provided she could find her board fast, she'd be okay. "How big are these waves?" She waved her hand and looked beyond the water below them to the waves out at shore.

"Ten feet," Newp said. "Are you sure…"

"Don't even ask me that right now." Frannie took off her shoes and grabbed the backpack next to Emmett, putting it on. At the last minute she reached down and tore the hem of her dress clear up to her waist. "Let's go."

CHAPTER 49

She was prepared for the violence of the water, but it still caught her like a massive kick to the solar plexus. Frannie and Newp hit the waves and their surfboards immediately danced out of their hands. Frannie plunged deep into the ocean and fought her way to the surface in hopes of finding the 10-foot *oa* board. Her head burst through the surface and she breathed as she instantly scanned for Newp and the boards. She spotted her own and swam for it. The board bobbed on the water, nearly invisible, but within a few seconds she had reached it and climbed on top. She looked around and saw behind her where Newp was paddling up on his own borrowed chariot.

So far, so good.

As she floated for a minute, the helicopter hovered not far away and she and Newp waved at them.

It was hotter than home by about ten degrees and the sun beat down directly, so that it felt even hotter than LA. From their vantage point as she bobbed up and down, Frannie could see a man-inhabited paradise of beaches, bungalows, highways, and the towers of the downtown in the distance, and closer, just across the highway, the white-blanketed dome of the Hawaiian Village Hotel.

She and Newp touched feet for a second, drawing strength from one another, and then the they began to look back for a wave.

Suddenly the emergency left her and she shouted with a sudden, unexpected joy. "Newp! Can you believe this? That we get to experience this place this way?"

"What's that?"

"Surfing was *born* here. That's what Hooky was so on about. If you're a soul surfer, this is where you come home." Soul surfer—that was the surf nation word for those whose bones ached to surf and couldn't care less what the world thought.

When a wave came, they paddled and rose, and soon they were surfing.

These were not California waves. They were high and hard and Frannie had to catch herself.

Let the waves come. They were just waves. Feet forward, mind your balance, focus on the sound of the board sliding over the water. Water is water is water.

They were surfing in flippin' Hawaii.

They left the boards embedded in the sand and headed straight for the hotel. At the outer swimming pool of the hotel, they found an open gate and a plethora of beach towels, no one swimming in the enormous circular split-level pool. As soon as they reached the pool, Frannie noticed something else.

"Do you feel it?" she caught her breath as she leaned against the bar under its grass thatched roof, a place like Tarzan would build.

"Feel what—*oh,*" Newp said. They craned their heads around the end of the bar and looked to great dome. The voice came hissing, sounding both around them and inside their brains, distinct in Frannie's ear like someone whispering over her shoulder: *come… and see the future.*

"I gotta admit, I know this guy and even I feel the need to listen," Frannie said.

"It must be stronger the closer you get, like over there at the hotel."

"Think of the power," Frannie said, pointing and running her finger along the shape of the dome in the air. "the fact that he can control all of those birds. He must have built them from the Blanks somehow. Like he sucks in the potentiality and he spits out the birds." She looked back towards the hotel. "We gotta find my parents before we do anything else. Or at least I need to."

Newp took her hands in his and kissed her. Then he held her hands for a moment. "Of course."

They headed over to the hotel and found that contrary to Frannie's expectations, it was not deserted.

All around the lobby, people stood idle, waiting as though at a bus stop. She saw one family of four, the children sitting and trying to play a card game on a little lobby table while the mother hissed at them. The children seemed distracted by the game and from it as well. The mom would hiss at them to be quiet, them lose interest, and the children would lose their place in their game, and all of them would look up silently towards the dome, which whispered on.

"Here," the mother said as she brought cotton balls out of her purse. She went to the little boy and girl and stuffed the cotton in their ears, which took some time, then stuffed some in her own ears. Then she offered some to her husband, who sat in his suit on the lobby loveseat appearing agitated and nervous, and he shook his head no.

All the while the whispering continued. Frannie said to Newp, "I think she has the right idea." But why weren't they in their rooms? So it must be *worse* in the rooms. Was that possible?

Frannie approached the set of couches. "Ma'am?"

"Yes?" the woman looked up, instantly putting her hands on the shoulders of the nearest child, the bow. "What is it?" She looked Frannie up and down, and Frannie felt suddenly self-conscious about the torn, soaked dress she wore.

"Could my friend and I have some of that cotton?"

"Oh. Oh! Of course." She rifled through her purse.

As the woman handed over bits of cotton, Frannie said, "If it's the sound coming from the dome you're blocking—that's right, isn't it?"

"Yes." A vigorous, nervous nod.

"Why don't you go back to your room?"

The woman pressed the cotton balls in Frannie's palms and leaned forward as her voice took on a deeper tone. "It's worse up there."

Frannie put the cotton in her ears and gave some to Newp, who drew closer but was also exhibiting the same nervous tic turning again and again towards the glass walls through which they could see the dome.

With the cotton in her own ears she now heard the whole world at a distance. She sat for a moment on the loveseat. "I need to find my parents. They're still in this hotel. I'm pretty sure, anyway. You said the sound is worse up in the guest floors?"

"Oh, yes. Up there it sounds like an alarm going off. It shouts."

Frannie turned to Newp. "Could you go to the front desk and find out the room?" Newp disappeared and Frannie asked the woman, "When did it start?"

"Yesterday," she said. "We were… it drove us to the lobby. But we were strong enough to stop here. We just huddle. We go to the bathroom in pairs, you know?" She pointed across the lobby. "The bathroom's over there, by the way." Frannie took in the interior stone walls and the facilities.

"Has the hotel staff told you anything?"

The woman shook her heard. "I think—I think *they* don't know what to do either. They all try to act normal, except every now and then one of them breaks and runs for the dome. It's hard to ignore."

"Why haven't you left—driven away?"

"The car was totaled," the man interrupted, leaning forward on the couch. "Someone bashed into it. Now the roads are all blocked. We may try to walk tonight. Then again, we may go swimming." Then he laughed, and Frannie's blood ran cold.

"Frannie." Newp returned, raising his voice a little unnaturally, probably because of the cotton in both their ears. "Your folks are in Room 714." He held up a brass key. "I said we were family."

Room 714 was an empty wreck, the wind whistling and the ocean roaring outside on the balcony. The glass doors had been torn away and Frannie felt a sickness in her stomach as she touched the bed. The backpack squirmed and she brought Emmett out, removing the tape once more.

Emmett tore across the room, stopping at the end of the balcony and looking out. "Ohhhh," he said.

"What is it?"

"He calls to all the sons of Adam," the golem said. "Penamue demands and cajoles and he whispers and he pleads."

Frannie raised her voice. The whispering on the air had turned up around her and she found she had to shout no matter what. "What about my parents? Do you know where they are?"

"I have not that kind of knowledge," said the golem. "But smart men know how to hide"

"Frannie," New said. "Let's scram—there's nothing up here."

But Frannie held up a hand because she'd noticed a book on the table. KNOWING YOUR RESORT. She flipped it open, the shouting of the demon growing so loud she could barely move, it wanted to control her fingers. She flipped pages. There was a diagram of the dome and a history of its construction, map of the hotel, even a clever little feature with a hula girl named Maile who answered printed questions like "How much pineapple juice do guests go through every day?"

"How do you service all these rooms and towers without overwhelming guests?

"Why, that's simple," said Maile. "We use tunnels."

Frannie determined that she would put Emmett away no longer, instead letting him ride in the top of her pack. She headed straight down into the serving hallways in the back of the lobby, trailing a thin line of Emmett's blue mouth smoke.

A door: Maintenance and Service Only.

In and through. Down the steps until they spilled out into a concrete hallway painted shiny industrial gray. The hallway was empty, lit brilliantly with ugly yellow bulbs. It stretched on twenty yards or so, then turned black at a corner, presumably going on into infinite darkness.

Still at the start of the tunnel, Newp said, "Great idea, Fran, but…"

"Shh." She took the cotton out of her ears. The whisper seemed far away down here. She put her fingers to her lips, and they began to walk the length of the hallway in silence. They turned at the end, stopping to regard the utter darkness as the tunnel plunged on.

She breathed and found a light switch and flipped it.

Her heart leapt as she suddenly saw perhaps a hundred and fifty men, women and children in all kinds of dress, staring back at her intently. "Good job, guys," she said.

The people in the front nodded and a woman said, "What's going on up above?"

"Still the same."

"Frannie," came her father's voice, and she smiled as he pushed through, her mother close behind. "oh, I found you," she said, holding them both. "Oh, I found you."

"Why are you trailing smoke?" her mom asked.

CHAPTER 50

They stood near the front desk and Frannie tapped the glass, indicating the dome across the green. "We gotta get in there."

"That's insane," mom said. "Why would you need to do that?"

"Because it's my fault that he's here," she said.

"No, because your father's *fakakte* brother got you involved in his secret Kabbalah bullshit. Don't kid a kidder. You couldn't you fall in with a motorcycle gang like the other kids?"

Pop smirked. "What happens if you and Saul go in?" She looked at him and saw that his attention was perfectly held, he was treating her as a respected expert, a part of Saul's family business. His respect made her want to learn the world and repair it all.

"As far as I can tell," Frannie said, "the Book Man—that's what we call the guy gathering people in there—will somehow suck, and this will sound strange, but he'll suck the *future* out of people. But we need to get close to him anyway."

"It doesn't look guarded," Newp said.

"Well, why would it be?" Frannie answered. "It's like fly paper. He *wants* them to come. And then they stick."

Frannie and Newp laid out their arsenal: they had a dybbuk box, the golem, and a few medallions. Finally Frannie took her mom aside.

"Okay."

"Honey," mom said, hugging her. "Is there anything I can say to you?"

"No, mom," Frannie said. "Look—the thing we could use most is if you can get hold of Saul and Truly, who are probably going to be driving in soon. But look." She pressed her lips to her mom's cheek. "I don't regret being in all this. It feels like what I should be doing."

Her mother's fingers brushed her hair. "*Shalom aleichim.*"

Frannie and Newp stuck extra cotton in their ears and headed out the door at noon. As they walked along the flowery path towards the dome entrance, Frannie was struck by the normality of the scene—the feel of the grass under her feet and the smell of honeysuckle. As they got closer, Frannie regarded the curved entrance and saw more clearly the thousands of white birds, could hear the flapping, the whispering and form of them as they would flap and fold, aware of the rolling across the rooftop in occasional undulating waves of white.

Frannie looked at the few people still making their procession towards the dome and tried to match their expression—not blank per se, but expectant, curious, even hopeful. She reached the entrance with Newp and a bunch of followers of Penamue's call.

Birds also covered the door, which was glass with steel struts below a deep awning, but if the birds counted as guards, they were the only guards. Frannie and Newp let a couple of people go by and let the doors shut with them still on the outside. Frannie ran her hand along the line of little birds next to the door, not touching them because she had a fear that somehow he would feel her if she did so. "When we have the chance," she said, "draw out the box. Emmett, you still feel good about this?"

"I feel good about nothing," the golem said. Frannie took the thing at its word. The aluminum door handle was cold to the touch as she grabbed it, ran her other hand over Newp's neck for luck, and yanked the door open.

The dome was lit by the glare of paper, paper everywhere, dotted hundreds of times by the faces of the people who had answered the call.

Frannie, Newp and the golem on Frannie's back stopped at one side of the great circle fifty yards wide. Human beings lined the inside walls, standing still; Frannie saw the two who had entered ahead of them stop halfway through the space in the center of the dome and freeze as if stuck by an unseen force. The pair, a man and woman in Bermuda shorts and aloha shirts, stared ahead at what Frannie could only think of as an altar.

"Oh my God," Frannie said. At the far end of the great circular pace was a proscenium of white paper and on it stood the Blanks, the books tilted and open, and out of them flowed and flitted a steady stream of origami birds. And standing between the stacks of the blank books, in a cloud of paper, was Hooky Carmichael.

CHAPTER 51

But it wasn't Hooky at all; it was his body, his skin, bronzed and beautiful but churning from within with the movement of the unholy parchment, the converted potentiality of the Blanks in the form of Penamue's origami evil.

The pair in the Bermuda shorts looked up as the birds landed on their hands and necks, and then the man and woman were lifted bodily, angling limp from long tentacles of paper; they were flung back and placed against the wall with the others. They hung on the wall then, held there by flapping tendrils of paper, staring blankly.

The demon that bore Hooky's face turned his eyes now to Frannie and Newp.

"Hello again," came the voice, and no cotton in her ears would stop that coming through.

Frannie took Newp's hand and she shouted, "We have suit with you, Penamue of the Fallen."

The demon did not smile, but had something like amusement in his voice. "You think to blot me out with your Hebrew magicks. Is it not so?" He clapped Hooky's hands together with mirth.

"*Gey in dre'erd,*" she hissed. "Go to Hell. Newp, get the…"

She was rocked back as a paper bird landed on her forehead with an audible thwack, its beak digging in instantly and she felt the warmth of blood and the buzzing in her brain.

"What are you, Frances Cohn?" the demon called, and he may as well have been whispering in her ear. "What are you to be? What can we see? What does the paper find, what is the potential of Frannie—you call yourself Frannie, don't you? Let us look—"

A queen on a surfboard, no surprise there do I feel, a book and a magic lantern show, and the adoration of our kind, this could be your future— fame around the world, is this the costliest potential to lose? Is this the tastiest, let us look, let us look—

Or is it this Frannie, this Frances, whose eyes begin to wrinkle, in white hat and blue smock, and handling bottles of blood and needles and saws, a woman among dying men in a jungle—is this the future you will find most valuable, this Frannie who fixes warriors and sends the intact ones back into the fire, is this the most priceless and golden future, a Frannie who saves many and touches many, who clutches bottles of blood by day and poison by night to soothe and sleep—

All of this is nutrient to me, sustenance—

(Somewhere deep within the spell: *but what am I without it?*)

You rest—you rest—nothing but rest—nothing more for I will feed on it all—

Frannie saw with her eyes again, past the drizzle of blood, and turned her head to see Newp caught; still, mumbling something she couldn't catch, not that it would matter. It would be particular and personal to him and all the future him there could be. "Newp," Frannie growled, "It's time to—"

You sit by so many bedsides, your soldiers and your patients and your father and your husband—is this him? Perhaps this is him, and I can take away all of that pain, I can consume it, and all beyond is gloriously quiet, gloriously empty.

"*A beyze sho*! An evil hour has come upon you!" shouted a voice from behind her and Frannie felt movement at her shoulder, and a weight had landed on her head.

The golem was leaping over her, moving fast. She saw it flip and bash the drilling bird off her forehead. Frannie staggered back, her hand at her brow as the golem stamped the bird against the tiles of the dome.

"You must partake of your destiny," came the smoking words of the golem. "Thou shalt *choke*, you potentiality-eating devil."

Slow motion, then, Frannie moved, swatting the birds away from Newp's eyes—she ripped the box from the backpack and thrust it into Newp's hands even as she began to shout and birds began to descend from all sides, swooping in at the three of them, she and Newp and the golem.

Emmett hissed, moving fast, stamping, and then he was surrounded.

"Newp, ready?" Frannie called.

Newp knelt with the box, ignoring the birds. "Ready!"

"Cursed shall be you in the city, and cursed shall be you in the field," Frannie called, batting away birds as she shouted. She yanked her numerological medallion from her shirt and held it before her. "By the all-seeing God, by the Tetragrammaton, I—"

Birds sliced her hand and she grunted and kept reciting at the rapid cloud of birds that plunged at the golem.

For a moment, Emmett was lost in a ball of birds, paper lurching and flying. And then the room clapped with a crashing sound and the birds scattered and she saw smoke pour from the golem as he exploded.

Emmett lay looking at her, or rather his clay head did; the rest was bits, torn every which way. She grabbed the tiny still-smoking head and batted more birds with her other hand as he clutched Emmett's head.

"You belong not to this realm, you are lost," she shouted at the Book Man, "you trespass, you defy the laws of God and know not the love and guidance of your make, you—"

Newp crashed into her, falling and out of control, shoved by something, and she now saw that people were closing in on them. Penamue was moving the people under his control against her. Newp scrambled to retrieve the box as it clattered away from him.

The clay head in her hands, the size of a doll, spoke. "They cannot capture thee. They must not. For thy destiny is more than this liar can know."

She opened her mouth and closed it as birds sensed the opening and burst against her lips, and now the arms of entranced people were reaching towards her—she fell back and looked up at the ceiling as another bird plunged its beak into her forehead once more.

What do we have here, what destiny do we have to sustain us—

An explosion. Birds and flesh flew and Frannie saw someone step into the crowd. Two explosions—*BOOM*—*chak-ckak*. Frannie sat up and saw a black girl and a bald man wading through the crowd, Truly and her uncle blasting actual flippin' *shotguns* into the air.

"You two," Uncle Saul said. "Time to go."

Truly stopped and Frannie saw she had spotted Penamue and was screaming, tears running down her face as she began to blast away at him. And Saul was grabbing her, and they were running.

The birds surrounded them as they shoved their way through the crowd, Saul and Truly bashing the entranced people with the butts of their guns, pushing as the birds fluttered around them. Desperately Frannie found the glass doors where the people were three deep, and she heard Truly shout, "here!"

About ten yards over Truly had found an empty glass wall and she blasted it, sending birds and glass flying.

They ran.

In defeat they fled, hearing the whispers in their brain, the laughter of Penamue taunting their failure. They ran like baby turtles to the sea.

She crouched in the tiny cutting shells of the beach with her friends and felt the foam lap against her legs, which stung from hundreds of cuts. But the sting was nothing compared to the defeat.

The head of the golem lay in the sand, opening and closing its mouth, weak and mouthing,

Frannie looked up at her uncle, who knelt in the sand with her.

Uncle Saul touched the letters on the golem's forehead and ran his fingers along the word.

"*Emet*, truth," Saul said. "You have served with honesty and truth, mighty clay warrior. And we thank you." Saul took a stone and scratched away the first letter. "*Mazik du bist*, ya great little devil."

The letters remaining made the word *Met*.

Frannie sobbed as the warmth of the golem's eyes and the smoke went out.

Met meant dead, and the golem was no more.

CHAPTER 52

Frannie looked away from the choppy waves, the sun beating down on her and causing blinding sparkles off the water. "My parents are inside the hotel. They're hiding in a tunnel with a bunch of others. The whispering is lessened down there."

Saul nodded. "Yeah, we found them after we finally made it in from the next town over."

Frannie chucked Truly on the shoulder. "Where'd you get a shotgun, Tex?"

Truly grinned. "Saul borrowed them from his helicopter friends."

"Sort of," Saul said. "Actually from some security people my friends know, it was a whole bit. Anyway—"

"That thing is using Hooky. Hooky's body," Truly said. "It had his face."

Frannie nodded. The beach was so deserted that the boards she and

Newp had ridden in on were still planted a few hundred yards away, like tombstones on a vast prairie. "In the name of all that's holy, what are we going to do now?"

"Frannie, we've tried everything," Newp said. "We're not getting near Book Man with chanting and a Dybbuk box."

Frannie held up a hand and wandered away to sit in the sand, looking at the ocean. Hawaii; hell of a place.

"If he keeps going, that dome will get too small," she heard Saul say.

"So you know a better spell, magic man?"

Saul chuckled. "I'm not a magician. This is Kabbalah, it's complicated and... I mean, I know this stuff, but I'm not gifted and I'm not a *rebbe*, all right? I'm just a guy who tries to guard the futures of men."

"I'm sorry," Newp said. "That's a lot, anyway."

"Yeah, but my point is: this is a *demon*."

Frannie took a stick and swatted at the sand with it. "He takes away the future." She stood up and they all looked at her. She rubbed her toes in the sand, feeling the heat against the pads of her feet. "He eats it. Gorges himself on the sumptuous futures of people. Golem said my future was different, though. He said that, right?"

Saul nodded. "Yeah, he said that."

"Can the Book Man... *choke* on loss?" Frannie searched for words, flipping through endless pages in her head from the past few days.

"How do you mean?"

"Something Emmett said: 'thou shalt choke.'"

"I don't know what that would mean," Saul said. "But you're the prodigy; what do you think it means?"

Frannie thought a second, looking up and down the beach. "Look around you. This hotel, that road, those cars moving up and down the highway. All these gentiles and Jews here, but there are bones below us. Captain Cook got here in the early 19th Century and there were 300,000 Hawaiians here, people with all their own laws, traditions, and kings. That was the early 1800s. But the *mid*-1800s there were just 30,000 of them left. By 1893, the land was taken by the Europeans and Americans—they call us *Haoles*—and the kingdom was all gone.

"So I'm looking up and down this beach and I'm thinking, what would they have become if all of that hadn't happened? Those gone souls, that gone destiny, all of that. You wanna talk about potentiality—that was a hunk of it. Let him choke on loss, these people were erased. May I have your *Luria*?"

Saul fished a book out of his shoulder bag, but as he handed it over, he said, "Frannie, what you're talking about—it's black work."

"We learned the rules of calling and banishment. And we're free to break the law to save a man's life," Frannie said as she took the book and started thumbing through it. "Newp? Run to the hotel. Find the hula dancers and the drummers, if there are any in the lobby. Bring them here."

# # #

Drums. Drums and dance. Four drummers pounded out a solid rhythm as tiki torches burned and hula men made them spin and sway, the fires tracing great circles in the air as Frannie stood at the water's edge.

"I bring together traditions under the eyes of God," she said. "By the one God and Tetragrammaton and by the kings of old, I stand at the water's edge. Listen, you kings! Look at your land that you have vowed to serve, think now on your losses, your many hopes, and weep not, but come!"

The drums pounded harder and she began to shout, running with the board as she shouted in Hebrew, the water cold against her feet. She felt the shock of cold and kept shouting.

"Ten Forces I call upon,

Keter, the will, in the presence of God who is Ehveh,

Chochmah and Brina, the wisdom and the mind, in the presence of God who is Yah and Elohim,

Da'at, the knowledge, in the presence of God who is Ehveh,

Chesed, the goodness, in the presence of God who is El,

Din, the judgment, in the presence of God who is Elohim,

Tiferet, the harmony, in the presence of God who is YHWH, the

Tetragrammaton,

Netzach, victory, in the presence of God who is YHWY Tzvaoh,

Hod, the glory, in the presence of God who is Elohim,

Yesod, the teaching, in the presence of God who is El Shaddai,

And Malchut, the presence, in the presence of God who is Shechina,

All of these each in the light of the Atzlut, the World of Spirit!"

Water splashed Frannie's face. "And by these I call ye strangers but sons of God!" She shouted as she paddled out beyond the breakers.

"Come ye bones in the deep, come ye bones in the mountains, come ye bones in the sea!" She saw a wave that looked right and paddled for it, chanting as the water splashed salty in her mouth.

She got on top of the wave and turned.

Blasts of something solid flashed from the north sky, shooting like stars. Water splashed up as each one hit. She saw them fall from the sky so fast that she could barely make them out, forms of unintelligible bone and moss streaking from the mountains and diving deep. Splash and splash and splash, the forms came from the mountains, and below her the water churned and she felt a great coming together, bones and flesh and moss taking form.

"Come ye old kings, and let us take back your land!"

She paddled and the wave broke and Frannie was up, and as she rose to her feet she danced forward and grabbed the front of the enormous *oa* board, perched at the edge, hang ten formation, and the sea gave a great rumble and opened up.

From the shore they saw it: Frances Cohn, guardian of the Kabbalah, hanging ten and flanked by twenty Hawaiian kings on surfboards of smooth *oa* wood, their hair on fire, their hips glistening with bright yellow feathered king's skirts.

On a great wave at Waikiki they made landfall with vengeance in mind, in search of battle without honor or humanity.

CHAPTER 53

The dome was alive with chanting now, as they people against the wall began to mutter. Penamue was pleased, fed but still hungry, and he was running his adopted fingers along the many lives on text filling in the pages of the Blanks when an explosion shook the building.

Birds scattered as the glass door flew off its hinges and Penamue raised a wall of dense paper even before he saw them all, sending birds and tendrils latticing before him as he called the humans to his aid.

The old Hawaiian kings strode in first, moving like lightning, swinging staffs with club ends, moving so fast that all one could see was the streak of yellow from their skirts and the flying of their clubs as paper birds flew, humans caught by great brown hands that bashed them this way and that.

"Who—" Penamue called.

Into the center of the dome came the girl called Frannie, holding a ten-foot surfboard like a weapon.

"Read the future, Penamue!" she called.

Penamue felt a shock as the invaders clapped their dripping wet hands onto the whipping paper tentacles, twisting the paper tentacles around their forearms, chanting as they sent their lost futures his way.

"Read it!" the girl called again. Penamue sent a pair of human boys after her and she beat them aside with the surfboard. "You want to eat futures, let me show you a thousand, three hundred thousand, let me show you children not born and marriages not made! Let me show you flowers not grown and surfboards not carved and holy untouched deserts turned to *Haole* farms! Choke on loss, you manipulative bastard!"

Penamue was losing his grip on the birds and the kings came closer, dragging themselves forward along his paper tentacles. He fought, trying to whip the tentacles way, and then he realized he was no longer in possession of them.

And then the girl was upon him and he was lost in a world, loss adding upon loss; no future, the ultimate future. No—it was too much, he was *choking.*

This is my curse, my leynendi toykheke,

And you shall grope at noonday!

No. He would take them. So much loss, he would take—

As the blind gropes in darkness! You shall not prosper in your ways: and you shall be only oppressed and spoiled ever more!

No man shall save you!

And Penamue screamed and wanted peace then, but found none, called for peace, and the girl, the accursed Blankguard, was holding an escape out for him. She held out a chamber of numbers that spoke to him of order, and a box that would *stop the noise*, it's tearing me apart—

"Run to your Hell! *Brenen zolstu afn fayer!*"

The box capped shut and Frannie put her foot upon it and strapped it closed with a metal cord carved with holy numbers.

She held the box aloft and set it before the altar next to the Blanks. She turned then to the kings.

There was nothing there, nothing but puddles of water and awakening tourists and a room overrun by lifeless origami sparrows.

CHAPTER 54

Into the depths the box went. For a brief time Frannie considered leaving it in Waikiki, but in the end, she carried the box with the engraved metal bands all the way back to where she could be nearer to it.

Off the coast of Laguna Beach, Frannie, Saul, Newp and Truly rode out in a boat borrowed from one of Hooky's Legion. She knelt in the boat and said a prayer over the box and then let it slide from her hands into the deep.

Afterwards everyone headed back to Café Monstro, but Frannie turned away as they ascended the steps. She went instead to Hooky's shack.

She had a few weeks of summer left and she'd be going back to school, Newp off to college. For now she had the beach, which was practically empty of surfers or visitors of any kind. There would still be some good waves though and she and Newp would have them practically to themselves.

The Blanks were in stacks at the café and soon would be back in their place, ready for the lucky few who were dredged in by the unconscious pull of them, just as she had been.

She was something else now. An *abba*, perhaps. She ached to know more. Ached to *learn*.

But not today.

Frannie stepped out of the shack to find Newp waiting for her.

She kissed him and together they bolted for the last swells of summer.

If you liked Surf Mystic: Night of *the Book Man*, you might also enjoy reading the following titles available now on Amazon from Castle Bridge Media:

Castle Of Horror Anthology Volume 1
Edited By Jason Henderson

Castle of Horror Anthology Volume 2: Holiday Horrors
Edited By Jason Henderson

Castle of Horror Anthology Volume 3: Scary Summer Stories
Edited By Jason Henderson

Isonation
By In Churl Yo

Please remember to leave us your reviews on Amazon and Goodreads!

CASTLE BRIDGE MEDIA
DENVER, COLORADO, USA

THANK YOU FOR SUPPORTING INDEPENDENT PUBLISHERS AND AUTHORS!

castlebridgemedia.com

Made in the USA
Coppell, TX
22 December 2020